Co

Contents

Dedication	3
Chapter 1	4
Chapter 2	14
Chapter 3	26
Chapter 4	29
Chapter 5	36
Chapter 6	38
Chapter 7	54
Chapter 8	57
Chapter 9	65
Chapter 10	71
Chapter 11	79
Chapter 12	81
Chapter 13	93
Chapter 14	96
Chapter 15	100
Chapter 16	104
Chapter 17	113
Chapter 18	116
Chapter 19	129
Chapter 20	131
Chapter 21	138
Chapter 22	141
Chapter 23	152
Chapter 24	154
Chapter 25	160
Chapter 26	162
Chapter 27	170
Chapter 28	172
Chapter 29	179
Chapter 30	183
Chapter 31	198
Chapter 32	201

Chapter 33   208
Chapter 34   212
Chapter 35   220
Chapter 36   222
Chapter 37   227
Chapter 38   234
Chapter 39   238
Chapter 40   242
Chapter 41   244
Don't forget to leave an Amazon review.   249
About the Author   250
Credits   250
Copyright   251

Dedication

It takes a village to write a book. Thanks to everyone like Elm and Nat who gave me great feedback and formed my beautiful cheering squad.
And to my Doodles, my number one fan.

Chapter 1

May 15th , 2015

Lia was nervous. She lifted her tattered carpetbag from the back seat of the yellow cab and stared at the house in front of her.

Instead of charging ahead, inertia held her stubbornly in place. She felt numb, the intense fear of failure and embarrassment weighing on her. Here she stood on the neat green lawn of a Mediterranean style house in Florida, thousands of miles away from her island home wondering why the hell she had thought this was a good idea.

Just two weeks earlier, she had gotten a phone call from a strange woman who had offered her the single greatest opportunity any novice writer could dream of and she had jumped on it. It had led her here. Lia had fantasized that this would be the beginning of an extraordinary career for her. She dreamt of book signings, major publishing deals, and a luxuriant lifestyle. And yet, here she stood, immobilized on a quiet street in the middle of a Florida suburb as the lawn sprinkler splashed her new clothes.

Born on the small Caribbean island of Barbados, Lia and many of her peers had grown accustomed to living obscure lives. There were only a handful of Barbadians who had broken into the nucleus of international fame, embracing the limelight and reveling in it. Like Rihanna and Sir Garfield Sobers and Austin Tom Clarke, Lia wanted to be one of them. But Susan Taylor didn't.

A New York Times best-selling author, Susan Taylor's seminal novel, 'The Unspeakable Truth' went down in history as the most famous novel by any Caribbean author. More than four decades later it was still in print, an enviable feat for any author.

The beautiful little island that was beloved for its white-sand beaches, tranquil blue seas, lush tropical foliage, and friendly people became the scene of an international crime. Long rumoured to be a slightly altered tale of an actual murderous political scandal that rocked the Caribbean, Susan's book was thought to be the reason she had never returned to Barbados after it was published. Barbados had endured its very own Watergate: the fallout from her novel had led to a shakedown in the political system, an international investigation and the disappearance of Susan, her family and a well-known politician.

Her name was now synonymous in Barbados and other Caribbean islands with being a whistleblower and squealer. Whenever people labeled someone as a "Pretty-Eyed Susan" you knew they meant that person couldn't be trusted.

And so Susan Taylor got her book published, people were outraged and she never returned to Barbados.

But what made her even more intriguing was the fact that she never wrote again.

Nothing. Not a limerick or greeting inside a birthday card was credited to her after 'The Unspeakable Truth'. Susan had lived her life cloaked in a haze of mystery since then.

Until now.

The call that had started this journey came from a lady named Ancil Adams. When she answered the phone, Ancil wasted no time explaining that Susan Taylor had chosen Lia to co-author Susan's memoir and wanted to start right away. Susan Taylor would arrange for Lia to meet important people in the industry to secure a publishing deal for her. And to sweeten the offer, Susan had agreed to pay all of Lia's travel expenses. The poor girl hadn't been able to sleep at all that night.

The next morning Lia told her mother everything as she scarfed down a cup of oats. Her mother, bleary-eyed and yawning, listened while she took off her work shoes. Her mouth hung open when Lia mentioned Susan Taylor's name and she instantly proclaimed that she was fully against it. Lia was an only child and she had long felt that her mother liked the idea of having her tethered to her apron strings at all times. Too often, Lia's innate sense of adventure was at odds with her mother's laid back attitude. Her mother resisted because Lia was only twenty-five and shouldn't give up a job she had for only two months. Lia listened quietly and, at the end of it all, the young woman admitted that her mother had a point.

Still, there was no way she was going to pass up an opportunity like this.

Lia and her mother were poor. And not in a charming "we-grow-our-own-vegetables-for-fun" kind of way. They were honest-to-goodness poor, complete with Salvation Army clothes and everything. And Lia was tired of it.

And so, like the stubborn wretch she was, Lia quit her job and made arrangements to leave the next week.

Lia wanted more than anything to be a writer – any kind of writer, it didn't matter – and the chance to write Susan Taylor's biography was something that could open massive doors for her.

Now, three thousand miles away from home, Lia looked around the beautiful middle-class neighbourhood, trying to drink in everything that had happened to her in the past two weeks. It was her first time in America, the first time anywhere outside of Barbados, for that matter. Her first time on a plane, even her first time in a taxi. This new surreal experience had engulfed Lia in an unexplainable and unimaginable way…it was just a lot.

The young woman had looked wide-eyed at everything that morning and tried to match her expectations – based on years of television watching – with reality.

"Excuse me…," the taxi driver alighted from the car and was now standing next to her. He jabbed his thumb over his shoulder. "The metre is still running and I've got to go."

She fumbled for a moment with the strange-looking bills she fished out of her pocket. At home, each monetary note was distinguishable by different colours. In America, they were all the same – a strange shade of pea green with lots of drawings on them. She paid the taxi driver who wasted no time in leaving.

Lia shuffled down the path toward the beautifully painted house clutching her carpetbag and a duffel bag filled with books. She raised her hand to knock but there was no need. The door swung open to reveal a plump, smiling, middle-aged lady wearing a pink blouse and a floral skirt.

Her eyes met Lia's and for a moment she regarded Lia in shock before a look of comprehension dawned on her face. She smiled again and leaned forward, grabbing the carpet bag in her left hand before reaching out to shake Lia's right hand with her plump one.

"Mornin'," she said cheerfully. Her Barbadian accent had lost only a bit of its island lilt, but there was no hiding where she was from. "You is Cordelia, right? So nice to meet you!" she exclaimed jovially.

Lia smiled warmly. "Yes, ma'am. But everyone calls me Lia."

The other lady's smile deepened, showcasing two glistening rows of straight white teeth. "I is Ancil; it is me who called. Come right in, dear."

Ancil ushered Lia down a pristine hallway, painted an elegant greyish-green that beautifully complimented the dark brown hardwood floors. Lia sniffed hungrily as she recognized the smell of chicken roti that wafted through the house. As she hustled along in Ancil's wake, the young woman looked in awe at the marvelous home, but was only able to take a quick glimpse at a sunlit living room painted in a lovely teal and an elegant dining room painted in a hue that she could only describe as "eggplant". She had never seen a more beautiful and tidy house in her life.

But the bright, effusive manner with which Ancil greeted her gave way to something entirely different as they reached the end of the hallway. There, she turned so abruptly that Lia almost bumped into her. The tone of her voice quickly went from chirpy air hostess to depressed mortician.

"Just one minute," she said in a low voice. Knocking lightly on the polished wooden door, she said softly and soberly, "Excuse me, Susan, but the young lady is here to see you."

"Good." came the muffled response.

Ancil looked at Lia before reaching for her small duffel bag. Lia smiled and said politely, "That's okay. I'll carry these with me."

"Oh, alright. I know you had a long flight so I gonna come back and see if you want some drinks and snacks after I put this bag in your room," Ancil said quietly as she turned to carry away the threadbare carpet bag.

"Thank you very…"

"What would happen…" the muffled voice asked, "if she came in here instead of jabbering out there with you?"

Ancil lowered her voice even further and placed a gentle hand on Lia's shoulder. "She a l'il rough 'round the edges, but she alright. You goin' see."

Lia hadn't even met Susan Taylor yet and she had already formed an unpleasant opinion about her. She looked askance at the door as the sound of the housekeeper's bare feet eased up the stairs to the second story. She wasn't sure she wanted to go in without an escort, yet she knew better than to do anything else that would increase the author's ire. She drew a deep breath and pushed open the door.

As soon as Lia entered the room, it was instantly clear to her that this was Susan's inner sanctum. Golden sunshine streamed through a wide picture window into the large room illuminating the light grey walls; a colour that merely set the stage to highlight the distinctive artifacts that harkened back to a historic Barbadian plantation house.

On one wall hung three large paintings – a group of field workers cutting sugar cane with sharp scythes and cutlasses; another with dramatic strokes and bright colours showed a pair of children playing marbles in a chattel village and the last was a marvelously realistic-looking rendition of waves breaking on the rugged East Coast of Barbados. Beneath the paintings, a charming set of polished mahogany chairs with latticed cane seats were next to a small table stacked with a collection of novels. A large bookcase filled with an eclectic mix of books stood next to the french doors that opened out to the expansive garden beyond it. On the other side of the room was a set of wall shelves filled with wooden figurines like cricketers posed with bat and ball, steel pan players and – odd, but looking like it was in its rightful place – a bottle of rum. The room was a sharp contrast to the contemporary style that pervaded the rest of the house.

And there, right in the middle of the room in a mahogany rocking chair holding a cup of ginger tea, sat the lady herself.

Lia was surprised. Light-skinned and long-limbed, Susan Taylor was remarkably unremarkable in many ways, her otherwise delicate features incalculably strengthened by her striking hazel eyes. It was easy to see why those eyes had been the catalyst for the less-than-flattering sobriquet. The power that reverberated from them was almost hypnotic. Lia wasn't sure what she expected, but somehow this waif of a woman clad in a beige cardigan wasn't it.

"Hello, Cordelia Davis," she said quietly, her eyes glued to Lia's.

Lia's inertia broke and she hurried forward, hand outstretched, intent on making a good first impression with Susan Taylor. "It's so nice to meet you, Miss Taylor. You can call me Lia."

"I don't shake hands," Susan said crisply. "That's how you catch things."

Taken aback by the prospect of giving Susan "things", Lia's hand fell back to her side and she smiled wanly. "That's fine, I understand; can't be too careful after all. Actually, I read in an online health journal…"

"I requested a biographer, not a fawning sycophant," interrupted Susan as she set down her teacup on the coffee table. "Now listen; if I want to know something, I'll ask you." She eyed Lia up and down, taking in her tall, lanky frame, the little freckles on her nose and her bright eyes. Susan huffed. "What did you say I could call you?"

The young woman pursed her lips uncomfortably. "Lia?" she replied, saying it like a question.

"Your mother gave you a perfectly good name. I have no idea why you would try to dismantle it. I'll continue to call you Cordelia. Now sit down." Susan jutted her chin to the chair on Lia's left.

Unnerved, Lia bit her lip and sat in the vintage mahogany chair. This is not going how I thought it would, she reflected worriedly as she busied herself unpacking a notebook and pencils from her duffel bag.

"What's your story?"

"Pardon me?"

Susan eyed Lia shrewdly. "I asked 'what's your story?' In other words, tell me about yourself."

"Oh...well I'm twenty-five years old and I recently finished a degree in journalism. I've been writing short stories for..."

"I know how to use the Internet, young lady, "Susan interjected. "You have all of that fluff on your Facebook page. Tell me about you."

Lia shifted in her chair. Susan Taylor was a crotchety, cantankerous old woman with bile running through her veins and it was all Lia could do to keep her nerves in check. The older woman picked up her teacup again and took a sip before she started talking. "I'm not sure why you assumed you would be given license to come here and pepper me with questions without preamble. I'm not entirely certain that you're fit for this undertaking as yet."

Lia took a deep breath, racked her brain and started again. "Well, what do you want to know?"

Susan huffed impatiently. "Did you have a happy childhood?"

Lia smiled. "Yes, I did. It was filled with lots of happy memories."

Susan scoffed and lifted an eyebrow skeptically, "Oh really? No embarrassing moments?"

Lia's face fell. The course of the conversation had veered sharply from "generic and harmless" to "discomforting and difficult."

She shook her head quickly. "Nothing really. I see everything in my life as a stepping stone, a chance to learn."

"Oh really? What did you learn when you were caught shoplifting? And exactly how did you use the stepping stone your mother provided when she lost her job because she had an affair with her boss' husband?"

Lia's face went blank. How did she know those things? Lia shot up from her chair, her body trembling. "You know what Miss Taylor? I left my job to come here. I fought with my mother to come here. I spent a quarter of my salary –

which I can't afford to spend on clothes – on this outfit because I wanted to make a good impression on you." She snatched up her belongings. "Short of weeping tears of blood, I don't know what it is you expected me to do, but I don't even want to know anymore."

A smirk lit Susan's face. "Finally, a little fire. You came in here pretending to be timid and weak; all I want is honesty. You expect me to share the most embarrassing, intimate details of my life with you and you come in here telling me lies? Start wrong and you'll end wrong."

Susan raised an eyebrow at Lia. "You seem to forget that Barbados is a very small island; everybody knows everything about everyone else. 'Yuh cuh' hide and buy land but yuh can't hide and work it' as the old saying goes." Susan said, slipping easily into Barbadian dialect.

"Is that why you chose me?" Lia asked, her defiance making her voice a little louder than necessary. "Because you figure that I've got dirty laundry?"

"I want somebody with a real-life to tell my story; somebody who might understand me properly. I sense that you'll do."

Shame wormed its way into Lia's stomach. Lia eyed Susan suspiciously, a sharp jolt of comprehension jarring her pride at the realization she had just made. "But why me? There are tons of other journalists; far more experienced and influential ones; what about someone from CNN or the BBC?"

"Bah." Susan dismissed the thought with a wave of her bony hand. "They have their biases about 'island' people... they'd never get it."

The older woman glared at Lia. "...and neither will the ones at home in the Caribbean. They too have their prejudices about me. No...," she said lazily as she sipped her tea again. "...you're nice and green and that suits me just fine. Sit back down."

Lia's cheeks burned as an internal battle waged within her. Her carefully planned speech about her writing trophies, her exhausting internships at local media houses and her zest for writing were all for naught. She thought fleetingly – very fleetingly – that she couldn't endure this woman for another minute, but then she snapped back to reality. The sound of her mother saying "I tell yuh so" screeched like nails on a chalkboard inside her head. Biting the inside of her lip, she sat back down, determined to see it through with the indomitable Susan Taylor. Barbados was "the rock" and Susan Taylor was obviously "the hard place". Never before had that adage seemed more apropos. Lia knew she was firmly entrenched between both of them.

Susan flashed yet another infuriating smirk at Lia. "That's settled. I'll tell you everything you want to know about me. The good, the bad and the real reason you're here: the scandal that rocked the Caribbean."

Chapter 2

1948 - 1955

I was born on the fifteenth of May, 1948 to Grace and Vincent Taylor in a village on the fringes of one of the largest plantations on the island. Back then, the island was very dependent on sugar production. Almost everyone lived close to a plantation of some sort, so there wasn't anything that stood out about my village other than the fact that it was large. Small quaint chattel houses with pitched gable roofs were clustered together a few kilometres away from the plantation house. Many of the houses – if painted – were wooden and coated in a pale chocolate brown or a putrid off-white. The village was tucked in on both sides by big green fields of fat sugar cane that were cut down to the nubs every year between May and June.

Every morning, lush green pastures would be dotted with black belly sheep, goats, and cows that grazed from sunrise until sunset. Their owners would stake them out on their way to the plantations to toil as labourers in the hot sun for deplorable pay in undesirable conditions. After school, children's laughter rang through the village as they gathered old tins, lost buttons and sticks to make whatever toys suited their fancy. Later, as the sun dipped low in the sky, men and women, backs bent from the strain of a day in the fields, would shutter their prized livestock inside stone pens. My village was an idyllic little place, really; you could leave your windows staring open and the door unlocked. Not like today;

you can't even have an idea without somebody trying to steal it.

Both of my parents were of mixed descent, even though my father's grey eyes and light brown skin made him seem a little more exotic than my mother did with her dark brown eyes and skin. I was the only girl, their fourth and last child even though they were both still relatively young. By the time I was born, my father was in his thirties and my mother in her late twenties. Both of my parents worked in the fields primarily because neither of them had gone to school past the age of twelve. My father cut sugar cane on the plantations and my mother dug potatoes and other crops. I remember going with them sometimes and it was something that I really liked, even though they detested it. The thought of one centipede bite or a scythe that went flying was enough to give them the nerves. If the wound didn't kill you, the infection probably would. We lost one of our neighbours to a rusty scythe when I was a child so I never had to look far for a reminder of what lockjaw could do. But I was young and didn't think it would happen to me; I loved the things you could find in the fields. I once found five cents in the cane rows, enough to buy something worthwhile during the fifties. In my childish wisdom, I spent it on sticky sugar cakes and tamarind balls for me and my brother. Other than that, I enjoyed spending my evenings making kites out of cane trash after school or playing marbles with my brother in the cart road in front of the house.

My family wasn't burdened with some of the trappings of poverty as many other Barbadians were at the time. My parents went to work every day and they ensured that their children had the best that life could afford them. We had shoes to wear every day, which was impressive when you consider that so many of the other children in the village went barefoot, even to school and church. We never lacked anything except my father's attention; mostly because when

Daddy wasn't working, he was gambling. It's only now – after going through life and seeing the many pitfalls with which it is marked – that I can truly appreciate that sometimes only my father's farts propelled him forward.

But in all fairness to my father, his father had left Barbados in 1912 to work on the Panama Canal and, like many of the other West Indians before him, he died. My father was still a child at the time and his mother found it hard to make ends meet while raising eight children on her own. I always believed that's one of the reasons my father gambled. He was lucky so it was a quick way to make money and it gave us a better way of life. And - I suspect - it also fed his desire for adventure.

My mother treated my father's gambling like an itchy rash on her backside; she never acknowledged it, but neither did she encourage it. She was a church-going woman and we knew she didn't like it; she lied mostly to herself to make herself feel better. She tried to be satisfied that at least he came home with the fruits of his luck rather than squander them on other vices like drinking or whoring. That was the good thing about my father; he picked his struggle early in life and battled that ship to shore.

But, as fate is wont to do, it's always the foundation that is laid that sets the template for your life. You'll see in due course how my father's gambling played a major role in my life.

My father had to move around with his gambling. As you can imagine, people didn't like playing against someone that won as much as he did. Eventually, he developed a reputation as a card reader and became a bit of a pariah in some circles. But he was jovial and popular and those attributes helped him keep his ear to the ground to find out where some sort of action was happening because gambling kept him "loose" as he liked to say.

In 1955, my father was invited by a friend to a house on the outskirts of Bridgetown where the players were known to have deep pockets. Back then, the bus system wasn't very extensive; sometimes you had to walk for hours to get to some places. That Saturday evening, as twilight came to a close, my father hurried up a long, dusty cart-road toward a great house in the south of the island. Nestled in the centre of a plantation that had gone to seed, the slightly unkempt property awakened something in my father. He said later that his very fingers tingled as he walked down that rocky lane and he instinctively knew that the night was going to be big.

It was just like many other great houses of the time. It was a large, square two-story home, built from big blocks of stacked limestone. It had a massive verandah with long, vertical shutters propped up on sticks like big, sleepy white eyelids. Hooded windows lined the façade of the second story of the building which was capped with two sloped hip roofs. The weather-beaten walls were flecked with woeful flakes of chipped paint. It was brimming with historical charm, with one notable update: electricity.

Crickets chirped sleepily in the croton bushes as my father made his way up to the big burnished front doors, his lean body casting long shadows on the moonlit verandah as he lifted the knocker.

"Vincent?" said a familiar voice.

The sound of footsteps intensified until the heavy mahogany door swung open revealing a smiling Norman Bailey, the friend who had invited him to gamble that night. Norman beckoned my father into the dimly lit entry hall. The great house reeked of old money and prestige. Modern fixtures cast flickering golden light on thick layers of dust that covered the artfully crafted mahogany bannister leading to the second floor. In a large room to the right, tall mounds of living room furniture hid beneath bedsheets and intricate seashell artwork hung on the walls. It was clear that there hadn't been a full-time inhabitant for many years. My father thought that it was a shame that someone would choose not to live in such a nice house that had electricity. He thought that he would rather live there instead of fumbling with smutty old kerosene lamps every night.

Norman pointed over his shoulder toward the dining room, indicating that was where they were headed. Tall, light brown and perpetually cheerful, Norman was my father's best, and most unlikely, friend. The only thing they had in common was their luck. Norman was very laid back and seemed to always have pure intentions. The same couldn't be said for my father.

Norman had been born into a successful merchant family, which at the time meant a social standing akin to that of a doctor or lawyer. His family owned a handful of grocery stores and a butcher shop and, like many shopkeepers, he had grown accustomed to having friends in high and sometimes questionably low places.

A flood of light emanated from the formal dining room that sat to the left of the entry hall. Jubilant voices chatted amiably and glasses clinked. Norman glanced over his shoulder anxiously, before lowering his voice and leaning towards Vincent. "Listen, I din' tell yuh who we playing because I din' want yuh to bring that leech Festus Broome wid yuh. He don' know how to behave properly 'round certain people."

Vincent cocked an eyebrow at him. "Who is dese 'certain people'?" It was more than abundantly clear that Norman was on pins and needles to reveal the identity of their hosts that night, and despite his intrigue, Vincent didn't want to appear overeager.

"James Hackett."

"You mean de same fella that pushing fuh Independence?"

Norman nodded excitedly. "Yes...dat fella. Dese boys got a lot uh money and dem in a real good mood tonight, so mind yuh Ps and Qs."

Vincent shrugged casually, feigning indifference as he bent over to remove his worn brown loafers. He placed them neatly next to the row of shiny black leather wingtips and brogues that lined the wall. He had always wanted a pair of those brogues. For a long moment, those shoes mesmerized him; pockets of light danced on the soft leather, highlighting the intricate stitching and perforations that adorned those shoes. Something clicked inside my father that night. I don't think anyone knew what it was, but the sight of those shoes awakened a creature in him that even he didn't know was there. He stood up, smiling quietly to himself before he turned to follow Norman.

In the dining room, four well-dressed men sat around the large oval mahogany table, their good nature fueled by full glasses of twelve-year-old rum. Norman smiled and gestured toward the newcomer. "Dis is de fella I tell wunna 'bout. Vincent Taylor, dat is Elton Guthrie..."
Pudgy and pleasant, Elton Guthrie grinned as he reached over the table to shake hands.
"...Bruce Oxley..."
A Caucasian man with a shiny bald patch and startling green eyes rose from his chair and greeted Vincent.
"...Winslow Vaughan..."
Dark-skinned, young and handsome, Winslow turned and shook hands cordially.
"...and James Hackett."
Dark brown with patrician features and natural charisma, James Hackett instantly put Vincent at ease with his perfect handshake. Warm but not too warm, firm enough that it belied strength but not aggression, James was the kind of man who was born to be a politician. James adjusted his

trendy browline glasses before gesturing towards the antique sideboard behind him. "Want something to drink?"

"Yeah. Gimme whatever wunna drinking," Vincent nodded, hitching up his brown slacks higher onto his waist. He watched as James fixed him a generous helping of mahogany-hued rum that moved like liquid fire over the large chunk of ice in the crystal glass. He was suddenly regretting that he hadn't worn the clothes he usually reserved for church; he hitched up his pants to hide the hole in his shirt.

Vincent eased himself into the mahogany chair next to James' empty seat, sipping his rum slowly as he surveyed the room. Almost unwilling to put all of his weight on the chair lest he break it, Vincent felt a little out of his element with this crowd. It didn't help that an unexpressed fervor, a level of unparalleled zeal zinged through the air like electricity.

All of the other men were clearly well off, a fact that did little to quell Vincent's sudden unease. He had thought he was able to fit in practically anywhere, but he was a bit unsettled about this particular crowd. He wasn't sure if it was the social differences or the fact that he was new to the group, but he felt a nervousness that he hadn't known since he had courted his wife. He was popular around Barbados, well known for his stick-fighting abilities as well as his knack for gambling, so he certainly wasn't a man that usually lacked in confidence.

Generic small talk filled the room as the men spoke about cars and other innocuous topics. Only Vincent and Winslow Vaughan remained silent. Winslow sat quietly, shuffling the cards repeatedly, indifferent to all of the babble around him, while Vincent slowly sipped his rum and tried to take in everything.

There were many things Vincent enjoyed about playing cards, not the least of which was the money he was able to get out of it. No, it was more than that for Vincent. He was a hunter in the keenest sense of the word. He enjoyed the chase and the stalking that came along with it. He liked to watch people.

In a few moments, the game got underway and in just three hands, (all of which he took great pains to lose) Vincent was able to tell who was who around the table. He had played with Norman before and knew that Norman wouldn't have come along unless he felt he had something to gain by coming. With Norman though, gains weren't only measured by dollars and cents. Sometimes it was just a matter of circumstance, simply because Norman was the kind of fellow who realized that time and people were more worthy investments than money. It was clear to Vincent that even if Norman didn't win a red cent at this table that he felt the relationships worthy enough to give up a few dollars to secure them.

Elton Guthrie was an easy pushover, obviously there for the drinks and the company. He had played against these men before and still wasn't able to discern when they were bluffing. Vincent wondered if the other men kept him around because he was affable and easy to control.

Bruce Oxley was a shrewd character. He couldn't be easily bluffed but was a consistent victim of his own bad judgment when it came to placing his bets. When it all boiled down, he was the type of fellow who would always break-even which was a rare thing in a game such as poker where there was usually a clear divide between the winners and losers.

James Hackett, on the other hand, was a formidable opponent. He was the kind of fellow who would take all of your money and somehow manage to make you feel good about it. He made clever quips and poured the drinks, gently coaxing the evening along so it moved as smoothly as a door on a well-greased hinge. James was an adept player too. He was cautious but willing to take some risks, to the point that it was very hard to get a handle on his pattern. But Vincent liked that. James was a predator, not a scavenger.

Winslow was…unique. If there was a diagram explaining how to be a model poker player, Winslow Vaughan would be the pinup boy. He spoke very little, choosing instead to focus on his chain-smoking, displaying neither elation nor disappointment when it came to winning or losing, never allowing anything to distract him. Vincent believed Winslow's style to be almost identical to his, save for one thing: the purpose. Vincent played because he respected and appreciated the game. He found it fun and saw it as a hobby. Despite Winslow's feigned indifference, however, it was clear that he took everything about it personally. Winslow saw the game as something else to conquer. Vincent wasn't sure if that was because Winslow was a closeted control freak or particularly focused that night, but he would have hedged his bets on the former.

As the night wore on and the drinks soaked in, the men's interests shifted gears a bit and the conversation picked back up right where it left off before Vincent's arrival. The betting had remained relatively conservative until then, but Vincent could smell a change in the wind. He had already doubled the money he had brought and he could practically feel those supple leather brogues caressing his feet already.

Elton burped and rubbed his plump stomach. "Last hand, fellas. I gotta get home soon. So James, when you goin' hand in de resignation?" he asked in a typically twangy Barbadian accent.

"Tomorrow morning, before de cat could' lick he ear," James grinned.

Everyone around the table except Winslow and Vincent grinned broadly in return.

James studied his cards intently as a hazy cloud from Winslow's cigarette drifted past him. "Got some meetings lined up fuh tomorrow wit' de mayor and some other people.

Gotta get dese people on board before I head up tuh England to talk about getting Independence sorted out." He tossed two cards face down on the highly polished mahogany table and Winslow furnished him with two new cards.

Vincent's ears pricked up. James Hackett was leaving the Barbados Political Party? This was big news indeed. But if he was resigning, why would he still be going to England on an Independence mission. Unless...

"So you already picked a name for the new party?" asked Bruce, his green eyes locked on James.

"Winslow is who pick out de name...Democratic Progressive Party."

"I like it, James," mused Bruce, casting an eye toward Winslow.

So that explained why they were in a good mood. And it probably explained why the rest of them were all here. It made sense to book your seat on the gravy train early. Vincent wondered how he could make his reservation. But he didn't have to wonder for very long.

"So Vincent," said James as he studied his cards. "Norman says that you've played cards all over the island."

"Yeah... I does get around." Vincent replied easily, shrugging his shoulders.

"Well, I need a man like you that knows people in a lot of places to help get the word around about the new party."

"Oh?" said Vincent easily as he took a sip of his drink while he stared at his cards. He felt everyone's eyes on him, but he didn't plan to fall into their trap that easily. This had been forethought, plain and simple. They obviously needed a grassroots man to advance their cause. Well, that would be easy enough, but Vincent felt it would only be fair for them to advance his cause as well.

He shrugged again.

James continued, "For now, I'll need someone to do some community work on the weekends. You know:

spreading the word and such. The pay would be the same as what you make for the whole week at the plantation, of course."

Vincent nodded slowly before he looked up and met James' eyes. "Yes, that sounds doable." Bruce and James grinned. Elton clapped him on the back jovially.

It was Vincent's turn to play. He had required only one card to complete his queen-high straight and he had gotten it. He had won the last few hands and was intent on going home victorious that night. He had spent enough time quietly observing the other's playing habits and now it was time to turn the screws and have some fun.

He made a hefty bet and everyone folded except Winslow. Winslow hadn't taken any new cards at all and Vincent knew that the odds of him having started with a set of cards that would beat his straight were so slim they could hide behind a matchstick.

Winslow looked at the betting stack lazily, almost indifferently, before matching Vincent's bet, making only an incremental raise. Never one to walk away from a sure thing, Vincent pressed his advantage by doubling Winslow's bet, doing all he could to keep a smug grin off his face. Without missing a beat, Winslow matched it, obviously intent on putting an end to the charade. By Vincent's calculation, there was three weeks' worth of his wages to be won and he was practically giddy with anticipation. Winslow, on the other hand, remained unreadable, his eyes never wavering from the cards in his hand.

By that time the rest of the group had congregated next to the antique sideboard, pouring more rum and watching to see how the hands would go down.

"Queen high straight," my father exclaimed, laying down his cards with a broad flourish.

"That's nice," replied Winslow languidly. He too laid down his hand, spreading five cards of the same suite carefully on the table's polished surface. "But it seems I've flushed you out."

It was true. His flush had trumped Vincent's straight. Vincent wasn't a card reader; he was a people watcher and he used his keen observations to determine what kind of players people were. Finally, Vincent knew what he was up against with Winslow. Controlling and irascible, he probably hid his extreme motions behind thinly veiled indifference.

Vincent hung his head. His only consolation was that the loss of a new pair of brogues meant he had gained a place in the little gang.

Chapter 3

May 20th, 2015.

"Wha' she like?" Lia's mother asked.

"She's nice. I'm learning a lot from her."

"Really? Hmmm… well….. she didn't have a very good reputation here, yuh know. But some people mellow with age."

"Yeah… it's true."

"What did she tell you about…"

Lia cut off her mother. "I can't talk long though, Mummy. I don't want to run up her phone bill and it's nice of her to let me call in the first place. Plus I had a long day and I'm really tired."

"Alright, sweetie. Have a good night and send me an e-mail if you can."

"Bye-bye, Mummy."

Lia hung up the phone and reached over to turn off the desk lamp next to her bed with a heavy sigh. She didn't like the feeling of shame that crept through her chest. It was cold and uncomfortable.

Every conversation they'd had since Lia had decided to leave the island had ended in an argument. Despite having no friends in the country and feeling like she would never grow very close to Susan, Lia felt it would be better to face loneliness than negativity.

She closed her eyes and leaned back on the crisp new sheets that covered the bed in the guest suite and considered how unhappy she was. Susan Taylor was a litany of bad adjectives like 'contemptible' and 'ill-tempered'. Lia couldn't even think of decent euphemisms to describe the woman. Before they had retired for the night, Susan had asked Lia about her sex life, something that horrified Lia to no end. Having learned her lesson earlier in the evening, Lia had given a modified version of the truth and then escaped upstairs before Susan could pry further.

Lia was a great believer in the power of positive thinking and as she lay there, drowning in her desire for optimism, she endeavored to have a better attitude toward Susan the next day. "This is a good opportunity. This is a good opportunity. This is a good opportunity." Lia whispered to herself over and over in the dark.

The sound of muffled footfall broke Lia's quiet murmurings. She instantly stopped chanting and listened to the sluggish shuffle of feet on the carpet runner that ran the length of the upstairs hallway.

Susan.

The shuffling grew closer. And closer.

Then it stopped.

Lia lay still, afraid to even blink, lest she was overheard.

"Goodnight, Cordelia."

Lia held her breath, afraid Susan might hear the rapid thudding of her heartbeat. She didn't want to have to endure any more of Susan's questions.

Silence.

And then...

"Either you ain't got no good manners or you pretending to sleep. Which one is it?"

Embarrassed, Lia shook her head and exhaled loudly. "Sorry, Miss Taylor. Have a good night."

"Good," came the smug reply from the other side of the door.

Susan resumed her steady shuffling to her room and Lia resumed her chanting. "This is a great opportunity. This is a great opportunity. This is a great opportunity."

Chapter 4

1955

Growing up in the 1950s in Barbados was a unique experience, to say the least. By today's standards, almost everyone on the island lived in poverty – no indoor plumbing or electricity, no refrigerators or any real toys to speak of. And yet, no-one went hungry, everyone was happy and the rate of suicide was practically non-existent. Now we have all of the modern conveniences and technology you could imagine, and still, the human race has never been more miserable. It just goes to show that poverty puts your life into proper perspective.

Our days were repetitive to the point of insanity back then. Every day at the crack of dawn, the village would start to stir as though pulled by an invisible string. The scent of boiling oats, linseed, saga, and barley sweetened with bay leaves and brown cane sugar would waft through the air. We rose en masse to feed the pigs, sheep, and cows that shared the small patches of tenantry land that we lived on. Every child had their little garden plot to weed, zealously tending small crops of carrots, peas, and okras that had been coaxed into yielding by using copious amounts of sheep manure.

Many of us then walked almost a kilometre with our mothers to the standpipe to draw water before rushing off to school. Others would collect the eggs from the hens, a task that I wasn't particularly fond of. I would always coerce my brother, John, into doing it for me, a task that wasn't that difficult. He didn't even have the decency to pretend not to like it. All of the prepubescent boys in the area liked it.

You see, part of collecting the eggs sometimes meant sticking a finger into the hen to see if they were 'egg-bound'. That meant that the eggs were stuck inside them and you had to move your finger back and forth inside that bird to get the egg to come out, otherwise it could kill them. Initially, I was disturbed by how long John's inspections took. But eventually, I grew to realize that his indecent examination was preferable to me trying to do it quickly. For some reason, I couldn't stand the feeling of those soft, tight, squishy muscles on my hands even for a second – I felt like I was violating those birds. But John – and all the other village boys – reveled in it. When I reached puberty though, I had a much better idea of what made the chickens so appealing.

By the time the chores were finished, it was time to get a shower and run off to school. Country schools in those times were these boxy buildings surrounded by little fields that never grew grass until the summer months when the little feet that trampled them were absent.

We learned the three Rs - reading, writing and 'rithmetic. The teacher would pace between the desks, making us recite our tables or grammatical rules. We would sit straight as arrows, lest the teacher rap us across our knuckles for slouching, and repeat our lessons like little robots. We wrote neatly on our slates because we didn't have many books at the time. We used to be proud to show our teacher what we learned. We didn't do it for stars or special privileges. We did it because we knew it represented opportunity and a way to escape the plantocracy. Not to mention the fact that your parents would pour some lashes in your ass if they felt you were wasting the two dollars they paid for your education every term.

Sometimes, at noon you walked back home for lunch – the School Meals Service came into being later (you got lunch for a whole week for literally a few cents) – and then back to school to finish off the day. That's if you wanted something hot and fresh and had the luxury of having someone at home to cook for you. Otherwise, you stayed at school and ate the food that the Barbadian heat had warmed for hours in your lunch-tin. Rest assured it would be covered with a layer of sweat so thick that you could wash your hands with it.

Perhaps the only variation to the days came during those lunch hours. That was when the real action happened. Many a friendship – and rivalry – was made during that time. There was a thriving black market for snacks at school and it was during these times that you could get a full measure of a child's social status and their interpretation of it.

Same-sex schools were the norm back then, but my brother's school was only a stone's throw away from my school. In fact, we shared the same schoolyard to play in so we still saw each other during breaks. Norman Bailey's boy, Kenneth, was in my brother's class and was always the one with the most coveted snacks. As a shop keeper's son, he had his pick of expensive treats to eat for himself that many of us would have had to share with our entire family. He didn't suffer the indignity of things like kerosene lamps or sticking his fingers up a chicken's backside. But Kenneth took his wealth in stride; to his credit, he was always willing to trade. To his discredit, he took pleasure in carrying out barters where he always came out on top. He was the only one who made better trades than I did.

Somehow he could take to school a single candy apple and return home with a bag of marbles, a spinning top, and a homemade cricket bat. Perhaps, he liked those little knick-knacks because he spent so much of his spare time measuring out flour and rice in his father's shop. And then there were others for whom trading was almost a contact sport.

Joan Mayers' father was a farmer and a drunken one at that. Many of us had homemade snacks, but Joan's snacks were always far and few between in terms of frequency. Plus, the uniforms Joan wore were always full of little rips and tears that came from shimmying up fruit trees to get the snacks that she brought to school. Joan spent many a lunchtime without a meal. Sometimes the other children would give her a bit of this or that depending on who she hadn't pissed off that day. She didn't take the "never bite the hand that feeds you" adage too seriously. It was often said that her mother did special favours for men to make ends meet since her father was such a louse but, admittedly, the veracity of those statements was never proven. But whenever in this world did we need the truth to continue to spread gossip? Curiously though, every new round of gossip always coincided with Joan having a proper lunch to eat. Poverty and those rumours put a humongous bee in Joan's bonnet and she became an unpleasant child that I formed a long-standing rivalry with. But not through any fault of my own.

I was the palest person at school and these hazel eyes that seem to waver in colour based on my mood or the ambient temperature didn't help. Throw in my curly hair and I hit the trifecta. That was all you needed to be deemed good looking back then. I'll be honest with you; I felt that my nose was too broad and my limbs were too long, but none of that mattered. There was a little rhyme that many of us grew up hearing and, sadly, it formed the basis for how many Barbadians perceived each other.

"If yuh white, yuh alright.
If yuh brown, stick around.
If yuh black, stand back."

Joan fell squarely into the 'stand back' category. I felt that she was actually a very pretty girl, even prettier than me.

She had beautiful smooth ebony skin, full lips that looked like they were hand-crafted by an artisan and wide brown eyes that added more piquancy to her already striking looks. Her only bad feature was her perpetual glower. She was at her most breathtaking when she smiled, a marvel that I witnessed a handful of times (usually only after she had gotten someone in trouble with the lies she told).

My brother John said that Joan was jealous of me because of my features and because her dresses had holes and mine didn't. I believed him. He was my older brother after all and Joan had a nasty habit of always trying to get me into trouble.

Initially, Joan's resentment for me simmered quietly like a pot of linseed on a cool night. She'd stick out her foot and trip me up if I ran past her or hit me with a wad of paper when I wasn't looking. Nothing too overt, but I knew that the perfect opportunity was the only thing holding her back.

One sticky day in May 1955 changed all of that. It was my birthday too so it was a bit of a pain for it to be so unpleasant. It was one of those relentlessly hot afternoons that turned heat into a hazy, shimmery cloak that covered everything in sight. The heat caused the wind to retreat and leaves in the trees stood still. Flies buzzed by so lazily that you could have mistaken them for small hummingbirds. The smell of cheese that had melted and turned greasy wafted from at least five lunch tins and hung in the air like an oily cloud. The teacher talked slower than usual and the children blinked in slow motion. Very few things could have dragged us out of that heated stupor – except for the thing that had lain in Kenneth's lunch box all morning.

At break-time, word spread like cane fire between the two schools that Kenneth brought to school a cold Coca Cola that day. My entire class lurched into a frenzy of excitement. Being as savvy as he was, Kenneth saw his opportunity and decided to up the ante: he spread the word that he was only willing to share half of his coke with two people. Some of us had never even tasted Coca Cola. The tension was palpable that day. Not even on the New York Stock Exchange had there ever been such fervid anticipation about the day's trades. Practically every boy and girl was eagerly awaiting Kenneth's judgment.

He certainly took his time packing away his slate and chalk that day. He took particular pains to ensure that each page of his Nelson's West Indian Reader was free of creased corners before he lazily put it away. Meanwhile, the rest of us chattered ad nauseam in the schoolyard, comparing our trades and even willing to collaborate in an effort to share the spoils of this one sip of Coca Cola.

But we all figured we knew who would get half of the Coca Cola that day. It was well known that the only thing Kenneth loved more than popcorn was a tamarind ball and it just so happened that Joan Mayers had both of those snacks that day. For some inexplicable reason, fortune had smiled on her that day and provided her with two worthy snacks to trade. She sat smugly under the shade of the bonafice tree practically brimming with confidence that she would be victorious. I, on the other hand, felt I didn't have a chance with my crumbling biscuits and wilted cheese. I couldn't even team up with John unless Kenneth fancied two sets of crumbling crackers and wilted cheese.

A few moments later, Kenneth sauntered out of the classroom and straight into the waiting crowd of potential traders. My brother, John, hustled past him on the school steps, straight past the melee, straightening his khaki shirt as he went. He winked at me before he leaned over and said, "You feel like drinking some Coca Cola, Susie?"

"Seriously?!"

John grinned broadly in reply.

"Kenneth really say that he woul' take all of de biscuits and cheese fuh some of de soft drink?"

"You crazy? Even I don' wanna eat that greasy cheese."

Confounded, I looked over his shoulder towards the mob that surrounded Kenneth.

"Then why would he share the drink with us?"

"Boys will be boys, Susie."

Even more confused, I asked, "What does that mean?"

"That there are some things a boy wants even more than popcorn and tamarind balls."

Moments later he emerged – Coca Cola still intact – walked straight past Joan Mayers (she was so angry that she turned purple) and over to us.

He cracked open that Coca Cola and each of us took an achingly sweet sip from the bottle before he told John, "Remind me again wha' time you say to come and help you collect the eggs."

John winked at me again. "Happy birthday, Susie."

That was my first lesson in understanding the way boys' minds work. What girls found to be revolting and unpleasant, boys found good enough to trade for a Coca Cola.

Chapter 5

May 21st, 2015

Lia's conversations with her mother were becoming more and more tiresome.

"How much longer you got tuh stay there?"

"Maybe two more months or so; I'm supposed to meet with her editor and her agent in the next few weeks so I want to do that before I go."

Silence.

Even over the phone, Lia could tell that her mother was pursing her lips. Lia's mother could tell that Lia was rolling her eyes in response.

"You know Lia, I really don't know what you think going tuh come uh this. You give up a good job and now have tuh come back here an' start all over again. It ain't like you gine write a best-selling novel. Lightning don't strike twice in the same place."

Lia shook her head disgustedly. "I'm grown up now and I'm tired of just getting by. What's wrong with me trying? And what's wrong with you supporting me?"

"Lia, I just saying…"

"Stop. Just stop saying. You always do this. This is just like the full scholarship to the college in Kansas that you made me give up just because you didn't think I'd be able to handle the cold."

Lia's mother exhaled impatiently. "Lia, I only want you tuh make good choices an' not run 'round behind people like Susan Taylor. You think you can hitch you cart to she horse?

The woman can't even come back to her own country because..."

"Because she spoke up! That's the problem with too many people. They're too passive and they don't like change."

"Lia Davis, I tired telling you that there is more to life than doing things just for the sake of doing them." She heaved a sigh and when she spoke again her tone was calm but distant. "For right now, do what you want to do. I goin' catch the bus to get to the hotel for the late shift, so I gotta go. Take care, sweetie."

Before Lia could respond, her mother hung up the phone. The dim light of the single bedside lamp illuminated the left of her pretty face, casting a golden light on one side, leaving the other in darkness. The dial tone singing in her ears, Lia sat motionless for a moment before a single tear escaped the corner of her eye.

Slowly, she hung up the phone and curled herself into a ball on the crumpled bedsheets.

And, just outside her door, an aged pair of feet quietly shuffled away.

Chapter 6

1955

I don't know if you know this, but many of the political parties in the Caribbean were borne out of unions that championed worker's rights. The majority of the islands at the time were still under British rule, and as such, despite the assertions of freedom and adult suffrage that were touted, many Barbadians still felt as though they were living in a colonialist state. Low wages, appalling working conditions, nonexistent labour laws and a lack of representation by Barbadians of African descent were the catalysts for the 1937 riots that started the labour movement on the island.

So it was a natural progression for the people who fought for the country's rights to assume the roles of heir apparent during the democratic shift that occurred in the 1950s and 1960s. The time was ripe for change.

Around that same time, my father had already infiltrated the motley crew that gathered once every other week at the old great house.

James had indeed gone ahead and started gathering support for a splintered political faction. He had grown tired of the other party's laid back approach and didn't feel that it was worth his effort to waste any more time with them. He gathered the most tenacious members and outspoken public detractors under his wing. Perhaps it was ambition or a general concern for his fellow Barbadians, but whatever it was, James showed that he was a motivated and generous man. You could tell that he had great plans for the island. He wanted to make education and public health services free – radical ideas that were practically unheard of, but would certainly cement his place in history if he managed to get it done. Education and health care were two major dents in the pockets of the underprivileged at the time and James had intentions of bridging the gap between the rich and poor on the island. He believed that was the only way the black Barbadian populace would ever be free. Many of us agreed.

He spoke to my father frequently about these things as time went on because they spent so much time together. Sometimes my father helped him with his political work but in general, he became James' Man Friday. My father washed his car, chauffeured James to meetings on weekends and ran errands for him. James was a man of his word – in exchange for helping him out, he gave my father a hefty salary that allowed us to live more comfortably than we did before. My father even talked about buying the land we lived on, things were so good. The majority of the property in Barbados was owned by white people who held on to it with an iron fist. Back then, everyone lived on what they called tenantry land – land that you paid rent for every month or year. That's how chattel houses had come about in the first place. All of the houses could be easily dismantled by separating them into four walls and a roof. The prospect of building a home with an actual foundation was giddying.

My parents were practically beside themselves with excitement at the prospect. Freedom was within their grasp.

Each of the men present at the first poker game now had a place in the little group: James, Winslow, Bruce, Elton, Norman and of course, my father, Vincent. There were others as well, but those were the men I heard the most about. James, Winslow, and Elton were members of the party but Norman and Bruce both had business concerns; Bruce owned a large sugar plantation and Norman had his shops. Neither of them wanted to ostracize their customers. Plus, Bruce was white. No-one felt it was a good idea to have him too visibly involved in a cause that championed getting away from under the thumbs of other white people.

And so, as time went on, my father helped them reach out to the island's populace. Elections were due within the next year and, despite their differences, they shared a common goal: to ensure victory and install James as the premier in 1956.

Each of them possessed disparate personalities that seemed to have no earthly business being together: Elton was easy going and affable; Bruce was blunt and wise; Winslow was quiet and brooding and James was the glue that held them all together. James was especially useful in keeping the peace between Winslow and Bruce. The metronome to their little orchestra, James had a way of guiding everyone along beautifully that never ceased to astound my father. He was enthralled by how easily James managed to quell the tension that often arose between them. Bruce once told Winslow that he was a "mongoose in a chicken coop" and they had almost come to blows over it. James had easily deflected the argument by insisting that Winslow come along with him the next day to meet some officials for discussions which he "wanted some help with". It had been enough to calm Winslow down and in that fashion James kept watch over his little group when they socialized.

And so, the next day Vincent went with James and Winslow to meet the vestry. It was a Saturday morning and I remember getting anxious when I saw my father dressed in his church clothes. My mother had starched them until you could cut cheese with the seams. I panicked, thinking I was going to be left at home while everyone went to church. I raced around the house looking for my church dress. Daddy laughed when he realized that I thought it was Sunday and told me he was going to a meeting.

That meeting turned out to be a pivotal moment in the history of the political movement in Barbados. My father came home beaming: the Democratic Progressive Party was now officially registered and would indeed be contesting the 1956 general elections. James had declared Winslow as his second in command, a fact that Bruce groused about, but the others tried to brush off in the spirit of celebration the bigger picture. I'm sure there was a celebration in every party member's home that night. James had sent a bottle of sweet cider for our family and we danced and laughed all night long.

The next day, the men gathered to celebrate at the great house, which meant that cards and drinks were in heavy rotation. That's just how they chose to relate in general though.

Occasionally they would gamble, but mostly they sat around and talked about practically everything. My father lived for those times; he finally felt he was among his contemporaries and in some ways he became a better man for it. He stopped gambling in unsavory places and when he wasn't with James and the others, he came home.

I was only seven years old at the time, but my mother always commented that he came into his own around that time. She said that Daddy felt that he had arrived and his ambitions were finally going to be realized. She never found out what his ambitions were though; she went to her grave suspecting that he never found out either.

I believe my mother also had her ambitions which were never realized for many reasons: marriage, children… never mind being black and poor during the 1950s. She was sharp as a tack, my mother, quick to catch on to anything and very good with numbers and reading. Many of the more progressive moves our family made came about through her recommendations where she often had to take my father 'through the back door' as she often put it. He was the type of man who had to hear gentle roundabout suggestions often before he finally surmised that the entire thing was his idea before putting anything into action. My mother would just nod, exhale a long breath and go back to peeling whatever was in her hand when he did.

I often suspected, even though she was good at hiding it, that she resented having to "take her place in the home" while my father ran rampant. That fact caused some friction between them.

My mother proposed that it may be a good idea to start saving some of the extra money my father was making towards my secondary education. Up to that point, many girls weren't educated past the age of eleven. My father immediately countered that school was expensive and he'd rather put John through the best secondary school his money could afford at the time. To put it bluntly, my father would rather light cigarettes with his money than fritter it away on a girl's education. As much as I looked like him physically, I was all of my mother when it came to personality and behaviour: she was willing to keep the peace for a while, but she would fight to the death for anything she believed in. I started hearing the same argument over and over again.

"But she's a bright girl."

"She's a girl."

"So?"

"Wha' she going do with education? De most that going come of it is being a school teacher and with the connections I got, she could get a teaching job easy so."

"You connections? We ain't got the next ten years put way in we pocket, Vincent. Susie is only seven and you ain't know how this politics thing going work out."

My father would huff impatiently. "So you saying I is a fool? I is man and I say that de little girl don't need no lot of schooling. Just relax yourself and stop doubting my plan."

"You ain't got no plan."

The argument would spiral out of control from there. Eventually, my mother stopped bringing it up. And if I knew Gracie Taylor as well as I knew I did, it was because she had a plan and she wasn't wasting her time talking to my father anymore. So on the outside, my father's life changed. He got a new job and a gang of new friends. My family ate meat twice a week instead of once a week but otherwise, the change for the rest of us was minimal.

Every day was the same. Even the conversations lacked any variation.

"Susie!"

"Yes, Mummy?"

"You give the sheep water?"

"Yes, please."

"You and John get the chicken eggs?"

"Yes, please."

"Good. Tell your brother to stop eating the sweet biscuits and the two of you get ready for school."

I blame John for that last part mostly. He was too predictable.

Without modern conveniences like supermarkets and fast food, your life was spent in the vicious cycle of surviving. Half the day was spent working to grow or buy food, a quarter of your time went toward preparing every meal from scratch and the rest of the day went towards eating and sleeping. In those days, fast food meant bread and that yellow tallowy butter that smelled like hot grease and tasted like bat guano.

I spent the majority of my time with the youngest of my brothers, John. We were fairly close in age (him being eighteen months older than I was). My two older twin brothers Samuel and Eli were considerably older than us (while we played, both of them apprenticed as carpenters, working long hours and we hardly ever saw them). Most evenings after school we spent hours playing marbles in the village cart road until it grew dark. A neighbour would watch us until my mother came home from the fields. Dressed in a long cotton dress and garden boots, she would amble up the lane shortly before sunset toting a sack of grain or ground provisions on the crown of her head to cook for our dinner. She was a strong woman, my mother, a good match for my father in many ways. As a child, I was fascinated by how easily she and the other women could carry such heavy loads on their heads like massive crowns, their backs and necks holding strain and never once bowing under the pressure, no matter how great the distance they traveled with that weight on their heads. Some of the other women cracked open a tin of corn beefed and served it up with Eclipse biscuits after a long day.

But my mother gave no quarter to such things. No matter how tired she was, every day she came home and cooked something for us to eat. And thankfully, my parents' hard work provided us with more than enough wholesome food. With my twin brothers and father out most of the day, it was primarily Mummy, John and me that spent a lot of time in the house together.

In those days, the doors were made from wooden planks, lashed together with cross boards. The bottom half of the door would swing out horizontally and the top was propped up vertically by a piece of beveled wood that held it open. My mother would sit at the back door peeling cassava and yams, her bare legs resting on the soft-stone steps as sandflies buzzed around her, and listen while John and I took turns reading 'Tom Sawyer' or 'Huckleberry Finn' in the sputtering light of the kerosene lamp. I took to the reading, but John didn't. Like most boys his age, he would rather have wiled away the hours making a toy car from the bits of wood Samuel and Eli brought home for him. In time, I gravitated to the classics like Shakespeare, which I still love. And it was through my love for books that I also discovered my love for writing.

But I digress. One afternoon, as I was about to eat my creamed yam and gravy, my father came bustling in. Even at seven years old, I could tell that something was amiss. I seldom saw my father during daylight hours.

He rushed into the house clutching his hat, the wooden floor creaking and the beaded curtain swinging frantically in his wake. Breathless, he panted, "Gracie... Grace...a big hurricane coming. We gotta get to de church now."

Instantly there was pandemonium in the house. My mother rushed about getting a change of clothes for all of us, worrying aloud that the twins still hadn't come home yet. My father ran straight to the one bed in the house that everyone slept on, ripping open the seam above a bulge in the side of the mattress and dragging out a small bag of money. My mother hedged, pretending to "study her head" before we left the house. I knew she was trying to stall and wait for my brothers to come home.

My father grabbed me, tossing me on his hip as he yelled again, "Gracie, come! Norman bring me here in de pig-van. We gonna take all of you to de church and then look for de boys. Just leave everything and come."

"But, Vincent..."

"NOW, GRACIE!"

We bustled outside with nothing but the clothes on our backs and my mother's canvas grocery bag to find Norman waiting behind the wheel of the small green Austin A60 truck he used to transport pigs to the slaughterhouse. My mother and I sat in the little cab next to him while my father and John jumped on to the open back.

The wind whistled in my ears as Norman sped that little pig-van up the road. He told my mother that the system was moving rapidly and had foregone the usual rigors of development. Let me put it in perspective for you. Normally tropical disturbances start just off the coast of Africa and drift westward toward the Atlantic. As they go, they collect heat from the ocean which allows them to build up strength. They go from tropical depression to tropical storm to hurricane. Then hurricanes start from category one and can go all the way up to category five which can cause incalculable damage to life and property.

This particular hurricane, christened with the name of Janet, didn't develop off the coast of Africa. It started off the coast of Barbados. It didn't start as a depression. No, that would have been too easy. Janet came to us as a category three hurricane. It was at that time that - as you young people like to say - "shit got real."

The hurricane hadn't made landfall yet, but I could already see the toll it had taken on Barbados. Normally we were lucky. Barbados has a unique geographic position; we sit to the right of the chain like a wayward child separated from its peers, while all of the other islands form a tidy row to the left. Most tropical systems don't get the chance to build up enough steam to even make a dent on Barbados because the warm water in the Caribbean Sea is the fuel that propels most hurricanes forward.

Our island neighbours were well versed in hurricane preparation, but we lacked their experience. So we did what people do best when faced with an unfamiliar situation: we panicked. Throughout the village, people could be seen scurrying around like rats in a cane-fire. Mothers ran with their children while fathers feverishly boarded up windows and doors hoping to lessen any potential damage.

Even the air smelled different; it smelled like fear.

Everything about that night is still etched in my memory. Maybe because that's the first time in my life I came to know what it felt like to worry. I think that from the time a child experiences fear, they leave a little bit of their childhood behind and dip their toe into the turbulent waters we call life.

Men, women, children, and donkeys packed the churchyard. The braying and shouting were almost deafening. Back then donkeys were used primarily to pull carts and they represented a significant investment, so it stood to reason that people would try to find refuge for their animals at the church too. It was clear that there wasn't space to park Norman's pig-van. Just like the Christmas story, there was no room at that inn for us.

We bypassed the church and instead found shelter at my school because the church was packed beyond capacity. That was a good thing. Halfway between the church and the school, we saw Samuel and Eli running helter-skelter to get home. My mother wept with joy, she was so relieved.

I was struck by how unfriendly the school looked that night. Usually, the room was bathed in sunshine that streamed through the open windows, desks and chairs were neatly arranged in rows and the smell of food and the sound of children's laughter always hung in the air.

Not on that night.

The only thing that remained the same was the limp Union Jack that hung from a small pole at the front of the classroom. It stood sentinel, moving only when a gust of wind issued from the open door to let in new arrivals. Other than that it stayed still, watching over the room.

The wooden desks had been shoved together in clusters to make room for families. Adults talked about the storm and worried aloud about the fate of their homes. Babies cried. Older children sat together in little huddles unsure of what to do with themselves. The wind started to pick up, incrementally at first so that you weren't exactly sure if it was getting louder or if it was your fear playing tricks on you.

And then we waited.

It was torturous, cramped inside that room with so many other people. A little girl about my age from a neighbouring village caught my eye and I longed to go to her.

But somehow I thought my mother would find it inappropriate for me to run around playing and singing at the top of my lungs while facing the possibility of mortal peril. Joan Mayers was there too. Even in that situation filled with fear and uncertainty, she didn't want to be pleasant to me. When I arrived, she stuck her tongue out at me when no-one was looking. After that, she kept her back to me as she played with a little bag filled with beads and string.

The night wore on in the same fashion: murderous sounding winds and crying children created a cacophonous rhythm broken only by the intermittent sound of debris or falling branches. All night long, we lived through that agony, each of us dealing with our demons – the children hated being in a cramped space among so many strangers, the adults hated not knowing what they would be going home to. Some of them didn't know what had become of loved ones who hadn't made it home in time. Some of them were painfully aware that their homes wouldn't withstand the storm.

And so we continued to sit there. Only our fears and Janet kept us company through the night. Eventually, I huddled closer to my mother and drifted off to sleep.

At some point or the other, a loud crash jumped me out of sleep. We found out later that one of the pear trees in the schoolyard had fallen onto the roof of the school. I had been brave up to that point, but that sudden noise did me in. I started crying so bitterly, it was shameful. John had woken up too and now he held my hand as I just sat there and wailed.

The next thing I knew, the roof started leaking. Well, a leak sounds like a steady drip. That was more like a little indoor waterfall. Everyone sitting directly under the hole screamed and scattered, abandoning any items they had brought with them. Looking back now I'm surprised that was the only thing that woke me up. Janet was an unholy monster; that pretty name belied the danger that she was.

The wind was howling so viciously that you could hear it whipping the trees outside left and right. My father and twin brothers joined the other men in doing their best to seal the massive gap that formed in the school's roof, lest we be drowned inside the school. They used Samuel and Eli's tools to cut up school desks to patch the roof as best they could. The rain beat down on their heads with a torrential fury and I worried that the rush of water would carry away my brothers. I cried harder.

My mother drew me onto her lap, then dug through her big canvas bag and pulled out an old utility bill and a pencil. She kissed me on my cheek and was amazingly calm as she said to me, "Susie, it's just some wind and rain. You know that Mummy and Daddy and your brothers will always protect you. Don't you?"

I felt completely justified in crying up until that time. I nodded bravely through the tears that ran down my cheeks and wiped the snot that bubbled from my nose. Mummy smiled as she handed me the paper and pencil and said, "How 'bout if you write a little story for me? Tell me a story 'bout a brave little girl and all of her adventures. Is a real good way to work on joining up your letters. Ah, that's mummy's sweet girl - so brave."

And there, in a school lain under siege by one of the most powerful threats of nature, I started to write. It was the first time I wrote something other than what my teachers asked me to do. When my pencil crossed slowly across that page, everything else around me dissolved and I smiled. It was a very basic story; certainly, I wasn't deemed a child prodigy thanks to a single tale about a little girl who could fly in a magical pink dress. Now that I think of it, it's amazing how such a simple thing has always managed to bring me such joy. After that, I kept a journal. It was always a hodgepodge of things: what happened during the day, reminders, story ideas, short stories, drawings of dresses I day-dreamed about…anything that came to mind. In those days, such whimsy was frowned upon and snuffed out at the first sign. But my mother delighted in it and encouraged it.

As she read my story back to me on the night that Janet raged on, she became my biggest and most influential supporter. She rose her voice enough to compete with the howling outside as she read it back to me, smiling broadly in complete defiance of the hurricane outside. Her pride in my ability calmed me and after she read to me, I drifted off to sleep again.

By the time we came out the next morning, it was clear that something terrible had happened and we had been spared. For the most part, the church survived the ordeal, save for the damaged roof and a broken window.

The scenery right outside the schoolyard was a testimony to what the country had faced. Hurricane Janet was like a lazy maid with an out of control vacuum in her hands. She went through every nook and cranny of the island, uprooting the weak trees and plants, handpicking the poorly built houses and tossing them aside, casting nary a thought to the families she was displacing.

Long strips of galvanized roofing sheets, bent double like horseshoes with the nails still in them, littered the schoolyard. The tree that had fallen on the school was merely a shell of its former self. Janet had stripped it naked, tearing off most of the leaves and branches and leaving just the trunk lying there. It wasn't hard to imagine some other little girl going outside of her church or school and seeing those leaves and branches and wondering where they came from.

The survivors gathered en masse to clear up the schoolyard as best we could with our bare hands and limited tools. We found the pig van hidden beneath a pile of leaves and loose branches, spared from any major damage.

We piled back into Norman's van later that day and drove back home. We were very hungry, having depleted our meager food stores overnight. We were some of the only ones who decided to leave. Some families were so fearful of what they would find when they returned to their homes that they started to make themselves comfortable at the school, setting up stations for laundry and cooking.

Anticipating that we would have sought shelter at the church, Norman's family had spent the night there and he was eager to get back there to make sure they were alright. That drive was perhaps the longest journey of my childhood, literally and figuratively.

Familiarity with a thing tends to change your perception of it. You never notice a long distance that you travel frequently because every detail has already been etched in the dark recesses of your mind. That day, everything was different for me. I noticed how different the mood was as people gathered around broken and bent homes. Some were crying. Some couldn't find a feeling for their heart to settle on, and their emotions ran the gamut between confusion, despair, and sadness. Massive mahogany trees that served as landmarks were missing, throwing off my sense of direction. I saw how naked and lonely many houses looked without their roofs and windows. Hurricane Janet had stripped Barbados of its dignity with her vicious passing.

We couldn't take the usual route back to our house. Between the downed trees and fallen houses, many roads were impassable. Twice we stopped to help. My brothers still had their carpentry tools on them and they came in quite handy for cutting up trees to clear the road. My mother and I would help too. We worked together with other women and girls to grab hold of those freshly sawed chunks of damp wood and toss them to the side of the road while the men did the sawing. After that we piled back into the little green pig van, damp and covered with sawdust and splinters. My brothers and father sat on the back while Norman, my mother and I got into the cab in front.

We made a brief stop at the church and you could see the weight leave Norman's shoulders when he was reunited with his wife and son. They had survived Janet too.

We were almost home when we came upon the strangest sight I had ever seen. There, in the middle of the road, lay a whole house that was literally upside down. Many chattel houses in those days rested on a hollow foundation of soft-stone rocks to prop it off the ground. Chattel houses were meant to be moveable back then to allow slaves and plantation workers to easily dismantle them and take them elsewhere in case the plantation owner told you to carry your backside off their land. And boy did Janet move that house around.

It wasn't particularly damaged as far as we could see from our vantage point, which is what made it so strange in the first place; it looked like a toy that a gigantic child had dropped in the middle of the road. The tip of the pitched gable roof lay on the grassy rut in the middle of the cart road, surrounded by all of our neighbours who surveyed the house incredulously.

My mother broke down crying as soon as she saw it. At first, I couldn't figure out why. Then I realized it was our house.

Crying was a wasted activity; nothing could be done about it now, but that didn't stop me from crying too. My mother wiped her face hurriedly and gathered me in arms. "Alright, Susie, it done do...it done do." That was how she rallied her strength. She was ready to get to the work of rebuilding already. Only our sheep and pigs, safely locked inside their pens were saved. My father's cousin who lived around the corner promised to look after them until we got back on our feet.

All of us, Norman included, got together and packed up whatever belongings we could salvage from the house. Despite the appearance of no damage, there was plenty of damage. Everything inside had been tipped and piled carelessly into one corner of the roof. My father entered by kicking out the eave window. I could see a jumble of bedsheets covered with clumps of the soft grass filling that made up our mattress. My yellow church dress was covered in bits of broken brown glass that used to hold my mother's witch hazel. Rice grains, plates, toothpaste, clothes... everything sat in one big heap. I was aghast. I asked, "Daddy, where are we going to sleep?"

We didn't have to ponder that too long. Norman graciously offered to let us stay with him and my father accepted.

Chapter 7

May 23rd, 2015

A knock sounded on the door. Susan and Lia paused their interview as Ancil brought in a tray with a teapot, a single teacup, a bottle of Sprite for Lia and a plate of molasses cookies for Lia and Susan to share.

"Thanks so much, Ancil," Lia said. She rubbed her eyes wearily before reaching forward to open the soft drink.

"Tired, Lia?" Ancil asked.

"No, I'm fine," Lia said with a big yawn. Despite her fatigue, she didn't dare complain with Susan so close by.

Susan said nothing, sitting quietly as she poured a stream of ginger tea from the willow patterned china teapot. She was deep in thought.

"Do you like Shakespeare?"

Whenever she asked Lia a question, it always caught her unawares. The timing of her questions, as well as the questions themselves always struck Lia as strange. Lia had assumed they would go straight back to Susan's tale about a pet monkey her brothers had. Lia glanced up to see Susan staring at her.

"Umm...well, I've read a few for my English Literature classes at school but not a whole lot of it."

"Hmmmm...," she sipped her tea again, inhaling the aroma and savouring it as her mind wandered. If there was one thing Susan was fond of (other than putting Lia on the spot) it was tea.

"Well, we can fix that," Susan said setting down her cup and easing herself out of her antique chair.

They were in her plantation room (the older woman called it 'The Barbados room') whenever they did the interviews. It was practical: Susan was always referencing a book or some other kind of Barbadian memorabilia that she kept in the room and truth be told, Lia also liked the room. It reminded her of home and in many ways that made the interviews easier. Somehow that room created a safe place that allowed both of them to relax a little.

The room had lost the effervescence of daylight and now a quiet calm settled over the Florida suburb that Susan called home. The cicadas chirped quietly just outside the French doors making a symphonic melody that threatened to lull Lia's tired mind to sleep.

In the dim twilight, Susan wandered over to one of the bookcases and selected a leather-bound volume with the words 'William Shakespeare's Tragedies" inscribed in gold letters on the supple burgundy leather.

"King Lear?"

Lia snapped her eyes open. "No ma'am!" she said, too quickly and too loudly.

Susan turned around, looking askance at Lia. She sat back down in her antique chair before she held out the book. She gazed at Lia, her face pensive as she said, "I want you to have this."

The young woman took the book carefully. It was perhaps the first sign Susan had given her that she might have a heart beneath her crusty armour. All along Lia had assumed that Susan just took great pleasure in being mean to her. Maybe she was wrong. Lia smiled warmly at Susan.

"Thank you so much, Miss Taylor. This is such a wonderful gesture. I'm sure that..."

"Relax yourself; it's an old book, not a vital organ. One of King Lear's daughters is named Cordelia too. You never know...maybe it's where your mother got inspiration for the name."

Susan sipped her tea again. "Perhaps you'll gain some appreciation for it instead of chopping it up and calling yourself 'Lia'. Now...back to 1955."

Lia sighed and picked back up her notepad. Now she was certain that Susan liked being a bitch to her.

Chapter 8

1955

Hurricane Janet was eye-opening in many ways. It drastically changed the atmosphere in the country. Some of the poor who were already oppressed felt even more downtrodden due to the worsening of their economic conditions. Some of them had no house and work in many industries screeched to a halt. Not exactly the most desirable position for people who were already living hand-to-mouth.

Others were so traumatized they stayed in the shelters for many months after the hurricane hit, afraid to see the state of their own homes after they heard what had happened to the homes of others. It took some getting used to in many ways. My school was closed for over two months but even that hiatus wasn't enough time for things to normalize. It's miraculous just how foreign a place can feel once a tree or even an overgrown shrub is gone – it disorients you and makes you a little less comfortable because the unfamiliar is something that human beings aren't altogether comfortable with.

We lived at the Bailey house for almost three months after hurricane Janet hit. The money my parents had saved towards buying our tenantry land was not enough to repair our house. They resolved not to spend a bad cent while we were there so as not to wear out our welcome. In many ways, it completely changed my life. And not just for social and economic reasons.

The first day we were there, my father took John and me aside and told us that we were to help in any way possible and never complain. I can still remember it like it was yesterday. We went around the back and all three of us crammed inside the outhouse so my father could speak to us privately. It was a rickety old thing made of vertical pine boards that had been weathered and aged until they turned a dirty shade of dark grey. I always hated outhouses and to be cloistered in there with two other people was my worst fear come to life. Firstly, it smelled to high heaven. Secondly, outhouses are home to a couple thousand cockroaches and I never liked them. I practically tried to squeeze myself between John and Daddy just so that the ones that scampered up the walls wouldn't touch me. You could barely see anything in the weak light that came through the dusty little peephole on the outhouse door and I couldn't stop thinking they would find a way to crawl all over me and run straight into my nose or ears. Oh gosh, those things still make me anxious.

Anyway, my father spoke to John and me with that quiet ferocity that parents use to let you know they mean business. He didn't want to sour relations with Norman. Whatever the Bailey family asked, we were supposed to do as quickly and efficiently as humanly possible. John and I nodded solemnly in the pitch-black outhouse and said "yes, please" before we shuffled back outside to start our self-imposed indentured servitude. My parents went to the plantation as usual and the twins continued their carpentry work. John and I traded our morning chores of egg collecting and animal watering for flour weighing and searching for rotten produce before the shop opened.

John was a natural at it, which might explain why he eventually became a shop keeper himself. I, on the other hand, had no real talent at the time other than reading and cooking so Kenneth took me under his wing. He showed me how to keep ground provisions fresh by digging a hole in the dry dirt and leaving them overnight and how to infuse oils with herbs so they wouldn't grow mold. The three of us walked to and from school together and spent every evening in the shop sweeping up spilled flour and weighing out twenty-five cent portions of salt pork. That forged a friendship between us that lasted for many years.

It started on the tenth night we were there. As I alluded to earlier, I had a certain knack for fixing food that bordered on prodigious. My brother always whispered that my soup was better than anything Mummy ever made, but he wasn't so drunk as to ever say it loud enough even for the floorboards to hear. All I did was throw in some extra thyme and a pinch more salt. I was a bit of a food snob and I found meal times at the Bailey house to be…hmm…what's the word I want to use? I'm tempted to say torturous or excruciating, but I'd have to mash those two together and multiply it by ten to give you a gist for the kind of madness that used to happen in that kitchen.

Mrs. Bailey was a wonderful woman. She came from one of the other islands and was part Carib. Boy…was she beautiful. Sloe-eyed looks gave her the countenance of a fallen angel. She had a melodic, soft voice with a lilting accent and a sheath of satiny hair that flowed down her back. Yet, somehow this gentility and refinement couldn't extend itself to her hands. Had it not been for her sweet demeanor I can't imagine how I would have choked down that food under any circumstances.

Mrs. Bailey's meal repertoire was limited at best. She "specialized" in two meals so awful I'm surprised her son made it past infancy: fried biscuits and fish with dumplings. Borne out of her frugality, she had invented both dishes using damaged or slightly expired ingredients from the shop. Never one to throw away anything, she had decided that in the case of the fried biscuits, it was best to steep stale crackers in water overnight until they turned into a slimy version of their former self before doing them a greater indignity of using perfectly good herbs and seasonings to flavour them, rolling them into egg-sized lumps and deep-frying them.

Yuck.

She had the audacity to serve that glop with scrambled eggs. It always bothered me; why couldn't she just fry up the eggs with the herbs and seasonings and serve them with the expired biscuits? I tell you, it drove me insane.

As for the fish with dumplings that caught me unawares because it was a misnomer. The first time she talked about making this meal I had already had the fried biscuits so I can't say I was too keen on any more of her innovations. Still, I had always been a sucker for dumplings so it was easy to build up a modicum of anticipation for dinner that night. Imagine my surprise when I opened my eyes after saying grace to see this nondescript puddle of greyish mush staring back at me with not a single dumpling in sight. It reminded me of a small washbasin filled with muddy clothes except the clothes were actually boiled sardines. Mrs. Bailey had stewed down cabbage (of course it was spoiling) with some sardines ("only two weeks past the date" according to her) to come up with that ridiculous concoction.

I forced that down, never daring to look around to see how my family was faring with their helpings. It was entirely unfair to have to sort through slimy rotten potatoes all day and then be fed that muck.

By the middle of the second week, (during which time I realized those two dishes were practically all she cooked) I couldn't stand it anymore and I started hanging around the kitchen in the afternoons when Mrs. Bailey was cooking just to see if I couldn't interject and preserve the dignity of a few innocent sardines.

It wasn't to be though. One evening after dinner, my mother overheard me telling Mrs. Bailey that maybe she should replace the sardines with tuna and to use potatoes instead of cabbage and that I would make dinner instead. My mother took matters (and my ass) into her own hands and told me in no uncertain terms that what I was doing was rude and was a poor way to repay hospitality.

The sun was making its descent in the sky as I took my singed bottom outside and wandered down to the little copse of trees behind the Bailey house. As much as my backside burned, I remember that day very well. That's the first time I remember taking note of how the average day transforms into night. Daytime is always bright and saturated with vivid shades of blue and green, highlighted with splashes of other colours, all of them so highly pronounced it's almost too overwhelming to take them in. But twilight is different. I remember being amazed by how the golden light softened the bright green grass that was coming alive with the nightlife. The crickets chirped ever so quietly at first, tentatively as though they were making sure the humans went to bed before they came out. A little later, the dew blanketed the world with delicate silver droplets that glistened in the moonlight.

That's when I became poignantly aware of the world around me. After that, I started noticing all of the nuances that we take for granted. I started to truly understand writing; how describing the things I saw in my head made all the difference between creating an enchanting scene or writing utter dribble.

I was reflecting that maybe I might have fared better if I had suggested I would just "help" Mrs. Bailey when something landed on my head. Reaching up, I was shocked – and more than thrilled – to realize that it was a sweet biscuit. I glanced up and saw Kenneth smirking down at me from the cover of the tree branches above.

He beckoned me to climb up, looking around quickly to make sure the coast was clear. I made my way up the golden apple tree carefully, knowing the roughness of the tree bark would easily tear the hem of my dress if I wasn't careful. I didn't need another cut ass that evening.

"Wha' you doing up here?" I asked him breathlessly as I settled into the forked branch next to him.

The gentle glow of the sunset highlighted the sparkle in his eyes as his face lit up with a roguish grin. "I always come up here to eat on evenings." He held out a piece of cheese that had been roughly broken off a big block. It was warm and flecked with bits of lint. "Sorry about the fuzz; I keep it in my pocket," he explained as he dusted it off before handing it to me.

I said thanks before tossing it in my mouth, lint and all, choking slightly on it as it slid down my throat. Kenneth chuckled lightly.

"Mummy's food isn't the best, but me and Daddy are accustomed to it." Kenneth shrugged self-consciously. "Daddy always gives me snacks every evening but tells me to go outside and eat so I don't hurt her feelings."

I took another biscuit he offered and we both munched quietly in silence before I turned to him and asked, "Is that really all your mummy can cook?"

"Well... no. It's just that we had so many expired biscuits and sardines that Mummy is making those two recipes until they run out. Daddy lets me eat the fresh biscuits though. You're lucky. A few weeks ago we ate fried ham all day, every day for three weeks. At least now there's variety."

I laughed. Kenneth's eyes lit up mischievously as he contemplated me quietly for a moment. "Be honest: if someone had a gun to your head and threatened to shoot if you didn't eat one, would you choose the fried biscuits or the fish dumplings?"

"I'd eat the bullet."

Our eyes met as we tried to stifle our laughter but it didn't work. Kenneth and I broke into a fit of giggles.

He smiled broadly, staring at me for a while. It made me a little nervous to have him watching me like that. I turned away and looked towards the horizon. The sun was setting just over the vast cane fields in the distance. It was late October and by then the land was stripped bare of canes and stretched as far as the eye could see. It was amazing to see it from that height and take in the majesty of the sunset from such a miraculous vantage point.

"Did you ever notice how the sunlight changes from white during the daytime to that pretty gold when it sets? The way it paints everything in the world in a colour that isn't orange or yellow or pink but a soft blend of all three?"

Kenneth raised one eyebrow at me thoughtfully, both surprised and confused by what I was saying. He turned to the cane fields and a look of awe and comprehension dawned on his face before he smiled broadly.

"Yeah. I don't think I ever noticed that before, you know. Did you read that in one of those old books I always see you with?"

I laughed. "No, I noticed it right before I climbed the tree."

"Hmm..."

"What?"

"Are you sure you didn't read that in a book?" he asked me again.

I glared at him and said haughtily. "I told you I didn't."

Satisfied, he nodded sagely and then surprised me by saying, "You should write down the things you say. You describe something really hard in just a few words. It would have taken me about ten hours to explain that sun thing."

I felt quite pleased with myself at this nice compliment from a boy. A blush crept up my cheeks and he didn't even try to make me feel embarrassed about it. He just took two more broken crackers from his pocket and handed me one.

We sat there as quiet as anything while the light

waned and the crickets turned up the volume on their chirping but little did Kenneth realized that he had watered the seed that my mother had planted in my mind. Writing was my gift and when someone is truly talented, their gift comes so effortlessly that it's easy to take it for granted. Even now, decades later, I still can't believe that Kenneth honed in on that aspect of my personality so easily. At that moment something clicked between us. Just like the knack that Kenneth saw I had for writing, our friendship came to us effortlessly.

Chapter 9

May 28th, 2015

"I've never liked any of this American food," Susan said distastefully as she and Lia settled into their booth.

After almost two weeks of being cloistered like nuns in a fancy abbey, Lia had finally been able to persuade Susan to go out for a meal. Even the taciturn Ancil chimed in, telling Susan that she had brought "de poor girl all de way from Barbados to keep she lock up like a zoo animal." Begrudgingly, Susan had agreed.

Lia wondered why Susan was happy to stay holed up the way she did. Ancil was the only one who ever left the house regularly, except for every other Tuesday when she took Susan along with her to do the grocery shopping. Lia thought bemusedly that Susan must be so controlling that she didn't even trust Ancil to get the right fruit without her supervision. Susan was just as bad when it came to choosing a restaurant.

"I'm not going anywhere with those little ends of food that they want to sell you for a hundred dollars. And I don't eat snails. Or anything endangered. As a matter of fact..."

Susan's list of demands had continued for the entirety of the twenty-minute drive. The only interjections came from Lia. She looked around wide-eyed as Ancil drove, relieved and excited to finally get out of the house to see the city. In Barbados, the small highways that ran through the country were bordered by houses, brightly painted rum shops and fields of green sugar cane stalks. Sometimes drivers and bicyclists stopped to let black-belly sheep, chickens or goats cross the busy motorways.

The highway in Miami was quadruple the size; a broad never-ending stream of traffic that raced along, bobbing and weaving at a frenetic pace and there wasn't a single sheep in sight. Noisy motorcycles whizzed by, their riders revving the heavy engines as they went. The buildings that fringed the highway were huge; tall gleaming towers of steel and glass that reflected all the lights around them luminescing with multi-coloured brilliance.

Everything amazed Lia.

"People don't walk on the highways here the way we do at home."

"FOUR hours to drive to Disney World? At home, it takes two hours to drive around the whole island."

"Really?! They only sell FURNITURE in that building? I thought it was a mall."

Lia's steady stream of questions and exclamations continued until they got to the restaurant. Susan had responded to all of them without complaint, apparently resigned to letting Lia have her night out as agreed.

They sat in a big booth at the back of the restaurant, a little secluded from the rest of the patrons. Susan insisted that they get seats as close as possible to the kitchen. Lia would have rolled her eyes if she wasn't so happy to be out. They could hear the clatter of dishes and the clanging of pots.

The unassuming little Italian eatery boasted a wide array of salads, chicken, fish and pasta dishes spanning the course of eight large pages. Yet, Susan took issue with everything on it. By the time the waitress came to take the order, Susan had finally determined that the only thing she could eat would need a few minor changes.

"Yes, I want this one right here. For $27.50; see it? Good. Now...instead of fried chicken, I want grilled fish. I don't like pasta so bring brown rice instead. No broccoli; I want a garden salad, but replace the tomatoes with croutons."

The waitress nodded. "Of course, ma'am. I'll just need to let you know that..."

"Don't tell me about paying for no substitutions; tell your boss I can take my business elsewhere."

The waitress pursed her lips before smiling tightly. "Of course." She arched a perfectly plucked brow and turning her attention to Lia.

"And what can I get for you, ma'am?"

Completely embarrassed, Lia fumbled with the menu before stuttering. "Just the chicken pasta, please."

"Any special requests?" the waitress asked as her manicured nails skittered across the page, scratching down the order with the merest hint of hostility.

"No." Lia coughed slightly, clearing her throat. "It's fine just the way it is."

The waitress scooped up the menus. "I'll be right back with your order."

Around them, families laughed and chatted over their meals while waiters and waitresses bustled about with trays full of food and drinks. Small tea lights floated in the little glass bowl on the table washing Lia and Susan with warmth, giving their eyes a catlike glow. Those four golden eyes met and surveyed each other, old and young eyes locked in a non-confrontational assessment of each other. Lia watched as the steady little glimmer highlighted the worn lines of Susan's hands and the angles of her face. That's when it struck Lia that Susan was human. As much as they had talked for hours about the details of Susan's life, they had always done so in a very controlled environment – Susan's environment. Now, here in this place, Susan's lithe frame was more pronounced, her vulnerability more tangible. Lia wasn't sure why but for the first time, she felt like she truly saw Susan.

Susan's face gave nothing away. She just stared into

Lia's eyes, staying silent and unwavering as she did.

The waitress returned with a basket of breadsticks, deftly pouring olive oil and balsamic vinegar on a small serving plate before whisking herself off to the kitchen again.

Lia cleared her throat, glad for the slight reprieve in Susan's examination of her. Suddenly, it dawned on Lia that her insistence to get out of the house might very well be her undoing. Susan never failed to pepper her with questions about her personal life and it certainly wouldn't be any better now that they had to find the way to pass the time during a three-course meal. Not to mention the interminable waiting between servings. Lia sighed. Something changed in Susan's eyes when she heard it but, intent on not giving her any leeway, Lia determined to take charge of the situation.

"So...have you come here before?" Lia asked lightly as she sipped her mineral water. It fizzed gently; she enjoyed the sensation as the bubbles tickled her nose.

"No."

"Do you like Italian food?"

"I like Barbadian food."

"So where do you like to eat?"

"At home."

"Oh... then do you like..."

"Cordelia," Susan interjected, "Relax. I'm not going to ask you any personal questions."

And for the first time, Susan Taylor smiled at Lia; a small smile that softened her features and made her beautiful. Lia smiled too. She was torn. Despite Susan's crotchety nature, Lia was quite drawn to her. There was something about her that drew Lia in. Yes, Susan had a brusque way with words, but Lia suspected that her gruff manner was just a smokescreen that could not adequately mask the goodness inside her. There was something intangible about Susan that always kept Lia curious. Lia shrugged. "No...I just asked. We talk a lot about your life in

Barbados but I have no idea about your life here in America."

Susan squinted at Lia as though she was mocking her. "I'm old; not much life left to have."

Lia laughed again. "There must be something you like about living in the States after all this time. How do you spend your time?"

Susan turned her eyes towards the large picture window and the big buildings that surrounded the restaurant with lights that twinkled like captive stars. Lia saw it again then; the look in those bright hazel eyes that was neither sad nor reflective, angry nor resigned. Around them, the din of the restaurant continued, oblivious to the older woman's deep thoughts.

"It's funny you should ask that," she said, her shoulders sagging in resignation. "Many years ago, I told someone that all we have in this life is time. No matter how you look at it, you have to decide whether you'll use it to love or hate, work or sleep, be happy or bitter."

Lia sat, spellbound, afraid to even breathe wary of interrupting what appeared to be the first emotional crack in Susan's armor.

"I made a lot of mistakes and was short-sighted about too many things. Sometimes it was my youth, other times it was my pride that caused me to focus on the wrong things. But of all of the mistakes I made, only one was made out of fear and it's the biggest regret I have."

She shook her head slowly.

"In this life, we are supposed to make mistakes; it's how we grow. I can't belabour that fact. How else would I know that love is meant to be cherished and that it is people and not possessions that must be guarded above all else? No...regret and mistakes are not the same. There is only one thing that if I had to do it over completely, then I would."

"What do you mean?" Lia asked.

The silence settled around them like a thick bubble,

ominous and sad.

The waitress chose that moment to return with their meals, her heels clicking merrily on the tiled floor as she walked. She set both plates in front of them.

Lia had to ask something that had been bothering her since she had arrived. "Miss Taylor, I can't help but notice that you seem very different from how you describe yourself as a child. You seemed like a straightforward, intelligent little girl who loved the people around you. And now...there are some inconsistencies in your personality."

Susan smirked."Do tell. What are these inconsistencies you speak of?"

Lia blushed and shrugged. "Well...it's just that..."

"You're wondering why I'm a bitch."

Lia bit her lip and started playing with her food.

Susan shook her head slowly and sighed.

"I guess I've had a few disappointments too many."

Lia raised an eyebrow at Susan. "We all have. But why have you stayed here for so many years? You've even got a Barbados room at your house that you hardly leave."

Susan shrugged. "It's like home without being home."

"Why didn't you go back? Why is it that no-one visits or calls? Did you ever get married or have children? What have you been doing all of these years? I mean, I just have so many questions."

Susan gave her a cheeky wink. "That's why you're here, isn't it? We are unraveling my life bit by bit and eventually, you will know everything you need to."

Susan snapped open her napkin.

"We're here to eat, not gab. Now, let's enjoy our overpriced meal."

Chapter 10

December 1955

We moved out of the Bailey house in December 1955 and I think each of us mourned a little for the loss of our extended family. I was going to miss helping out in the shop and playing with Kenneth after we swept the flour and rice off the stone floors. John said he would miss the bartering and hustling that came along with shop life. Daddy said he would miss sitting around and drinking with Norman. No-one said anything at this but I'm sure we all thought the same thing: Daddy had been sitting around drinking with Norman for years. The only difference is that he could drink much longer because Mummy could no longer lock him out if he took too long to come home. My mother, Grace in name and nature, was a good guest and thanked Mrs. Bailey for opening up her home to us, but I could tell that something was amiss and I soon found out what it was.

A few days after settling into our new home (which looked everything like the old chattel house, just with slightly newer siding boards) I noticed how restless she was. I paid it no mind until one evening when I got a splinter in my finger and went to get her to take it out.

I had just put my hand on the door to pull it open when I heard my parents' voices.

"Susie is a bright girl; always coming top of the class, always reading and trying to figure out things. She should be able to go to secondary school."

"Grace...don' talk madness. We got three boy children and we couldn't afford for Samuel and Eli to go to secondary school. I gine see at least one of my boys going to school past 10 years old."

"Vincent, John is a good boy, but he ain't interested in school. He smart enough and everything, but he would be better off learning a trade."

"Why you confusing me with this all of a sudden?" my father asked irritably.

"Because we got to start getting things in order if we want Susie to go to secondary school. It is bad enough that I does work in the fields and you is a driver; you know that is the first question on the test she would got to do and she can't get around that."

I heard my father sigh impatiently. I could imagine him throwing up his hands in anguish the way he usually did when he was flustered. "Send she school to learn what? Ain't nothing to gain from giving girl children no lot of schooling."

"That ain't true. She could be a teacher or a secretary or something like that."

"She could be all of them things without me wasting so much money. My son could be a doctor or a solicitor. Oh dear..." his voice rose an octave. The floorboards quivered slightly in the verandah and I knew he was hopping lightly on his toes. "You could imagine me telling Norman and the other fellows that my son come back from over and away and now name Dr. John Taylor? You hear the punch that name packing? Compare a doctor to a teacher and tell me which sound better to tell people."

"But Susie could be a doctor too."

"Gracie, you making my head hurt me. You talking like you crazy now. I ain't got no money to send school the little girl. That is the end of that. I going by the shop and play some dominoes."

I scampered from the door so he wouldn't see me lurking. By the time I ran to the back of the house, shimmied over the fence and pretended I had been playing in the backyard, my mother was peeling potatoes with a solemn look on her face.

"Mummy, you okay?"

"Yes, Susie."

"You're sure?"

"Yes." She stopped peeling potatoes for a moment and stared out the wooden window. "I just wish that everyone could be treated equally. I wish that money didn't equal patience and understanding. I wish..." she shook the raw emotions out of her mind and smiled at me. "...I wish that you would help me peel these potatoes so I could start the gravy."

"Okay. But I have a splinter in my finger."

She wiped her hands clean on a cloth before taking a bit of candle grease from a little jar. She heated it in a spoon over the stove and then blew on it a bit before pouring it on my finger to ease the splinter out.

I dipped my hand in a cup of cool water for a few minutes to let the burning settle down. Then I gathered some potatoes in the bowl and started to peel. I watched my mother as I did and I suspected that some of her restlessness came from being at the Bailey house. Even I had noticed that Mr. Bailey tended to have discussions with his wife about business and household matters. At our house, Vincent Taylor didn't believe in a whole lot of discussion.

As a pile of potato skins gathered in the pig bucket, Mummy started to sing:

Blessed assurance, Jesus is mine,
Oh, what a foretaste of glory divine.

I glanced up because I knew what that meant. She had resigned herself to not hurting her head with what she couldn't have. We slipped back into our usual routines and I didn't hear my mother say anything else to my father about my education.

The only thing that changed slightly was our meals. That was the last evening we ever ate store-bought English potatoes. After that, we only ate rice or the sweet potatoes, eddoes, and yams that my mother took John and me to dig up at the plantation. My father never liked those other ground provisions but whenever he asked when next he was getting English potatoes, my mother always said they were too expensive and she was doing her best to juggle the money. He'd grumble about the British's taxation on poor black Bajans, noting bitterly that the Queen never drove a stroke in her life and was surely eating more than her share of potatoes.

A few months later, I found a bag of coins stashed away in a small potato sack in the corner of the cupboard. When I asked her what it was, Mummy shushed me and stuffed it back behind the cast iron pot. "That's your future; put it down."

I'll admit that I was glad to go back home even if I did miss Kenneth a lot. Mr. Bailey's shop was on the main road and, as such, didn't have the same atmosphere that our village would. I missed watching the sheep come home on their own every evening, their feet trotting a familiar path. I missed pitching marbles with the other children in the cart road every evening. But most of all I missed Saturday mornings. Clanging bells and creaking cartwheels would wend their way through the village heralding the arrival of various vendors plying their trade. You'd smell the salty rawness of fish caught at daybreak by the fish vendor who bellowed, "Fish! Fresh fish!" in a lively staccato. His cart would be piled high with frays, jacks, reef fish, flying fish or pot fish, the shiny scales glistening in the early morning light. Seawater mingled with blood dripped through the bottom of the wooden boxed-cart on little toes that squealed when the cold drops spattered their feet.

His haggles would play out the same way they had played out the week before for everyone except Joan's mother. Her parcel was always specially wrapped and she just sauntered up, collected it and then pranced off, her big backside swaying defiantly as she side-looked everyone who tittered at the exchange.

The bread cart would be close behind, the yeasty scent of loaves and buns warming your stomach with the sweet aroma. That little white cart was handsomely decked out. It was always well painted and the little glass windows in the rectangular case were always wiped clean of fingerprints before the cart arrived in every village. It was no wonder to me that the lady who pushed it was so plump and good-natured. I would have been plump and happy too if I could have my fill of jam puffs, sweet bread, and rock cakes. But those sweets didn't matter to me as long as my mother bought me a turnover. That lady - Mrs. Williams I believe her name was - made the best turnovers I ever had. They were shaped like small loaves, only big enough to fit in the palm of your hand. The sides were soft and sticky and the top was baked to a crusty golden brown. The insides were filled with the perfect blend of grated coconut, sugar, and spice. My mouth is watering right now, thinking about those turnovers. Any time I misbehaved all my mother had to do was hum softly under her breath, "Saturday gine soon be hey" in a singsong voice and I would straighten up so fast it would give you whiplash.

I'll tell you, those turnovers were enough to power you through all of the Saturday chores. Mummy usually bought seven, but I could only ever eat one turnover when she bought them. The other six would be divided equally among the entire family for a treat after Sunday lunch. Mummy would store them in the pantry and that sugary aroma would hang in the air making that entire Saturday totally maddening.

I'd spend the rest of the day doing whatever chores my mother needed to be done whether it was shelling peas, cooking or helping with the laundry (not just mine, but all of the laundries for the entire household. Daddy said that no son of his would ever sit over a jukking board.) I could never understand that to be honest. My mother worked just as hard as Daddy and still did all of the cooking and cleaning. One day I remember asking, "Mummy, do you think you work hard?"

She was taken aback. "Yes, chile. You can't see that wid yuh two pretty eyes?" She gestured at the soapy tub of warm water that sat between her legs filled with dirty clothes. Another identical tub behind her held yet more clothes soaking in grated blue soap. They smelled sweaty and looked grimy until Mummy and I got our hands on them. After the wash, they always smelled like fresh sunshine and lavender.

"Yes, please."

I scrubbed Eli's church shirt more vigorously. "So how come Daddy and the boys don't help with things like washing and cooking and cleaning? It's four of them and only two of us. And after they finish with the pigs on Saturday mornings, they get to go to the shop and play dominoes."

My mother's hands stilled. Her brown skin looked distended and milky after being submerged in the soapy water for so long.

"Susie, I always say you could ask me anything once you don't be rude. You father would pour two lashes in your ass for asking that question. I gine tell you not to ask those kinda questions in front he. But, I will answer you. This is a man's world. Men running de government. Men is de doctors and lawyers. But dem foolish because they can't do it without them wives."

"They can't?"

"No. They make all the laws in the world and run all the governments, but they come home to a hot meal, a clean house, and good-behave children. You know how hard it is to get all of that right?"

I nodded sagely as my little fingers seized up like claws. I flexed them a few times, then squeezed soapy water from Eli's shirt.

"Men can't chew cane and whistle."

I crinkled my brow.

She laughed. "Dem can't multi-task, Susie."

"Oh." I laughed and plopped the shirt into the basin of clean water.

We continued in silence for a few more minutes until I said, "So if women can multitask and my school marks are better than John's, why Daddy don't want me to keep going to school?"

She arched an eyebrow at me. "Always use the Queen's English, Susie: 'Why doesn't Daddy want me to continue going to school?'" Mummy shook her head and sighed so deeply I thought she'd use up her lifetime quota all at once.

"Because he believes a woman's place is in de home no matter how bright she is."

She looked at me then. "My parents stopped me from going to school because them say I gine end up as a maid or in de fields. But them spend all them money sending Wilbert to school."

"Uncle Wilbert went to secondary school?" I asked incredulously. My uncle had nine children (I doubt he was aware of that fact because he could barely count that high) and worked for the government cleaning up donkey poop from the alleys in Bridgetown. Either it was a more specialized job than I realized or my grandparents indulged him when they could have smoked kippers with their money.

"Yup. Total dimwit. Talking 'bout how Wilbert gine be a solicitor, he just want training up properly."

Our eyes met and we broke down laughing. "See? Good times make light work. We done this first tub already and we ain't even notice it."

She winked at me.

"You don't worry though. I ain't born rabbits and mongoose. All of my children gonna get the same chances as each other, cuz my girl child is as good as de boys or even better."

Chapter 11

June 1st, 2015

Lia got a little homesick every morning when Ancil started making breakfast. Every day Ancil made a hearty broth from oats and sago with a heavy helping of cinnamon and sugar. The aroma would waft up the stairs, under Lia's door, and into her nostrils, gently breaking her slumber. There was something about the simplicity of it that Lia savoured. She was never one for routines, but in some ways, she felt she would never tire of that broth. It was homey and familiar and helped to bridge the divide that spanned the Caribbean Sea.

In other ways, Lia felt that broth was a delivery from the devil himself. She would sit on the steps by the back door, shaded by a bush with soft pink begonias that bordered the walkway, and drink that concoction. When she did, her mind would wander back to Barbados. She would think about her ex-boyfriend. She would think about his new girlfriend that she had briefly shared him with. She would think about the shame she felt in the pit of her stomach knowing that she still thought about him every day. Lia didn't know why. She just knew she wanted it to stop. There was nothing to be gained by wallowing in something that gave her nothing but heartache.

When Ancil had first invited her to write Susan's story, she had seen the opportunity as a chance to get away from him for a while. It pained Lia that the distance she had put between them only made her miss him more. She thought she had nothing to lose, but when she was so far away she couldn't even pass through his neighbourhood to buy salt bread and accidentally see him. She thought about how much she wanted to call him and tell him everything that happened during the day. She wondered if he would be happy for her when she got her book published. Those wistful thoughts would brew in her mind until the sago and oats grew cold and gelatinous at the bottom of her bowl.

By the time Ancil returned to the kitchen with Susan's breakfast dishes, Lia would feel worn out.

One day, Ancil asked her if she was feeling sick. Lia shook her head and changed the subject as fast as she could. "How long have you worked for Miss Taylor?"

Ancil glanced behind her. "A long time. Since 1967."

"That's a long time indeed. You've been her helper all of those years?"

Ancil nodded and smiled. "You could say so. Now I think you should get started on your day. She waiting for you." Ancil turned away and began washing the dishes, humming a little tune that sounded like a hymn.

"True."

Lia headed out of the kitchen but paused at the doorway. "Oh, so that means you've been living in the States for a long time." She shrugged and laughed. "I dunno why but I thought you were here for less time than that."

"Hmmm? Oh no, Miss Cordelia. I've been in the States for twenty years."

Lia stared at her, the cogs in her brain turning sluggishly. "But I thought you said you were working for Miss Taylor since 1967. That's closer to fifty years."

Ancil glanced at Lia and then shrugged her shoulders. "Yes, but it's getting late. Get going before she comes looking for you. That ain't goin' end well if she does."

Lia headed down the corridor. Ancil was lovely indeed but Lia wondered if she struggled with memory loss.

Chapter 12

June 1966.

The years rolled on with a placid pace that defied the changes that swept through my family and the nation on a whole. There was a lot of infighting within the West Indies Federation government that Barbados was a part of. In 1966 it was disbanded and Barbados became a self-governing entity that was still ruled by England. Samuel and Eli remained carpenters and John and I both attended secondary school. My father was astounded by the fact that my maternal grandmother had left an inheritance for me to study. He had never known her to be a wealthy woman and neither could he understand why I was the only one she had left anything for. The potato sack at the back of the cupboard disappeared and I didn't know it was possible to love my mother any more than I already did.

I'm not sure how or why, but I ended up losing my virginity to Kenneth Bailey one day after picking cherries in the gully. Yes, yes, I know – ironically, I let him pick mine too. I was eighteen and I don't think I'd say that I was in love with him or anything at that time. I would say that what we had was unlike any relationship I have ever experienced in my life. Up to now I still haven't met anyone that I connected to in the way I connected with him. He was the only person that truly understood me, one of the only people who encouraged my dreams of being a writer and the first boy I ever kissed. I suppose that losing my virginity to him was a simple marriage of trust, complete inhibition, and raging hormones.

Truth be told, it wasn't a complete surprise to either of us. In those days, parents used to leave their children to roam free with nary a care, because children always came back home safe and sound. A group of us always went to the gully some evenings to play games after school, but the size of the group varied according to the day. On Friday evenings, Joan usually went with her mother to drag her father out of a rum shop so he wouldn't fritter away all of the grocery money and Daddy had started sending John to apprentice with Samuel and Eli every day after school. The other girl that played with us sometimes had to help her mother cook for her six younger siblings so she seldom showed up.

When Kenneth and I were alone, there was no pressure to be anything or do anything I didn't want to. I always walked with a book of some sort. Yates, Sherlock Holmes, Shakespeare, many stories and poems accompanied us. Kenneth didn't care much for books. He always said he was only interested in reading the shop's ledgers. As the heir apparent to the Bailey Grocery Store chain, he felt that distracting himself with any other reading was a frivolous pursuit.

That was one of the only things that separated Kenneth and me. But I still couldn't fault him. Even though he didn't like books, he didn't mind if I read to him while we sat in the gully. We would lay entwined together on the soft mossy ground, him absent-mindedly curling my hair around his fingers as I read.

Otherwise, our friendship was underpinned by one key thing that always kept it fresh: curiosity. His leaned more to nature and how things worked. Mine was far more random, but we were both curious nonetheless.

As we grew older, the allure of climbing trees in the gully and playing two-person cricket grew old and we started kissing to break the tedium. At first, I didn't think much of it until I kissed Dwight Alcott a few weeks later. Dwight's kiss was so sloppy and disgusting I decided there was no point in reinventing the wheel. After that, if I wanted to kiss, I usually sought out Kenneth. He didn't rush it the way Dwight did. I can see now in my old age that a kiss isn't a simple thing; it's perhaps the most intimate experience that any two people can ever hope to have. It manifests itself from deep within and doesn't hide what's inside someone's heart. It lays bare a person's intentions, their motivations and character all in one dandy package.

After that, we progressed to other things. I can't remember whose idea it was for him to suckle my breasts (I'm lying – it was mine) but I remember being so nervous for a boy to see those two little things that had barely settled themselves on my chest. Whenever we were feeling frisky we walked a little deeper into the gully, chatting non-stop as we went. We talked about everything; school, friends, parents, siblings, ambitions. Nothing was off-limits between us.

Kenneth and I had found this little nook that overlooked a small stream. It was absolutely beautiful. Just against a big rock wall, there was a shallow cave that opened up right next to a tree that had the most beautiful yellow flowers. Cat-tail tree I think you called it – I can't be certain. When the wind picked up and shook the blossoms loose, they fell so softly and sweetly around you that you could lose yourself in that place. The flowers would drift down from the branches like wispy pieces of silk and blanket the floor of the cave with those downy yellow petals.

That particular time started just like any other. We were sitting at the mouth of the little cave, the gully full of life all around us. Everything was lush and green and cool, the scent of nature around us was intoxicating. Flowering plants, damp grass, fallen nutmeg and mace that we had crushed with our feet as we walked made a gentle earthy perfume that enveloped us. Insects buzzed and birds chirped. Bajan green monkeys wandered about on all four legs, their long, slim tails erect and proud as their little ones hung upside down clinging to them.

I can still remember what I was wearing: a red shift dress with big sunflowers on it. It was an old church dress that had faded because I had worn it so much. Kenneth was wearing a plain grey buttoned-down shirt and black pants. He had eased his hand under my dress and was caressing my belly softly while I told him that I had gotten in trouble with my father.

"Daddy is just so old-fashioned the way he thinks. I mean...he doesn't drag down the boys the way he does with me...it's just so...vexing." I whined. "When I told him that I wanted to write books, he asked me 'you making sport or you joking' because those were the only two options he could imagine. He says this is all Mummy's fault, sending me to school and putting ideas into my head. Insisting that he has to pay full price for me to go to school and I should be sensible and get a real job or he would ring a lash in me." I sighed deeply. "I'm too old for a cut ass if you ask me. Know what I mean? Normally Mummy doesn't say a word, but this time she told Daddy that if he raised a hand against me that she would chop it off for him." I giggled lightly before a droplet of water fell from the roof of the cave onto my forehead.

Kenneth propped himself up on one elbow and gently brushed the water away, ever so silent as I kept babbling on. I loved the feel of his hands on me. His palms were calloused from all of the lifting and scrubbing he did at the shop, but his touch never betrayed the hardships his hands went through. Unerringly tender, he had a languid approach to everything he did, careful but passionate. His fingers traced soft cascading circles from my navel to my chest.

He was completely engrossed in what he was doing until I slapped him. "Kenneth, did you hear what I said?"

He didn't even pretend that he did. Instead, if anything he seemed more intense, more concentrated on the mission he had in mind. "Susie...," he started, his voice soft and measured, "You're the only girl I ever met that's so down to earth. I never have to think before I talk and I really like it. A lot."

Never before had I heard Kenneth speak like that. Almost like he was in a trance and wanted to say everything that was on his mind before he lost his nerve. He was always so easy going that to feel that palpable pressure surround us was too much for me to digest. To be honest, I was a little afraid to hear what he had to say. I had that funny feeling that you get before you broach the unknown and I wasn't keen to find out what it was. So I did what countless people have done since the dawn of time. I avoided the situation.

"Kenneth... I know what you're going to say and I feel the same way too."

His face went blank. "Really?"

"It was bound to happen though, wasn't it?" I said, as I slid onto his lap, his hand still under my dress. I kissed him softly, my tongue sliding between his lips for the merest moment before he pulled away.

"But Susie... I..."

"Shhh..." my skin prickled under his touch as I brazenly guided his hand under my dress, moving his hands further down.   "Touch me."

Up to that point, the most Kenneth and I had done was kiss and touch each other above the waist. This was brand new territory and whatever reservations he had were quickly silenced by the feeling of my body beneath his hands. I imagine no amount of fingering chickens could have prepared him for that.

His breathing laboured and intense, Kenneth leaned his head toward mine again, kissing me with a hunger that I had never known him to have before. His tongue caressed mine so seductively that my body hummed with feverish anticipation that coursed through my every nerve. I ran my hand up his arm, savouring the firm muscles beneath my fingers that coiled and tensed as his fervor grew.

His arm curled around my waist and his other hand caressed me so gently and so sweetly that I could hardly breathe. Never before had I experienced such feelings – my centre throbbed with desire. Anxiety had long since abandoned me, only to be replaced with a heady confidence. I felt beautiful and free in the moments that followed.

Afterward, I lay huddled against Kenneth until the sun painted the sky in shades of tangerine and pink. I was sore in some places but the rest of my body felt relaxed and at ease. Oddly enough, I felt more nervous afterward than I did during or before. I was afraid that everything between us had changed after what we did. So I did everything I could to keep the conversation neutral. His sweet kisses punctuated my sentences as I talked non-stop about the new Shakespeare story I was reading about the king and his three daughters. Normally, Kenneth would have poked holes into any aspect of the story he found laughable. That evening, he didn't. He just held me until the first chilly drops of rain splashed us, chasing us from the gully and back to our homes.

Night was drawing close when I eased into the house. I saw when my mother squinted her eyes at me in a funny sort of way. She hadn't lit the kerosene lamp yet and the weak light in the house made that squint even more sinister. My insides squirmed. I felt like she could see right through me.

"Susie...," she said quietly. My stomach clenched. My mind raced over the possibilities, wondering what fate lay in store for me.

"Y-yes please, Mummy." I stammered.

"Go and hot some water."

I rushed off to do as she bid. Was she going to scald me? I started sweating. The moisture in my mouth evaporated, leaving it parched and itchy. That moisture found its way to my palms, soaking them in a slick sweat that made me drop the kettle twice. That quiet voice, so controlled and polite, was the most dangerous of them all and I feared for the safety of my little red ass. My chest vibrated so intensely with every thud of my heart that I didn't even hear her when she came up behind me in the kitchen. I screamed and dropped the matches when I turned and saw her standing there.

She said nothing at all as she went to the cupboard, rummaged through the tea tin and took out the small paper bag filled with the mysterious leaves she had been brewing for herself for years.

Since I was a little girl, I remember my mother going into the backyard to gather these different cuttings. Just behind our paling, lots of bush grew up wild around the house. Not until I was about ten did I even come to recognize how different each of these plants were. That was also around the time that I realized that my mother fertilized and cared for these same plants that I thought were just growing wild. She cut little bunches off each of them and each of us would get this "bush tea" as she liked to call it.

She cut nettle for my father to ease the pain in his hands, wonderworld for the scaly patches that erupted on Eli's and John's skin when the weather got dry, bay leaf for Samuel just because he liked it, mint for me because I sometimes got sniffly, and a prickly green plant for herself.

Whenever I asked her what it was, she always said, "When you get older, you can get some too."

I had sipped her tea once when it was steeping. It smelled like damp crabgrass, tasted bitter and green and left a chalky feeling on my tongue. It was atrocious. I suspected no amount of honey would have made it any more palatable. I never tried sneaking her tea again.

Now she took two mugs, mine and hers, pinched a portion of dried leaves into each and poured hot water into it. In a few minutes, she strained them off, gave me my mug and said that from now on we would both drink that tea every morning.

"Susie…"

I gulped again. It turns out that my childish palate wasn't to blame; the passage of time hadn't improved the taste of that slop. The tea was hot and bitter on my tongue and burned my stomach as it went down, but I didn't dare protest.

"Yes please, Mummy."

"…next time you playing the fool in the gully, try and knock the blossoms out yuh hair. You must still hold yuh head high out in public."

My face burned red, but I just nodded like a fool.

That was the thing with my mother. I don't think it was the blossoms that gave me away. She took just one look at me and knew what I had been up to. Mummy probably told herself that "it done do" as she liked to say and she may as well make sure I didn't have any other concerns to plague my young life. It also explained how she had managed to make sure I was her last child.

After that day in the gully, Kenneth was a little clingy, to say the least, and I didn't know how to deal with it. I became completely distant for a few reasons. Firstly, he was my best friend and we should have never let it go that far. Secondly, I felt wordless pressure emanating from him every time he looked at me. Every glance, every touch from Kenneth felt too intimate and while he walked the plank of change masterfully, every one of my movements felt like a treacherous misstep. I needed time to roll everything over in my mind. By the end of the first week after the tryst in the gully, I was just overwhelmed and took to avoiding him every time I could.

Looking back now, I know he felt the sting of my rejection very deeply. Kenneth remained friends with John and still visited our home to see him (and hoped that I would make an appearance), but I always went to feed the pigs or stayed in the bedroom whenever he was there. I was young and inexperienced about those things and I made foolish mistakes. Instead of secluding myself, I should have tried talking to him about my feelings. That was, of course, if I could have figured out what they were. All our lives he made fun of how springy my curly hair was and the strange things I said. He teased me about every little thing, so I never once imagined that I was anything else to him but "one of the boys".

I was conflicted because I thought that my first time should have been with someone I was married to and in love with. Or at least that's what the church said. I worried that it had changed our friendship and that's all he wanted me for. But most of all, I felt lost without my best friend.

Maybe two weeks passed before I finally went to his house to visit him. It was the end of the academic year and maybe the loneliness of the long summer vacation that loomed ahead of me made his absence even more glaring.

It was the last day of school and I stopped by the shop on the way home. It was packed with children who had saved their pocket money that term to buy some sort of reward for their hard work plus the ones who had learned nothing but felt they were due a reward for sticking it out in spite of the hardships. The little black and white Zenith TV set on the shelf over the bar was blaring the scores of the England vs West Indies test match at Lord's after the teams went to tea. I looked up and saw Garfield Sobers sitting next to Muhammad Ali. The men crowded around the set said,

"Ahhhh!" in unison, clinking their glasses at the mere sight of so much sporting excellence in one frame.

I greeted Mr. and Mrs. Bailey as they bustled back and forth serving the spirited crowd of school children. Kenneth parceled out flour at the back of the shop in preparation for the afternoon rush. His hands and apron were smeared with long streaks of white dust that shook off of him in little clouds and settled on the floor around him like a powdery halo. My breath caught in my throat. That image flicked a switch in my brain and took me back to our childhoods when both of us would pack out the flour bags every evening after school. We would stand side by side and laugh as we worked, trying to see who would stay the cleanest by the time we were finished. Kenneth usually won because I was always so dusty that I looked like a ghost. In that instant, I didn't see someone who threatened what I knew about life or relationships. I just saw Kenneth and I was ashamed that we had ruined everything that was once so simple and pure. My heart sank when I saw him; I'll never forget that look on his face. I knew then that I had hurt him by not speaking to him.

He glanced around and immediately stopped short when he saw me. Our eyes held each other's for a long moment before I jutted my head to the right and made my way back through the noisy children, walked around the side of the shop and headed toward the back. Kenneth was already there pacing the neat vegetable rows in the kitchen garden.

"Why are you avoiding me?"

"I just had some work to do for school and...."

He raised a finger and cut me off. "That's not what happened so don't start with that rigmarole."

My blood ran cold. "But, it's just that..."

He grunted angrily. "No buts, Susie! You just up and disappeared after what happened and whenever I went to see you, you never came outside."

The cold in my chest intensified. I felt horrible.

"I thought I had hurt you. You made me feel like I raped you or something. And then I started worrying that I had gotten you pregnant." He scrubbed the top of his head roughly and started pacing again. Kenneth looked at me like he couldn't believe what he was seeing. "I'd be really mad if you kept this up and wouldn't let me see my baby, 'cause that just ain't fair."

I bit my lip and suddenly I couldn't bear to look at him. The speech I had planned in my head evaporated under the heat of Kenneth's anger.

"But I'm here to talk to you now," I whimpered as tears rolled down my cheeks.

"Why didn't you want to talk to me before?"

I stared at the ground and shrugged miserably.

"Why do you want to talk to me now?"

"Cause I miss you," I wailed. I stared at the ground, ashamed of my feelings and the crying that accompanied them. Kenneth's feet shuffled uncomfortably as he seemed to consider what I was saying.

"Hmmph," he grunted noncommittally. The pacing resumed.

"Susie..."

Kenneth put a finger under my chin and gently raised my head until I was looking at him. He squinted his eyes and inspected mine and maybe he saw enough melancholy there to convince him that I wouldn't do it again.

He was thoughtful for a moment before a smile lit his face. "I think a hug would make both of us feel better." I nodded, glad that our little rift seemed to be healed.

He pulled me to him and we embraced for a long time. When we pulled apart, the dark blue pinafore of my uniform was covered in the white powder that blanketed his apron. He grinned and looked at me. "I hugged you on purpose. Oh, well...since you're dirty, so you may as well come and help me pack the flour."

I slapped him and laughed as he swaggered back to the shop, pleased with himself at his cheeky trick.

Chapter 13

June 18th, 2015

"Seriously? So how do you send e-mails? Don't you use Google?"

Lia was horrified to find out that Susan Taylor didn't have internet service at her house. In the month that she had been in the reclusive author's Doral home, she had been so busy talking to Susan that she hadn't found the time to browse the net as she usually would have. That morning, Susan had said she wasn't feeling well and had remained cloistered in her bedroom. While helping Ancil tidy up the kitchen, Lia had asked Ancil for the modem password, only to find out that there was none.

Ancil laughed as she swept the floor. "Miss Susan don' need de Internet to read books or de newspaper. De paperboy does bring de paper and she publisher does send new books all the time. And I don' need no internet either."

Lia frowned. "So...you guys don't buy anything online? Groceries, clothes, anything?"

Ancil laughed again at Lia's chagrin. "I guess this is an old fashion house, young lady."

Lia's breathing quickened and her chest grew tight. She hated to admit it, but her internet withdrawal was more severe than she realized. No contact with the few friends she did have made her feel isolated and homesick. But more importantly, not being able to spy on her ex-boyfriend's social media pages to see if he had broken up with his new girlfriend was excruciating.

Just before she had left Barbados, he had started posting daily inspirational memes about the importance of self-love. Lia smelled a change in the air and any day now she expected him to update his relationship status. The thought of having to wait weeks or months to find out was enough to give her cold sweats.

Lia sighed. If nothing else, she was learning the incredible virtue of patience in Susan's home.

She stared out the window, fidgeting with the wet sponge in her hand. The dishes were clean, but she stood rooted by the sink, trying to figure out what to do with herself. Maybe she could go out and meet other people in the neighbourhood. What if she met the love of her life right outside the door? What if this was all part of her destiny and the metaphorical lemon that she had been sucking on so discontentedly was the precursor to the most glorious lemonade she'd ever had?

She smiled at the thought and fixed her gaze on passersby who made their way down the street. The sidewalks were coming alive with young children strolling hand-in-hand with their grandparents and elderly couples walking their dogs. Birds flew to and fro, squirrels scurried through the bushes and up tree trunks. Lia frowned when she smelled burning bread coming from the house next door. The little old lady who lived there sat in a rocking chair on the patio contentedly knitting a dog sweater. Lia had never noticed before how few young people she had seen since she had arrived. Wait a minute...

"Ancil...is this a retirement community?"

The older lady beamed widely. "Yes, ma'am. It real nice and quiet, ain't it?"

Lia groaned inwardly. She was more likely to get internet access than a date in this place. Lia mumbled under her breath, "I ain't able."

"Pardon?"

"I said I'll wipe the table."

Ancil handed Lia a cleaning cloth and started humming as she swept the kitchen.

Lia swept up bits of fallen oats from the placemats. "So where does Miss Taylor go when she wants to use the internet?"

"Hmmm?" Ancil was emptying the dustpan.

"I asked where Miss Taylor goes to use the internet," repeated Lia.

Ancil turned to her, puzzled.

"Hmmm...I can't remember Miss Taylor wanting to use no lot of internet, you know. Anything we want we does get from de store or she got a business manager who does handle everything else."

Lia quirked an eyebrow. "That's strange."

Ancil laughed again, her white teeth a stark contrast to her beautiful dark skin. "Lots of Americans got 'people' to deal with their bills and things as they like to say. You don' watch TV?"

Lia grinned. "That's not what I meant. The first day I was here, Susan told me that she had seen all of the fluff I told her on my Facebook page. So how does she know that if she doesn't use the internet?"

Something Lia said sucked the mirth out of Ancil in a hurry. Her smile vanished before she shrugged, snatched up her cleaning supplies and raced from the room.

"Hmmm..."

Ancil was certainly loyal but clearly, any sort of subterfuge wasn't her thing.

Chapter 14

July 1966

The end of the cane harvest and the dry season were upon us. Every morning before dawn, one man after another would join the mob of workers headed to the fields. They greeted jovially, ribbing each other about last night's domino games or the cricket match being played in some far-flung part of the world. Covered from neck to toe in layers of old clothes stuffed into their boots, they'd sing songs as the sun and temperatures rose, swinging sharp cutlasses at the cane, hacking off the trash and tossing it on the ground. Dray carts stuffed with thick reddish-yellow stalks rolled up the village lanes toward the factory all day long. It's possible that the men felt a different kind of relief that year when every field had been cleared. They all hoped it would be the last crop harvested for the Queen.

James travelled to England that same month and came back with the news that he had been successful in lobbying for our independence. No revolts or bloody wars like other countries. Time, perseverance and good planning were all it took.

November 30th, 1966 was set as the date for Barbados' independence from England and all hands were on deck. Two weeks later, Kenneth and I listened to the Rediffusion box as James welcomed the British royal family to the island. We could hear the crowd jabbering excitedly as the announcer described the plane landing on the tarmac of Seawell Airport. We bit our lips and squeezed each other's hand when we heard James say that he would escort Her

Majesty in the royal convoy. James gave Queen Elizabeth II a tour of the island and she bestowed several properties to the people of Barbados. The entire country fizzed with unfettered glee at the prospect of owning Farley Hill national park and numerous other landmarks. The independence wheels were fully in motion in a matter of days and every man in the DPP was hungry for the glory that came along with spearheading such a project.

James' little brood was intent on creating social equality through programs that allowed even the poorest of us to enjoy a better standard of living. As the most likely candidate to be the country's first Prime Minister, James felt the most pressure and was intent on going down in history with his initiatives. That prompted the unorthodox notion that reaching out to people at the grassroots level was the best way to have good solid discourse.

He invited anyone who wanted to voice an opinion to visit his beautiful home over the course of three weeks: field workers from the plantations, maids from the houses of the affluent Whites and factory workers. And they always had a lot to say, ain't that the truth.

Every evening after work, my father would ferry us there in James' car. The six of us worked about eighteen hours a day in those weeks. Everyone did their day job and still helped out with the independence campaign. It was especially hard for my mother. That back-breaking work in the fields coupled with cooking, washing, cleaning, looking after a family...I don't know how she did it. All she used to say when things got hard was, "Grace by name and Grace by nature." She didn't grumble about what was expected of her; she always said that complaining took energy she couldn't afford to waste. We would bustle around James' big kitchen with the fancy appliances talking non-stop while I helped her make sandwiches. Norman's wife would hand them out to the visitors (we didn't trust Mrs. Bailey to do much else in the kitchen). Other ladies would volunteer to do the cleaning so we could watch the meetings. Mummy and I would huddle under the big mahogany staircase and watch as the living room thrummed with the boisterous chatter of the masses. People took up every available space, even sitting in the massive window sills and on the floor.

I saw them all. The woman who had six children to raise and a debilitating factory injury which left her without legal recourse or any sort of social security. The families that had to choose between sending their children to school or feeding them. Many of them were eating for the first time that evening and covertly squirreling away a sandwich or two for breakfast. Not to mention the cost of food, books, and supplies that the children needed for school. All of these parents were saddled with the same fear. They worried that their children would be forced to perpetuate a cycle where they still lived in a socially acceptable kind of slavery. They didn't want rudimentary education, rock bottom wages, poor working conditions to be their children's reality.

James was a true testimony to yeoman duty. He listened to them all, nodding sagely as they postulated. He declined food politely, always saying he would eat later, but he seldom did, he was so focused on his work. He was a force unto himself; powerful yet endearing and I couldn't help but notice how enthralled my father was by James. He watched him carefully and, in time, my father started to adopt his mannerisms: gentle nods of the head while he pretended to listen patiently, small gesticulations while he spoke. He even went as far as trying to substitute his lackadaisical saunter for James' upright stride.

When James wasn't engaging constituents at his home, he spent countless hours at our house with Elton, Bruce, and Norman. Winslow was usually absent, a fact which Bruce was quick to point out and James was equally quick to discount. According to James, Winslow's work took place primarily behind the scenes. As a lawyer, Winslow's main concern was drafting the legislation and preparing the necessary paperwork. Winslow was snowed under with incredible amounts of research which had to be finished in the very near future. Bruce grumbled whenever he had a chance and Elton shrugged good-naturedly. Norman and my father didn't seem to be bothered either way.

I guess each of them had found their coping mechanisms for the incredible amounts of stress they were under.

It was around this time that James started to cut back on his drinking considerably. He claimed that alcohol made him feel light-headed and short of breath, a notion which my father summarily dismissed as pure nonsense. Don't get me wrong; my father was dedicated enough to his Christian duty that even though he never went to church, he always gave up alcohol at Lent as his penance for Jesus' sacrifice. The only downfall was that he became a hypochondriac every Easter, catching colds and fevers at an alarming rate. And, just like Jesus, he soldiered on bravely for forty days and forty nights, never wavering even though he always complained about the mysterious maladies he contracted because he had "no rum to kill the worms".

In spite of my father's assertions, he could do little to persuade James to have more than one drink at a time. James would always say, "No, Vincent, I'm good" as he stubbornly nursed Kola Tonic and soda water until the ice melted and the wet ring around his glass dripped off the table and onto his slacks.

James' days were always the same: helter-skelter schedule, poor eating habits and long meetings with barely any breaks in between. But, as with anything else, some things break themselves.

Chapter 15

June 12th, 2015.

"You had all day to frolic and play the ass yesterday. What's the hold-up now?" Lia sighed, closed the door and rushed to sit in her usual chair in the Barbados room. After a whole day of rest, Susan should have been fresh and cheerful. Instead, she was more cranky than ever and had insisted that they start two hours earlier to make up for lost time.

The sun was only just coming up over the pretty garden beyond the French doors. Even though Lia had already had breakfast and a shower, she still couldn't suppress a yawn as she opened her notebook.

And although she hadn't had the chance to use the Internet the previous day, she hadn't been "frolicking" as Susan had assumed. It was hard to frolic comfortably in a senior citizens' community.

The only good thing about taking the day off was that Lia had taken the chance to review the copious notes she had been making on Susan. There were over one hundred pages and she'd realized that there were quite a few points she wanted to seek clarification on.

"So, Miss Taylor, I wanted to ask you a few questions if you don't mind."

Susan paused as she lifted her teacup to her lips and flicked her eyes in Lia's direction. "That's not the way this works, young lady."

Lia wasn't surprised. As a matter of fact, she'd been

expecting it. Susan's controlling nature showed itself in spectacular form every time they met. Lia couldn't figure out what Susan had to hide if she was so keen on having her biography written. It was the most asinine thing Lia had ever heard, but she wasn't brave enough to tell Susan that. Instead, she had come prepared. She smiled sweetly. "Well... a life that's as rich and beautifully layered as yours requires a bit of extra shading to help one truly grasp the gestalt of it."

Susan barked out a laugh. A laugh so deep and human that it startled Lia. The grim facade fell away and Lia could glimpse the beautiful girl who had spent her youth dreaming big dreams, wiling away her days in a gully with friends and loving her family unconditionally.

"Alright, yuh win dah one," Susan said, slipping comfortably into a Bajan dialect. "Now...what's the burning question that made you stay up all night composing that little soliloquy?"

Lia grinned and then grew serious. "Well, it always kind of bothered me; I guess if you've got success at your fingertips that you'd want to grab it by the horns. I...," Lia blushed. "I've loved your book since I was fifteen and I've read it about twenty times. How come you never wrote anything else? How come you just stayed here and never left?"

A deep silence settled over the room for a few moments. Then Susan sighed. Her posture sank a little as though Lia had foisted a heavy burden on her. She put down her teacup, the smooth amber colour of the ginger tea reflecting the hazel in her eyes as Susan folded her hands on her lap.

"Cordelia, there's a Bajan saying that 'loose goat don' know what tie goat see.' Do you know what that means?"

Lia smiled. "Don't judge someone unless you're in their shoes."

Susan looked into Lia's eyes, an internal battle waging

war beneath the steady hazel stare. "It's...," she struggled for the words, her hands grasping for them in thin air as she shrugged her shoulders. "...it's not the same when you gain success for something that brought you shame or pain. If you work hard for something that you took pride in then... that's different."

Suddenly restless, Susan stood up and went over to the bookcase. She shook her head at the volumes, touched their long leather spines and toyed with the cricket figurines. Her body trembled as she spoke. " 'Pretty-Eyed Susan,' " she said with a sneer. "I know that's what people call me. Nobody wants to be called that anywhere in the Caribbean. I used to think that if I was ever published that I'd be revered and the world would bow before me. Look at what I got instead. That book cost me everything. All for my spite. All for a situation that I created."

Lia exhaled and bit her lip. She didn't realize she'd been holding her breath waiting for Susan's answer. Shame crept into her chest, cold and heavy as she chastised herself for even asking the question and for wanting to ask another. In a way, she could understand what Susan said, but still, she had to know.

"Miss Taylor, It's been almost fifty years. And you keep saying how much writing used to mean to you. How could you hate something that you used to love so much? Why haven't you written anything since then?"

Susan smiled bitterly as she turned to face Lia. "Have you ever been with a boyfriend that your world revolved around and then you suddenly can't bear to see him? The thought of running into him with a new girlfriend makes your stomach churn so much you want to vomit? What's the difference?"

Lia struggled for an answer. She thought about her ex and how anxious and sick she had felt yesterday when she couldn't use the internet to spy on him. Her cheeks burned with embarrassment because as much as she wanted to see him and know what was going on in his life, she also kept hiding from him in public. Behind columns, ducking into bathrooms, Lia felt like she was always on the run from something that she couldn't understand whenever she saw him.

The young woman met Susan's eyes and nodded once. If nothing else, the two of them could agree on that point.

Chapter 16

1966

Many Barbadian children born after 1966 took free education for granted but during most of the 1950s, there was no such thing. The cost per child of $12 a week plus $4 for extras was a major burden and the only way that many poor black children could afford to go to school was through scholarships. The only problem was that scholarships were purposely designed to keep rank and file Barbadians out of school. Children had to do an exam before the district vestry would decide if that child qualified. Take Samuel and Eli for example; my parents might have been able to afford to send one child to secondary school, but the bill literally doubled with a twin and they simply couldn't afford it. That's why Samuel and Eli became carpenters. Kenneth's father, Norman, on the other hand, was a member of the district vestry and a well-to-do merchant, so he could easily afford the fees. I don't think Kenneth ever had it in his mind that he wouldn't go to secondary school.

James Hackett set about to change all of that. No longer would it be a question of if a child went to school. Completing secondary school would now be mandatory and all Barbadian children would be able to attend school up to the university level for free. It heralded the dawn of a new era and I was envious of those born after me.

My peers had to face entirely different realities. We never assumed that we would enjoy a life of frivolity while we endured school until we reached adulthood. That's why as time passed, the little neighbourhood playgroup dwindled.

Some got married and moved away, many had children at a young age and some of us just grew apart from each other. When I was growing up, a whole set of us used to meet in the gullies after school to pick fruit and play games. We would climb trees and pick whatever fresh bounty was offered us: mangos, golden apples, cherries or soursops. I never appreciated just how wonderful those times were until I grew older. By the time I was a young adult, practically all of my childhood friends had fulfilled their pre-ordained destinies. Very few broke the mold and used their education to build lives that were better than what their parents knew, but many walked in their parents' footsteps and in some ways it was a little sad to watch. The children of crop workers also became crop workers. The children of drunkards got inebriated at little gatherings, treating their livers with disdain as their parents did before them.

That kind of existence was fine for some, but I wanted more than a quiet country life in Barbados. I talked about the fancy cars I'd drive, the beautiful clothes I'd wear and the amazing people I'd meet. Kenneth would listen to me talking and talking, laughing at the far-fetched and whimsical descriptions that filled my imagination.

He would often interject with a bit of dry humour that did very little to cut the wind that filled my sails. I always laughed when he did that. He made fun of my imagination, but not my dreams. Otherwise, he was supportive and encouraging and made me feel like I was the best at whatever I did. That's no small thing in a world where being black, poor and female are enough to condemn you to a life of low expectations and mediocrity.

That is why I was so irritated when my father came home one day and announced that I was to start my new job as an assistant secretary for the Democratic Progressive Party in the morning. I still had another year of school and was looking forward to getting a job with the national newspaper when I graduated. In those times, telling your parents about dreams when they found you a paying job was frowned upon. Mummy looked at him like he had sprouted two heads. Her eyes met mine and she said nothing but her shoulders heaved and she exhaled the way she only did when she was angry. So, I bit the inside of my lip, fought back tears and I nodded curtly before I went to iron my best dress. And just like that, I was finished with school.

In those days, you didn't need much in the way of qualifications to have those kinds of jobs. You got on-the-job training and that was enough. My mother passed behind me and stroked my curly head with a gentle hand as I ironed my dress. Small, salty tears fell on the polka-dotted pleats in the full skirt, moistening the seams and making the creases as crisp as new paper.

I spent the next day tottering around the DPP office in my good dress and my mother's too-small kitten heels learning how to take dictation, write shorthand and draft official letters. It was dull work but I soon realized that the lessons I was learning would be invaluable when I got my job at the newspaper. My attitude improved quite a bit.

Weeks went on and I settled into a routine. The lady who trained me, Mrs. Manning, was nice and it was wonderful to get some pocket money I could spend on anything I wanted. With my first paycheck, I bought my mother some fancy fabric so she could make herself a nice dress and every week I gave her money to help pay bills. Despite the long hours, sore feet and hard work I enjoyed those times. The downfall was that I only spent time with Mummy when we did our chores. We'd hunker over laundry or piles of potatoes to peel. She'd listen to me prattle on about all of the exciting things that happened during my day, laughing at the silly things I said.

"I got to open a letter from the British Parliament today. It was on actual parchment, Mummy. Parchment! And it smelled like Lux soap, just like everything else that comes from England."

"Mummy, I don't know why, but whenever I get correspondence - not letters, correspondence sounds far more British - I always read them with an accent in my mind."

She would tell me about her day. "All of that rich food the pastor eating got he guts so big now. Talking about a big guts, Nita daughter pregnant with a second child now for that married man. She mother wan' know how it is that my Susie don't get caught up with them things. Hmmph." Mummy would have a big self-satisfied smile on her face and she would prance up at how well she had raised her children.

For the most part, I was happy.

And yet, what made me decidedly unhappy was when my father was late in collecting me from the DPP office. It was the full stop at the end of a long cart road lined with bearded fig trees that swayed like wooden tentacles when twilight fell. The rustling vines grated against each other when the wind blew and in the dark, they sounded like the creaking floorboards of a haunted house. The untethered imagination that I held so dear became my undoing and I was terrified to walk that road after hours.

I sometimes took the bus, but mostly my father insisted on taking me home because he didn't like me walking that road alone either. The problem was that shuttling around James meant Daddy sometimes came to collect me at all kinds of hours in the night. I'd stay in the office alone while it grew dark with nothing more to do but practice my typing.

One night in particular, I was clacking away on the typewriter getting my fingers caught between the metal keys when I smelled smoke. My heart skipped a beat. My first instinct was to rush out before I was burned like a roasted breadfruit in that building, but I sniffed again and realized it was a cigarette I was smelling. I pushed back my chair, cringing as it scraped loudly on the parquet floor. I grabbed a heavy metal paperweight engraved with the likeness of Queen Elizabeth II and made my way down the stairs.

I saw no one as I eased down dark carpeted corridors and peeked into empty offices. The night was still and I could hear ticking clocks and the rush of wind through the eaves. The stench of smoke grew even stronger as I searched every room in the building. He's outside, I thought to myself. I braced myself, knowing that I only had the element of surprise on my side. I yanked open the heavy front door and rushed out into the night. The courtyard was completely dark, save for the flicker from the lone exterior light that cast long shadows across the facade of the DPP building.

I could still smell the smoke but couldn't figure out where it came from until I saw the bright orange tip of a cigarette materialize next to the hibiscus hedge. It bobbed around in the dark, rising to the lips of a tall, well-built silhouette who took a slow drag on it before he exhaled a long plume of smoke.

He turned to look at me but said nothing as he lifted the cigarette to his lips again.

"Who are you?" I asked, a mixture of curiosity and fear making me swallow a bit too hard after I asked my question. I squeezed the paperweight in my hands as I cradled it behind my back, ready to throw it or bludgeon him with it if he came too close.

"Who do you think I am?" came the reply.

I was taken aback. If he was a thief or rapist, he wasn't in any hurry to perpetrate his crime and if he had any legitimate business, he wasn't in a rush to carry it out.

"Sir, you're trespassing on private property and I'm going to have to ask you to leave."

"Is that so?"

I straightened up and said in a more convincing voice, "Yes, as a matter of fact, it is. I'll have to ring for the police if you don't leave right now."

He chuckled lightly. "You're Vincent's daughter, I assume. No one else would dare question me."

The man flicked the now tiny cigarette butt onto the gravel and extinguished it with his foot. He stepped into the light. He was handsome with noble features that didn't easily lend themselves to laughter or mirth. He surveyed me and one of his eyebrows quirked for a moment as he deliberated. He must have decided that I was worthy of an answer before he spoke again.

"Winslow Vaughan. I work with James."

I racked my brain. I had heard the name but I couldn't remember in what capacity. "I've been here for three weeks and I've never met you. What exactly do you do?"

"I make dreams come true."

That wasn't the answer I was expecting. I laughed. "Oh really?"

"Mother Goose couldn't do what I do."

I bit the inside of my mouth, but I couldn't stop the smile that played on my lips. "And just how do you accomplish that?"

"It depends on the agenda. For the DPP, I broker deals and arrange financing to ensure that we can afford our campaign and pay the uppity new staff members who ask impertinent questions."   One corner of his mouth rose in a smirk. "But for you... the agenda would be quite different."

Something about the way he spoke caused tingles to run along my spine.

Before I could respond, headlights illuminated the corner and Winslow melted into the shadows of the building in the blink of an eye. My father pulled James' car to a stop right outside the office. He jumped out and smiled at me before he said, "Evenin', Susie. Had a good day?"

"Yes, Daddy."

"Good girl. Hope yuh didn't mind the wait too much tonight."

I shook my head, glad that the darkness around us shrouded the heavy blush that stained my cheeks. I didn't know why but I was very eager to see Winslow Vaughan again.

Over the next few weeks, I made numerous excuses to stay in the office late, but it was all for naught. I didn't lay eyes on Winslow Vaughan again until a month later and even then we met in the most unlikely place.

Daddy was in England with James. It was meant to be one of the last such trips before Barbados became independent. I had left my mother grumbling at home about how Barbados' freedom was costing her a husband. I greeted everyone I met on my way to the bus stop: both old and young, dark-skinned and light-skinned. It was miraculous how differently the other villagers viewed me at that time. They saw my stiffly starched sheath dress, the stockings that clung damply to my legs and the curly hair that my mother had pressed into submission with the hot comb and somehow I wasn't little Susie anymore. My father's work with James had given our family an esteemed position in the village. I stood out from the girls who dressed similarly, but went to work in the sweaty garment factories and came home smelling like lye every day. I was nothing like the older ladies who were stooped from bending their backs all day to pull weeds from the plantation fields, enmeshed in a gentler kind of slavery than my ancestors. They still greeted me in return, but with looks that no longer met my eyes and smiles that were less kind.

I stood at the bus stop, fretting that the bus was late when I spied a little car cruising down the road. The top was off and I thought for a moment that the driver must be completely oblivious to the heat that held the day in a stranglehold. The car pulled to a stop in front of me and without even glancing in my direction the driver said, "Good morning. Get in."

I was taken aback by Winslow's brusque address. "Pardon me?"

He leaned over and opened the passenger door, but didn't answer. The other lady at the bus stop raised an eyebrow in disgust but said nothing. Part of me disliked his attitude but the other side of me was so intrigued by him that I did as I was told. I looked askance at him as I closed the door, but he said nothing as he made a U-turn and headed back the way he came.

"Good morning, Mr. Vaughan," I said politely. "How are you today?"

"I thought our little chat a few weeks ago was a hint that I'm not a man who's overly concerned with pleasantries."

"I'm quite well, thank you and how are you?"

He downshifted the gears as he turned left at the T-junction. "Emperor Selassie once invited a warlord to his home. Selassie's cooks prepared all of the warlord's native foods while Selassie wined and dined him all night long. The warlord laughed mirthlessly believing that Selassie had finally bowed to him. But as the warlord ate and drank, the emperor sent men to infiltrate the camp and bribe the soldiers with cash and gold if they would hand over their weapons and leave. The warlord returned to an empty camp. He was shocked at how cunning Selassie was to use diversionary tactics to essentially make him a political eunuch."

I stared at him blankly. "What does that mean?"

"That you should always pay attention to your surroundings. We took the left turn instead of the right we needed to take to get to the DPP building."

I was aghast. "But I'll be late for work. Where are you taking me?"

"I told the office manager that I'll be commandeering you today."

I raised an eyebrow at him. "And why do I need to be commandeered? And I'm surprised that you would risk speaking to Mrs. Manning like that. She's no sweetbread."

"Firstly, I give orders; I don't take them. Secondly, I need you to take some dictation for me. I have a feeling you'll be quite good at it."

Chapter 17

16th June, 2015

Lia was up to her elbows in soapy water. A strong stench of bleach hung in the air as Lia worked. The white tiles gleaming brightly in the sunlight that shone through the bathroom window. Lia's light brown skin was dry and wrinkled after all of the cleaning she had done in the past few weeks. She regarded her hands with disdain as she worked, marveling at how much they looked like Susan's.

It was another bothersome Tuesday when the other occupants of the house did their weekly grocery shopping and left Lia with nothing but her thoughts and a ring around the tub to keep her company.

She had insisted that she didn't want Ancil to clean up behind her and Ancil had agreed. The caveat was that the older lady wanted Lia to adhere to the lofty standards she maintained. Nothing but a good scrubbing on the whole bathroom every other day would suffice for her. On top of that, Ancil did spot checks every day. She would smile brightly as she inspected Lia's work declaring that she would pass by later and "brush up the little spots that Lia had missed." Lia was determined not to hear that comment again this week. That's why she had spent almost two hours cleaning the tiny bathroom in her room.

By the time she packed away the cleaning supplies, it was almost time for lunch. She thought longingly of the roti she had helped Ancil to make earlier that morning and smiled. Lia had a quick shower and was about to head downstairs when the phone rang.

"Hello?"

"You say three weeks ago that you did going write to me. Even a carrier pigeon woulda bring that message by now."

Lia laughed. "Sorry, Mummy. I didn't realize that Miss Taylor didn't have internet when I told you so."

"Those old people set in them ways. How everything going?"

Lia lowered herself to the floor. "It's good. I like it here. I think we should be getting close to the end soon and I'll be able to meet the publishers and agents after that."

"So you does write every day?"

"Well, most days. Not on Tuesdays though. I just finished cleaning the bathroom."

"Cleaning de bathroom? Cordelia Davis, you left a good job down here to go up there and be that woman's lackey?"

Why did I tell her that? Lia exhaled and said patiently, "No, Mummy. I clean my room because Miss Taylor's helper has a lot to do and it's not fair to give her any extra work. I want to do it."

"Hmmph...alright." A dramatic sigh. "Girl..."

Lia could tell that what was coming next wasn't going to be good.

"Things ain't so good since you left. I barely hanging on. My knees hurting so bad, joints just seizing up all the time. The bailiff wan' come get de furniture soon effin' I don't get the money to pay for it. This phone probably goin' get disconnect soon too."

Lia pursed her lips. She knew her mother didn't have the best job in the world. She worked as a cleaner at a seedy guesthouse in a run-down area of Bridgetown that her mother insisted on calling 'a hotel'. The area was always crawling with rowdy foreigners who got into bar fights and patronized the brothels that dotted the crowded street. Her mother complained about the pay, the 'guests', management, the smell of urine and everything else, but never looked for another job. She whined about her lack of prospects, but never once took a class to improve her educational status. And to top it all off, her mother made bad decisions that kept them in a cruel cycle of poverty. She gambled heavily, always chasing the 'big win' which never chased her in return.

Despite it all, Lia knew that she could have been left at a children's home after her real mother died - a fact which she was always reminded of.

Lia swallowed. "I...I left some money in a book under my mattress. You can use that to pay the bill."

"Lia, you just put such a big smile pon my face. Alright, love, I gotta run now. You keep good, yuh hear."

The line went dead.

"I'm fine, thanks for asking, Mummy," Lia said. She shook her head and put down the phone. No longer hungry, she lay in bed and stared at the ceiling.

Chapter 18

August 1966

After just a few weeks, I was completely infatuated with Winslow Vaughan. He was smart and worldly and the power that emanated from him was completely intoxicating. He held doors open for me and did everything with such passion and intensity that it was hard to ignore him. Not to mention the perks that came along with being beside him.

In short order, he imbued me with a facsimile of his authority at the DPP. No longer was I the little grunt who was stuck with the filing and unceremonious tasks that no-one else wanted. No sir. Winslow was very clear about the fact that he wanted things done in a timely fashion and therefore, as his agent, my instructions were to be followed to the letter. Suddenly, I was at the top of the heap and no-one questioned it.

No-one except for my father of course. Winslow's attitude had always rubbed my father the wrong way. And now that Winslow was spending so much time with his only daughter, my father just plain disliked him for it. Daddy mulled over the situation and in the end, he dealt with it the only way he knew how.

"Susie, you ain't to work at the DPP no more. Your mother and I decide to send you to secretarial school." My mother gaped at him, clearly intrigued by this brand new information.

I scratched my head. "But Daddy, I'm already a secretary. And remember when you said that you don't believe in wasting money to educate girls just so they can marry and breed?"

"Yes, but yuh doing so well at it that me and your mother t'ink you should go to school and get yuh certificate." My mother rolled her eyes and turned back to shelling peas.

I squinted my eyes at him, unsure of what I was being instructed to do. "So stop being paid to be a real secretary, so I can spend money to go to school and learn how to do work I already know how to do?"

My father shifted his feet irritably. "Listen here, Susie. I am man and I say that you is to stop knocking around Winslow Vaughan."

Stray peas hit the side of the bowl with a clatter. My mother's hands stilled as she looked up at my father.

My cheeks coloured. "But Daddy, there's nothing wrong with working for him. What's the difference between working for him or someone else?"

He turned to my mother and shook his arms at me. "This is exactly what I mean. Talking back and questioning my authority."

My mother cleared her throat. "Vincent, Susie being fair in she question. Wha' is the reason you don't want her to work with Winslow?"

"Because I say so!"

"Alright." My mother put the bowl on the table and heaved herself up to her full height. "Susie, go and pick some more peas for me, please."

I glowered at both of them, shame and anger roiling through me at an untempered pace, but I just bit my top lip and went through the door.

I think my mother knew me well enough to know that I wasn't going to pick no damned peas. I snuck back to the window and listened to everything.

"Susie is eighteen years old and I raise my child right. She ain't gonna let no big hardback man come up to she with no foolishness."

"Winslow ain't no sweetbread, Grace. That man had some of everybody round hey. He even had the one-eye snow-cone woman."

"So you saying that I raise my child wrong?"

"B-but no, all I saying is that he ain't no use and I want Susie to be able to walk and hold she head high."

"Vincent, sometimes you need to relax yourself. We done raise these children. All we could do is hope they stick to the teachings we give them."

My mother asked if he was going to keep me in the house forever before reminding him that she was my age when she had the twins. My father grumbled something about changing times and wanting more for me. My mother must have kissed him then because he said what he always said after she pacified him that way, "Alright, alright. She could stay but only because I say it is to be so."

I kept working with Winslow. Two weeks later, I was in his bed. Either my father was a visionary or my mother hadn't raised me as well as she thought. Whatever Daddy thought, I knew what I had with Winslow was real. I knew it because he didn't encourage mediocrity like everyone else did. He pushed me to want great things for myself. I came to realize that adult Barbadians were highly risk-averse.

Complacency and a fear of failure were the results of three hundred years of slavery and all of the mental sublimation that came along with it, kept them timid and guileless. Toss in a lack of education and it was a lethal combination. Winslow never fell victim to the psychological shackles that held everyone else in a steely grasp. He dreamed dreams that were so big, my imagination could probably only take them all in because I was young. Had I been a few years older, I suspect that the collective disappointments of the world would have tainted my ability to see life's unrestrained potential.

And then, of course, there was the sex. There was something about being with an older man that I found to be undeniably erotic. He was commanding and certain in his actions which translated to a physical satisfaction that's hard to explain.

I have to admit that after getting involved with Winslow, I didn't spend much time with Kenneth. Between my work and Winslow, days lapsed into weeks and before I knew it, a month had gone by. John told me that Kenneth had asked for me on numerous occasions and I kept thinking to go and visit him but I never did.

Until one evening when Mummy sent me to the shop. She left home to take produce from our kitchen garden to her elderly aunt. My brothers had gone with Daddy to help James set up a stage in Bridgetown for a speech the next day so I was tasked with fetching two tins of corned beef to make sandwiches for them by the time they got home.

The shop was almost empty after the evening rush. Just a few stragglers sat in the corner nursing bottles of lager.

Kenneth jumped up from behind the counter knocking over one of the weights next to the scale in the process. "Evening, Susie," he said, hurriedly dusting flour from his apron. I caught myself staring at him. It's strange how some time apart can make everything seem fresh and new. Kenneth had been a tall and gangly child, but that day I looked at him and saw a man. His face had lost some of its boyishness and his chin had the hint of a beard. Lifting heavy sacks of potatoes and onions had chiseled his form into that of a dark-skinned Adonis and I couldn't help but smile shyly at him.

I put my striped blue, red and white grocery bag on the counter. "Evening, Kenneth. I need two tins of corned beef, a pound of onions and a tin of biscuits, please."

Kenneth put the corned beef and biscuits in the grocery bag before bringing a handful of onions in his apron and tipping them into the curved tray on the heavy metal scale. He shifted the weight on the counterbalance, glanced across at me and smiled. I smiled back and asked, "Where's your mummy?"

"She's in the house looking at dress designs in a magazine. She says she has to look 'sprank-cious," he said bobbing his head and flapping his hands comically. "Whatever that means."

We both snickered at his silly impression until he cleared his throat and said, "I've been wanting to see you for a while now. I keep asking John for you and he says you're hardly at home these days."

I laughed. "You saw me recently. And John saw me this morning."

"I normally see you every day."

I cast my eyes downward and grinned guiltily. "Yes. I know. Sorry... I've just been busy."

"Doing what?"

"Just busy."

Kenneth tossed up his hands and said miserably, "I thought we were best friends. Unless you're a serial killer like Jack the Ripper and you've got bodies under your bed, I don't know what you've got to keep so secret." He nervously brushed away the light dusting of flour on the counter, then murmured, "I wouldn't like it, but you know I'd help you bury the bodies. I've missed you, Susie."

My conscience bit me then. I remembered the last time I had shut him out and realized that I had to do better. Kenneth was right; we were friends and I wasn't being fair to him. He would understand once I told him. I glanced over his shoulder and then behind mine and then over his again. I leaned in and said, "If I tell you, you can't tell anyone... ok?"

He nodded quickly and then leaned in toward me. I spilled the beans and told him about me and Winslow. His face was a mixture of confusion and disgust.

"Winslow Vaughan? That smokestack with a bad attitude? He's a playboy, Susie."

My face flushed. "How would you know? It's not like you've even met him."

Kenneth rolled his eyes and shook his head in disgust. "You can't be serious. Daddy is always telling me about the pretty young girls he's toting around. And I heard he was with the one-eyed snow-cone woman. He may be good at making deals, but he's not any use."

"If you were really my friend, you would take my side and not just believe everything your father shoves down your throat. That story is harder to swallow than your mother's cooking."

He recoiled like I had slapped him. He pursed his lips and shrugged. "Don't play you vexed at me when you in the wrong. Try and shut your nostrils before you inhale these goods. That will be ninety-five cents for everything. Are you putting it on your account or paying now?"

"Put it up your ass," I said angrily. I snatched my bag from the counter and stalked home, furious at Kenneth for saying what he did. But somewhere in the back of my mind, the seed of doubt finally burrowed down and rooted itself firmly.

I stalked home, feeling the rage that kept my blood simmering hotly beneath my skin. I could tell my nostrils were flaring again as I thought about what Kenneth had said; he always joked that they gave away my anger. I usually laughed when he said it, but tonight it only made me angrier.

"Always criticizing me," I muttered angrily as I walked. "I don't make fun of his ears."

In the time it had taken to walk to the shop and argue with Kenneth, the road had grown dark and still. I continued to walk and grumble to myself as I bustled down the narrow road. It was fringed on both sides with long wild grass with blades so thin they would cut your fingers if you weren't careful. I passed the bend in the road where the church sat on my right with its long wooden windows tightly closed, and its door unlocked. Pastor said the church was the community's refuge and as such, would never truly be closed as long as he could help it. The church's closest neighbor was the rum shop next door and as long as Joan's father could help it, the rum shop would never be closed either. Even if it meant propping up the walls using the bones of his vertebrae, he would do his duty. I continued past the shop and its patrons, who barely glanced up from their rum and cigarettes to pay me any attention. Dominoes clattered and bottles clinked above the chaos of rowdy voices. I heard a chair scraping the ground as someone said they were going home and they would see everyone tomorrow.

Just one more corner to go and I would be home. The stink of cigarettes faded away and the scent of freshly cut grass mingling with dew provided a welcome relief. The overgrown field ahead luminesced with silvery moonlight. The soft grass gave way under my feet as I stepped off the road and took my usual shortcut through that overgrown field. The little footpath was hidden from the main road by bush and bracken that grew past my head. Frogs hopped out of my way and crickets chirped noisily as I shifted the bag on my shoulder. I brushed a lady-of-the-night plant with my fingertips as I passed by, lighting up the air with the bloom's sweet scent. I inhaled deeply to savor the fragrance but something wasn't right. I sniffed again and wrinkled my nose when I realized that I was also smelling a cigarette. Before I could turn around, I felt a heavy thud against my back and I fell forward into the grass. My bag fell into the bracken; the tin of corned beef clanked to the ground and the onions rolled under a bush.

Two meaty hands grabbed hold of my arms and pinned them behind my back. A heavy mass settled on my back and legs completely immobilizing me. I didn't even have time to scream before he pulled the cigarette out of his mouth and pushed the tip towards my face. The glowing embers bounced like an orange firefly in the darkness. The smoky stench of tar and tobacco filled my nostrils when he brandished the cigarette mere inches away from my eyes.

"Scream and I gine push this inside you instead."

Somehow that one word - "instead" - made my limbs go numb and my blood run cold. That was what fear did to me that night: it crippled me and made me less than what I was. With a simple utterance, that strange man broke me and I became hollow in an instant.

I said nothing, whimpering silently as he yanked my dress up around my waist and pressed me further into the ground. My tears started. I felt the grass beneath my face, soft and damp. I felt his hand on my upper thigh, rough and warm. Rum and sweat eked out of his pores. I heard the clatter of his belt buckle against the zip on his pants as he started to undress. Something warm and fleshy rubbed against my leg and everything inside me cringed with a dark, sticky fear.

Then fate intervened.

A heavy crunching noise sounded behind me. He fell forward and I felt the full weight of his musty body on mine. I screamed. But he was still and for a moment I grew even more fearful.

"Susie?"

I broke down in tears as Kenneth pushed that man off my back and helped me to my feet. I started shaking and scratching my face and neck. Perhaps because I had already braced myself for what was to come, my body felt phantom pains that tore at my body and left invisible scars. Kenneth glanced at me for a moment but said nothing before reaching down to pick up the onions under the bush. He shouldered the bag, looked down at the man, bit his lip and turned back toward me.

He guided me back to the main road - the road I should have taken in the first place instead of that short cut - and then told me to wait for a moment as he had forgotten to pick up the corned beef. Leaving the moonlit path to return to the harsh neon streetlights was like being tossed into an alternate reality. It should have felt safer there, but it didn't. I latched onto him, wide-eyed and tremulous with fear.

"Nooo, Kenneth...no...no. Come and go home with me."

He looked me straight in the eyes and for the first time, the quiet and humorous boy was gone and the steel-eyed glare of a man looked back at me.

"Susie, I said I'm coming back. If there's one thing in life I want you to believe is that I will always come back. No matter what."

I nodded numbly. "Okay. Okay... come back."

He pressed his lips gently on mine, as gently as the moon that washed our skin with silvery light. There was no hurry nor passion; his kiss was merely comfortable and reassuring. I trusted him and let my hand slip away from his as he turned away and disappeared through the narrow overgrown footpath.

I paced. Then bobbed on the balls of my feet in the glare of the streetlight. Then paced some more until Kenneth returned. Neither of us uttered a word as we walked.

He put one arm around my shoulders and clutched my bag of goods with the other. The house was shrouded in darkness when we arrived; Mummy still wasn't back from her aunt's house. I sank onto the bed, the heavy mattress springs squeaking wearily as I did. Something - maybe regret or fear - lay heavy on my chest as everything played over and over in my mind. Kenneth quietly slipped away to the corner to light the kerosene lamp. My friend fetched water from the white enamel face basin in the other corner of the bedroom and tenderly wiped the streaks of mud from my face and arms.

"Susie?" he said tentatively. He held my head gently in his hands as he forced me to look into his eyes. "Please stop shaking your head like that and talk to me."

"Shaking my head?"

"Yes. Like someone has asked you a question and you keep saying no."

My lips trembled as I started to cry.

"Tell me what happened."

"He just came up behind me and pushed me down. He wanted to…he tried to…," I wailed miserably, unable to finish the sentence.

"Shh…shhh…it's alright. It's alright. He can't get to you again." He pulled me to him, trying his best to calm me as my body quaked with sobs.

We stayed like that for many minutes, just the two of us alone in the quivering lamplight on that old bed. His hands and body made strong by years of hard work, became a fortress of strength for me as he protected and reassured me that night. He was remarkably calm considering what both of us had just experienced and like osmosis, some of his calm seeped into me. I knew it was in no small part due to him that I was able to start the healing process.

"Did you follow me?" I asked.

He nodded, a blush creeping up his face as though he was embarrassed. "Yeah. I figured that if your nostrils flared anymore a stiff wind would pick you up and carry you away like Mary Poppins."

I laughed and cried at the same time, wiping away my tears as he grinned at me.

"Do you remember when we watched that at the Empire last year? You laughed so hard when the penguins started dancing."

I smiled at him, then looked at my hands in my lap. He stared at his feet for a moment before he said, "It's funny how easily we can see love in movies or books but it's so hard to see it in our own lives."

Surprised, I regarded him for a moment before I said, "I love the way you said that. It's almost poetic. I must be rubbing off on you." I exaggerated a big wink at him as he smiled broadly at me. "You know... I started writing a short story yesterday. I'm going to steal that line for my story to save you the trouble of having to write it yourself."

The smile stayed on his lips but left his eyes as he nodded numbly at me. I felt then that something was askew - like I was the one who had missed something.

"What?" I asked, my smile waning. "Are you upset because of what I said?"

Kenneth smiled warmly before pulling me to him and hugging me. "Nah. Besides, it's not about me right now. It's about you. What he tried to do to you was horrible but everything is going to be alright. You'll see."

I sniffed sadly as I pulled away from his chest and turned my tear-stained face to him. "Shouldn't we go to the police?"

He looked me squarely in the eyes and said, "We didn't tie him up or anything Susie. He probably ran away as soon as we left. Plus I don't think either of us got a good look at him."

My shoulders slumped when I realized he was right. "But what if he follows me again?" I asked as the realization sank in. I held tight to Kenneth's hands, suddenly trembling with fear. "What if he knows where I live and tries to come here and hurt me?" Inertia gripped me. I sucked in a breath, afraid to exhale.

At first, Kenneth said nothing. The steady chirping of the crickets outside my bedroom was the only noise we could hear. He chewed the inside of his lip, obviously weighing his thoughts carefully before he said, "Susie...do you remember when you were at the shop and I told you that you can trust me with anything? That if I had to do something to help you that I would?"

I exhaled and nodded slowly.

A gust of wind whooshed by the house. It made an eerie, ghost-like sound as it echoed through the timber eaves. It rattled the wooden windows and even in the dim light, I could see that Kenneth's attention was so unwavering that not even that infernal noise could shake his focus.

The lamplight flickered and caught his eyes and the fire that was reflected from them caused my breath to hitch in my chest.

"He's not an issue anymore. Do you understand?" Kenneth whispered.

I nodded again.

Kenneth pulled me to him and kissed me gently. We stayed like that until the wind wore itself out and the dark became impenetrable. That was the good thing about Kenneth. While Winslow was exciting and unpredictable, Kenneth was comforting and reassuring. He was just what I needed at that moment.

Early the next morning, as the sun dawned bright and clear on my little village, an unsuspecting passerby found an unconscious man with two deep gashes to the head lying on the grassy path just past the rum shop. The newspaper story was a heartbreaking piece of journalism. The victim was well-known to the area; a labourer at the nearby plantation who lived in a neighbouring village with his wife and children. His name was Simon Whittaker and the poor man had suffered broken ribs, blunt force trauma to his head and paralyzing injuries to his spine.

Everyone asked who would do such a thing. They tutted and shook their heads as they read the story or had it read to them, lamenting how our sweet little island was going to seed. Pastors prayed for Barbados' salvation and mothers chastised their children for taking shortcuts off the beaten path. Simon never told anyone who hurt him (not in the least because his jaw was permanently damaged) and the police were never able to get a concrete lead on the perpetrator. Mr. Simon Whittaker never culled another stalk of sugar cane again; he lived out of the rest of his brain-addled days in a hospice where his wife visited daily and fed him broth from a spoon.

Chapter 19

June 18th, 2015

"What did your parents say about what happened?"

Susan shook her head and lowered her teacup. "I never told them."

Lia tilted her head. "But why not?"

"You're such a clever little wordsmith. Tell me exactly how I should have framed such a declaration to my parents about their only daughter," Susan snapped.

Stunned by Susan's acidic retort, Lia sat back into her chair and waited a moment before she tried again.

"Ms. Taylor, I don't mean to be rude or forceful by asking that question. I just wondered why you didn't say anything to them about it."

"I never said anything to anyone about it until now."

Lia stared at her. "Never?"

Susan stirred her tea with a bit too much venom but didn't look up.

"I'm very sorry about what happened to you, Ms. Taylor. I'm only trying to understand how the situation unfolded. I apologize if my questions seem insensitive."

Susan heaved a sigh and shook her head. She smiled ruefully and looked at Lia. "Even though it was a near miss and it happened almost fifty years ago, it still does something to me. I don't even want to begin to imagine what would have happened if Kenneth hadn't come by. I'm sorry. It's a very difficult thing to discuss."

"But why?" Lia asked.

"I guess because I was raised in a time when women

were expected to endure. Men were always right. I wasn't sure how to explain it properly. I didn't know if telling would have done more harm than good. You can pick any one of those reasons and run with it."

"Reasons or excuses?"

Susan glared at her. "Young lady, you'll come to understand in your lifetime that life doesn't always hand us what we need. We fit within the parameters that the world delivers and we square away our differences in private. How wonderful for you that in your lifetime there are rape centres, helplines and TV shows like Law & Order: SVU. Back then, there was nothing of the sort. The school system never prepared me for such an eventuality and I never heard anyone explain how to be a victim. So I pretended I wasn't one and moved on."

Lia sighed and nodded her head. "I'm sorry, Ms. Taylor."

Susan sat up straighter and said, "Don't be sorry. I would never want such a thing for you, Cordelia. Try to avoid rape if you can. Be brave and speak up if you can't." Her voice wavered at the end and a tear slipped down her cheek.

The look on Susan's face touched Lia's heart. She got up and reached out to hug the older woman. To her surprise, Susan extended her arms too.

Chapter 20

August 1966

I can look back now and admit that sex probably accounted for eighty percent of my attraction to Winslow. Simply because, outside of the sex and his big imagination, Winslow was difficult to manage.

He was full of rich ideas about people who were lazy and unable to accept responsibility for their actions - all traits that he possessed in large quantities. One prime example was a deal that he made in 1960 which came back to haunt him in 1966.

My father had summed it up best one evening as he sat in his chair, back bent, his right elbow on his knee and his chin propped on his hand. His face bore the troubled look of one with severe constipation. "That boy, Winslow Vaughan, get send to the States to organize trade deals; just get good deals on rice and peas or something to feed poor people. That is all he get send to do. You imagine he come back talking 'bout how Barbados gine be making weapons with the Americans and Canadians?"

Unbeknownst to the other 230,000 Bajans he was representing, Winslow had convinced both the US and Canadian military departments that Barbados was perfectly situated for the sixty-five-foot HARP gun they were looking to construct. James was livid and so was the rest of the DPP, but there was no way to back out. Construction began in earnest as the party collectively swore under their breath. By 1963, the military and engineers had doubled the size of the HARP gun to one hundred and twenty feet and testing of the gun began. Massive tremors rocked parts of the island whenever the military fired that gun towards the Atlantic, leaving anyone with ill health nursing headaches and other maladies for days on end. The entire DPP practically held their breath for years, worried that this alliance would anger other military superpowers by harboring that piece of Cold War artillery. In 1966, when Winslow suggested that they secretly feed information about the project to the Russians and Cubans in exchange for money, James declared enough was enough and relegated Winslow to the dregs of the party. He was left to craft legislation and nothing more. Three months before independence and his dream of becoming a minister of parliament had been dashed. Winslow's mood worsened.

 His erratic behaviour, unnecessary stubbornness, and mercurial temper were hard to predict and even harder to understand. He was a stickler for respect and order but he never reciprocated. And then there were his dreams. They cast him into fits of despair like nothing else. Once he dreamed that someone stole his safe and left it open in the middle of a barren field. A great gust of wind sprang up, caught the bank notes like fallen leaves and swept them out to sea. He chased behind them like a man possessed, fighting against the raging black sea until it finally sucked him under and he and his money were no more. He woke up in cold sweats and had to drink three shots of brandy to settle his nerves.

 I often wondered if he was like Van Gogh, plagued by a genius so great that the weight of it was too much to bear. At first, I tried soothing him as I'd seen my mother do with my father. A quick kiss on the cheek and a word of reassurance. A hearty meal and a tender hug. These things seldom worked and only served to incite his wrath more because he accused me of trying to "dim his desire to incite change for his fellow man."

He was perhaps most enraged when he was around Bruce. He detested how close Bruce was to James. Winslow often complained that Bruce was not interested in helping black Barbadians, but was merely a figurehead that the plantocracy had put forward to ensure that everything James did was to their advantage.

As the weeks went on, I said less and less, sure that the stress of the rapidly approaching deadline for Independence was to blame for his mood swings. I played the dutiful wife, cooking his favourite foods at the great house and laying in his bed at his command. I was waiting for a version of him to surface that I had never seen, but desperately hoped was there.

In time, other problems emerged. I came to realize that Winslow had taken up with none other than Joan Mayers. Despite all of the years that had passed since those childhood rivalries, our rift hadn't mended and time had only served to deepen our mutual resentment.

Winslow said he needed another secretary and she came in the form of that dark-eyed grinch. Joan had grown up beautifully, I'll admit. Dark chocolate skin and beautiful eyes, her features were decidedly ethnic with those full lips and high cheekbones. And yet, her beauty could not distract from her perpetual grumpiness.

I never found out whether he initiated the affair or if she did it just to spite me, but that didn't change the fact that I was broken by it. She never hid it and took to dropping little remarks about how nice his body was or how much energy he had. The stress of it all gave me terrible headaches, but I was too afraid to confront him about her antics lest he throw a tantrum. So I did all I could to make her days miserable.

I put a dollop of mud in her chair so that it looked like she soiled herself when she stood up. I soaked the ribbons from her typewriter with extra ink so that her good clothes were spattered when she typed. Joan gave as good as she got, frightening the dickens out of me when she left a centipede in one of my kitten-heels and putting a slug in my lunch. The office became a war zone and eventually, it bled into our home lives too.

My anxiety at work was only matched by the anxiety I faced at home. Joan had slept with Winslow to upset me, but what drove me crazy was that she also harbored a deep love for Kenneth. I overheard my brothers say she was always loitering around the shop trying to get friendly with him. To compound matters, my friendship with Kenneth had become heavy and uncomfortable. There was something piteous about the way he watched me after I was attacked: the way one looks at a puppy with a lame leg or a butterfly with a torn wing. I could see how he saw me: a flawed human being with hurt in my past, a shell that thinly covered cracked emotions. That hurt me. Seeing myself like that in someone's eyes made me worry that all of the defenses I had built up were flimsy armaments that could never withstand any real rigors. I always pitied myself whenever he looked at me that way and instead of loving him for sympathizing with me, I resented him. If I was healthier emotionally, I would see it as a call-to-action and I could set about trying to repair the fractures that I had clumsily plastered over. Our relationship, while not broken, felt like a burden. I couldn't split myself in two so I had to choose. I decided to start spending more time with Kenneth. My rationale was that Winslow spent more time at meetings and was easier to manage. Kenneth spent his entire day at the shop so Joan had more opportunities to visit him there. I realized later that I started spending so much time with him to make Joan jealous even though I hated the looks he gave me. The conflicting emotions inside me warred. In the end, I told myself that he was my friend and I didn't want her to sully him too. My only consolation was that he never returned her interest and I giggled with glee at the way he always kept a polite distance from her.

And yet that wasn't enough for me; I rubbed salt in her wound whenever I could.

If we walked past Joan at the standpipe, I'd clutch Kenneth's hand, press my breasts against his shoulder and lean in to whisper the most banal sentences. "Mummy left some pepper pot for you in the conaree jar." His eyes would brighten - everyone knew how much Kenneth loved pepperpot - his face would break into a broad grin and he would exclaim, "You serious? I can't wait to get to your house." I'd smile at him and let him lead me home as the daggers from Joan's eyes pinged harmlessly at my back. It was a very wicked thing to do, especially because I knew full well that Mummy hadn't made pepperpot in weeks. Running interference between those two men and Joan became the rhythm of my life for months.

Outside of my problems, everything was moving along rapidly in preparation for Independence. Bruce and his caucasian friends donated money to the party to assist James with the food baskets he distributed every Tuesday. More and more people showed up every day asking for jobs, food, help with bills and all other kinds of daily troubles. The DPP couldn't sustain the altruism on its own. Winslow complained that every donation meant serious adjustments had to be made to the various laws that were being created. Simply because those hefty donations came at a price. Bruce and his friends were greasing the wheels of bureaucracy and making gentle suggestions for their own gain. James felt conflicted by wanting to help the poor while depending on the rich to do it. Elton lived for the imminent glory of having his name etched on history's page. My father and Norman loved being around power. Winslow wanted to be rich without having to work for it. The DPP was a tangled mess of agendas cleverly masked as a progressive institution.

It was a vividly bright Tuesday when James mentioned he was feeling poorly. I got him a glass of water and sat on the other side of his desk to take dictation for a note to the newspaper. He wiped his brow repeatedly as he spoke. He squinted at me with glassy eyes as he started to sway. I ran to get his secretary but I only made it as far as the door when I heard the glass break as it hit the floor. I looked back to see him clutching his stomach and vomiting blood all over his antique desk.

I jumped back in horror as that awful splashing sound filled the room. Bloody little droplets and undigested food trickled down the front of the mahogany bookcase and a bright red stain bloomed on the ornate rug under his desk.

We rang for the ambulance, but it was slow in coming, even for the future prime minister. Only three people at the office had cars. Elton and Winslow were out at separate meetings. My father was delivering letters in James' car and in those days there were no cell phones so the best I could do was call every single place I knew my father had gone to and hope to catch him. It was all for naught. My father couldn't be found.

James lay there unconscious as his secretary cried and fanned him with a folded newspaper. The room grew uncomfortable as everyone crowded into it offering suggestions and trying to direct things as best they could. James lay there like a bag of rotting potatoes and all we could do was stand around, wringing our hands and watching him.

I liked James as a person, but it wasn't just the thought of a nice person dying that scared me. James was the father of independence and I couldn't imagine it carrying on without him. Perhaps everyone had that same idea. Anxiety shrouded the room as we all waited for a miracle. I stood there watching him grow pale and everything inside me coiled up. I thought of other girls not being able to go to school because "boys were better". I thought of the woman with six children and three limbs who now sold nuts at the market on weekends but still couldn't make ends meet. I thought of my family and how freely my mother sang now that she wasn't managing a shoestring budget. Yes, I complained about not being able to go to school, but I had a job - a good job - and it was all because of the man who lay before me with blood and stomach acid clotting on his chin. I didn't even want to think what would happen to my family if anything befell James.

The wail of the ambulance siren shattered our anxiety but could it weaken the rusty scent of blood that rent the air or strengthen the slow breaths that wheezed out of James' mouth? Was it too late?

The gravity of the situation was too much for me to bear. I fainted.

"Susie...you alright?"

"Where is he?" I asked as I blinked slowly to let my eyes adjust to the light.

"De ambulance come. He gotta ulcer so they gotta operate."

I said nothing else as my father drove home. My entire family spent that whole night in stir. The new Rediffusion box screeched out white noise all night long and no-one complained about it keeping them awake. We knew there would be no broadcast, but the steady hum of that static dead air was better than the nervous silence that filled the house.

By the time morning broke, all my mother could do was make Daddy a cup of tea before he rushed down to the hospital to find out if James made it through the surgery.

Hours later, Daddy returned with good news.

My family and the rest of Barbados breathed a little easier again. Or so I thought.

Chapter 21

June 17th, 2015

Lia bounded down the stairs, sleep-deprived but happier than she had been in all of the weeks since she had been in the United States.

Ancil shelled peas and hummed hymns at the kitchen table as the sweet scent of boiling oats topped with cinnamon and brown sugar filled the kitchen. Lia greeted Ancil with a cheery "Good morning!" as she pulled up a chair at the table and poured herself a cup of tea.

"Wha' happen that you in such a good mood?" the other lady asked, smiling at Lia.

"Well..." said Lia with a smug grin, "you'll be happy to know that I have finally finished plotting the entire outline for Miss Taylor's biography. Ancil, my Bajan flower, my eminence is imminent."

Ancil stared at her with one eye closed, the way she always did when something confused her. Lia laughed. "It just means that my ship is on the horizon...my fame is approaching...I'm going to be a famous author." Lia sighed deeply and gazed out the window as though the white sails of her glorious ship were billowing over the rooftops.

Ancil laughed. "Don' discombobulate my brain with dem big words, Miss Cordelia."

"It is absolute genius, the way I've plotted it out. I thought that instead of just doing it chronologically from her birth, I'd start with her at this point in her life and then work in her story along the way. I even started writing the first chapter last night." Lia did a bouncy dance in her chair, drawing a little cackle from Ancil.

"You done eat so quick?" Ancil asked just two minutes later.

Lia feigned horror. "Ancil, my greatness won't make itself. The sooner I talk to Miss Taylor, the sooner I finish my notes. The sooner I finish my notes, the sooner I write the book. The sooner I write the book, the sooner I'll be so famous I'll have to schedule my fan club meetings at the National Stadium."

"Alright, Miss Cordelia. You get along then. No, no - leave the bowl, I goin' wash up. You goin' need that extra ten seconds fuh you greatness."

Lia skipped lightly down the hallway, buoyed by the prospect of creating her very first novel. "My first best-selling novel," she corrected herself.

She knocked on the door and entered when she heard a gruff response. Susan didn't look very pleased to see Lia looking so pleased.

"Hmph, you've got firecrackers in your underwear? Why are you so uppity today?"

Lia laughed. "No, ma'am. I finished the outline for the book last night and I'm just very happy to go over it with you." She waved eight sheets of scribbled notes gleefully.

"You're getting ahead of yourself, young lady. Shouldn't you hear the whole story before you start planning it?"

"Well, I've heard a lot of it already, but I was thinking that if I had a better idea of how I'd like it to go that it would help me to ask better questions."

Susan didn't respond. She just kept stirring her tea.

"Which brings me to another thing: can we meet your publisher soon?"

Susan heaved an irritated sigh. "One thing at a time, Cordelia."

"My mother always tells me that. To be honest, I'm more of a planner. I guess it's a sort of coping mechanism or something. But..."

"Cordelia."

Lia gulped. She knew that tone. "Yes, Miss Taylor?"

Narrowed hazel eyes stared at Lia. "Stop talking and start writing."

"But..."

Susan eyed her stubbornly and said, "We haven't finished 1966."

Lia bit her tongue and resigned herself to tackling the outline the next day. She picked up her notebook, ready to do Miss Taylor's bidding once again.

Chapter 22

September 1966

Winslow often brought me to the house to play the waitress for his meetings. I would bustle around making finger sandwiches, frying fishcakes and topping up everyone's drink while he schmoozed with bankers and captains of industry. I saw us as what you'd call a power couple, both young and good-looking with the world on a string. He would hold court in the dining room where flickering kerosene lamps and candelabras illuminated the burnished wood furniture and fine crystal. Winslow said he needed a "more intimate atmosphere" for such delicate meetings. That may have been true, but I knew that he still hadn't paid to reconnect the electric service.

The juxtaposition was amazing to behold. James' spirited meetings were held in a bright room crowded with people while humble food was passed around on enamel dishes. They were good salt-of-the-earth people with no greater ambition than fair treatment. The meetings that James moderated with the poor blacks were shrouded in hope tinged with a bit of depression.

When that group spoke about a lack of opportunities, low wages, and substandard conditions, it forced me to reframe my concept of life and expectations. I could never imagine being submerged in a life where I did nothing but work, cook, clean and look after children. Winslow's moody meetings were one-on-one affairs fueled by brandy in a hazy cloud of cigar smoke. The business owners he met with were quick to point out that higher wages for staff meant higher prices for consumers which meant that Bajans of every rank and file would be back to square one by the time you accounted for the price increases. Even I could admit that when you framed it like that they had a good point. It was clear that some others simply didn't like the idea of paying blacks too much money. Some opined that they wouldn't be able to remain viable because there were rumors that the flood gates of trade would be thrown open to the USA after Independence. Many worried the Americans would bring their budget-friendly operations to offer lower prices and competing brands. All of this talk was fueled by massive changes that James had instituted. The three-hundred-year-old port at Carlisle Bay had ceased operations after the development of the Deep Water Harbour at Pelican Island a few years earlier. The new habour was how Barbados demonstrated to England that the country could support itself after Independence, but thus far trade with countries outside of Europe wasn't that robust. Business owners had grown comfortable with the status quo and they didn't want anyone to trifle with it. The rumours made the merchants fearful that the United States' aggressive efforts would completely dominate trade. Not to mention the rumours that the country would soon eschew the usage of the Eastern Caribbean banknotes in favour of a Barbadian currency that would be tethered to the American dollar.

Many of these were fears which Winslow himself tended to propagate and then brush off as though they were of little concern to the average businessman. Their eyes would widen and they would worry aloud that these factors spelled their imminent demise.

But Winslow had a plaster for every sore. The script seldom varied but one particularly memorable scene played out on a warm September night with a rotund merchant who owned a pharmacy and dry goods store. A man who clearly lived too well, Mr. George Best generously filled out his clean and immaculately pressed shirt jack. He pouted like a sullen child as he wiped his flushed face with a crisp white handkerchief.

I had a good view of the visitor and Winslow from my post in the darkened alcove across from my lover's chair. I had heard this spiel too many times to count but I had never seen someone's face get that red before. Winslow listened, feigning sympathy as the merchant did little to hide his greed and indifference toward the poor. He complained about the pitfalls of being in business while Winslow leaned back in his chair, sipping his twelve-year-old scotch as though deep in thought. I knew better. He had practiced this routine until it was as smooth as the ice that cooled his liquor.

"But how can I keep my doors open when the Americans flood the markets?"

"Ah, don't worry about that, Bessie. Better paid staff will be more motivated and they'll produce at much higher rates. Profits will skyrocket. You'll be rich before 1970."

"Produce what?" the guest asked indignantly, his drink remaining untouched. "Everything I sell is imported. There's no wiggle room for me. Furthermore, I've heard that when this independence thing is settled that import licenses are going to be handed out like Christmas toffees. We're already autonomous. We've got our own money, and we never even took Grant A when the British offered it. Explain why we need to spend a bundle on a new flag, new police uniforms for the bobbies and all of this lot when we've got a premier running the government and everything else."

Winslow shrugged lazily. "I have no argument with what you're saying, Bessie. I can see the issues that the proposed minimum wage would have on your business and its bottom line."

The unsuspecting pigeon stared at him, his anxiety practically leaking out of him as the candlelight illuminated the sweat that beaded his brow.

The ice cubes in Winslow's glass clinked gently,

thinning the amber liquid as he took his time swirling it, pretending to weigh his next sentence carefully.

"We are creating a system of unparalleled social services for Barbadians: free health care, free social support services, free garbage collection, free education up to the tertiary level. I'm sure you can appreciate the burden of all of these services on a young government."

The man stuttered, spittle flying from his lips as he said, "Y-yes…but what about me? You're going to put me in the poor house with these Robin Hood tactics! You want me to pay my staff twice what I usually would; I can't afford that. And opening up trade with the Americans? I'll be just like these unwashed masses in two months."

Winslow's face steeled and he fixed the man with an unwavering stare. "Your staff has been unwashed for years. We can't wrap up the Independence referendum without the support of these same people you're trying to fleece. Barbados is in a horrible financial consortium with the other islands that should be abolished. The country will remain a part of the Commonwealth nations, so all ties to Britain won't be lost. Opening up trade will give rise to other businesses and offer the people more competitive prices on goods."

The man huffed impatiently as he stood to go, obviously not too pleased with how the meeting had gone. "I'll mull this over and get back to you."

"You'll do no such thing," was Winslow's languid reply. He took a sip from his glass as he stared at the gentleman from upturned eyes. "The existing legislature will be dissolved on the tenth of October and I've got many other meetings before then. You talk to me now or you don't talk to me at all."

"I'd rather deal with James on these matters, not a greenhorn like you with no manners. You don't know how to talk to people or how to be a good politician."

Winslow smiled up at him. I shivered. I had seen that

smile before.

"Despite what you think, I know quite a lot of things. For example, buggery is still a crime and should anyone else learn that you have carnal knowledge of your shop assistant, Frank, I suspect that a wage increase will be the least of your problems. People wouldn't want to catch any homosexual diseases from someone selling pharmaceuticals. I know that your wife wouldn't be too pleased to learn that news either. You might also be interested to know that the opiates which you intentionally mislabel and import for your own usage are against the law as well."

The man's face paled. His breathing grew shallow and a cold tension settled over the room as Winslow walked to the sideboard and refilled his glass from the crystal decanter.

Bessie eased himself back into the chair and his tone softened as he tried a different tact. "Look...you're a man who likes nice things. What if we split the baby?" The chair scraped the mahogany floor as he edged closer to Winslow, his confidence worming its way back into his spine. "There must be give and take in these situations."

"I'm glad you realize that," said Winslow crisply. "What will you give me if I don't take your fat ass to prison?"

"How about this?" Bessie asked. "A thirty percent wage increase instead of forty, but the government will charge double the tariffs on any competing imports in the category. And I'll tell you what: I'll even set you up with a nice watch. You should carry something more befitting a man of your taste...a Rolex maybe?

Winslow sat quietly, pretending to contemplate both sides of the situation. He nodded thoughtfully as though he had resigned himself to logic, never once letting on that he had no authority to dismiss the forty percent wage increase James had always intended. "You're right, we have to protect Barbadian industries. That seems fair. Rose gold oyster inset, black leather straps and the little window that shows the date. I like those."

The man stared back at him, confusion clear on his face.

"The watch," Winslow replied, as he stood to escort the gentleman to the door. "And make sure it's here by the middle of next month. I'd like to wear it to the flag-raising ceremony."

But sometimes, even Winslow couldn't find a way out of the holes he dug. Just two months before Barbados was set to raise its very own flag for the first time, Winslow received a visit from a man named Ignatious Grimes. Short and wiry with light brown skin and steely grey eyes that could penetrate a lead door, Ignatious Grimes gave me the shivers from the moment I laid eyes on him. He walked slowly, intentionally so, as though he presumed the world would wait until he arrived before starting the proceedings.

He had been the last mayor of Bridgetown before being unceremoniously booted out in a landslide election. I'm not sure why, but no-one ever called him Mr. Grimes or Ignatious. It was as though everyone secretly knew that tampering with his name would be akin to sacrilege. They balanced their fear of him by only calling him by his full name.

It was a dark and stormy night when I first happened upon that strange little man. I suspect he waited until that infernal weather hit the island to make his appearance - in the time that followed, I came to realize he had quite a flair for the dramatic.

Winslow was giving me some of the sweetest, most intense sex I've ever had. The rain pounded on the roof of the great house, its steady rhythm making the experience even more enjoyable.

So engrossed were we, that we never heard the squeak of the front door's hinges or the groan of slow footsteps on the creaky stairs.

A few minutes later, with a heavy grunt and shudder as sweat beaded his brow, Winslow uncoupled and collapsed in a heap next to me. That's when I saw him. As worn out as Winslow was, my blood-curdling scream was enough to make him sit bolt upright. He spun around and saw the little man, sitting calmly in an antique winged back chair. His eyes never left Winslow's as he stared at him over steepled fingers.

Winslow jumped up, grabbed the sheet to cover himself and barked, "How did you get in here?"

"The same way you got into her; the entrance was open," he replied in a deep, clear voice that had no business coming out of such a small person.

My cheeks flushed angrily. I said nothing, waiting for Winslow to hit him or drop an expletive-laden rant at such rude remarks. Instead, Winslow asked angrily, "What do you want?"

"The same things you want. You may already know of me, but I'll go through the protocol nonetheless. My name is Ignatious Grimes, former mayor of the city of Bridgetown. I'm a misunderstood visionary and I've decided that you may be deserving of my tutelage."

Winslow squinted at the little man, "Oh...you're the one who did up all of those faulty land deeds."

I bit my lip as I stared at the former mayor who also happened to be Joan's uncle. What they lacked in physical resemblances, they certainly made up for with their shared haughtiness and nasty glower. A few years earlier, many of the city's residents had signed land tenantry agreements with the handful of whites who owned the bulk of property in the island's capital. The residents, mostly poor and uneducated, had been so desperate to own the land their little chattel houses sat on, that many of them had resorted to eating only one meal a day just to make the monthly payments. A foolhardy thing considering the back-breaking work that many of them undertook in the hot sun. Many of them dreamed of carving a foothold for their children by at least bequeathing them with a property of their very own.

Those poor people had been unable to afford the solicitor's fees to secure the necessary deeds after the high cost of paying for the land. In came Ignatious Grimes, a fellow coloured man who happened to be the mayor and a solicitor. Many tenants felt they could trust him to represent their interests. It turned out that Ignatious Grimes' only interest was his own. Every last one of the agreements that he prepared included clauses that said that the tenantry agreements were made between the signatory and the landlord's estate and were non-transferable. In short, dockhands, seamstresses, and other hard-working people put their X on contracts that expired the same day they did. Ignatious Grimes had been in cahoots with the rich white people all along. When the city residents found out, they had rioted, threatening to burn Bridgetown to a smoldering heap of ashes and nailing the mayor to the pyre. My aunt Millicent had been one of his victims. Ignatious Grimes' actions left her delirious and she spent the rest of her life in Jenkins subsisting on a diet of horse pills and electric shock therapy. Elections had come around and Grimes had been ousted in favour of his opponent, but the damage had already been done.

Winslow glared at the ex-mayor as he pulled on his drawers, "For the last time: what do you want?"

"I understand that you are in charge of the legislative duties related to the independence effort."

"And?" Winslow asked as he lit a cigarette.

"And it would behoove you to accept my guidance on the matter. The inept tactics which you've employed to bribe business owners are more befitting two-bit criminals and pickpockets."

Winslow bristled but composed himself with a weak chuckle. He shook his head as he puffed on the cigarette before he passed it to me. "You're the one who got caught and thrown out on your ear. If this place operated how America does, you would still be in prison for what you did. I don't need your help."

"I never offered you my help; I pointed out that you need my guidance. There's a substantial difference between the two. I'll explain the difference as soon as you pay her and she leaves."

Unbidden, tears stung my eyes at the insinuation. I opened my mouth to tell Ignatious Grimes just what he could do with his explanation, but he held up his hand to silence me as he continued to stare at Winslow.

"You think too small. You're doing all of the grunt work with the legislation but you'll get none of the glory when it's all said and done."

"And none of the blame either," the younger man retorted as he resumed his position on the bed.

Grimes cocked his head to one side and contemplated Winslow for a moment. "We are perched on the precipice of a critical juncture in our island's history. Do you have any idea how important Barbados was to the world at one point? We are called Little England for a reason. Centuries ago, this island was the epicenter of the slave trade. Every enslaved man, woman, and child that made it to the new world passed through this place. This country was a stud farm where the whites took the choicest negroes and forced them to procreate to improve the quality of stock that was shipped off to the new world. Not to mention that we were critical to the merchant trade in terms of rum and sugar production. Now we are about to seal the deal on one of the most peaceful transfers of independence known to man. Many other countries have fought tooth and nail for it. Barbados is like a well-behaved teenager; we built up a little port and handled our pocket money properly to show that we could manage our finances and now our grand ideas have found favour with the Queen. For a small island, we have a powerful reputation on the world stage which...how should I say... you're not properly leveraging."

Winslow lifted an eyebrow at him. "James' cabinet is already full."

"Bah. James is playing the hand he's been dealt and the deck is stacked with jokers."

Winslow smirked.

"Drafting legislature is a good task for a spineless lackey but in the end, there will be nothing left for you after that ink is dry. Plus, being James' whipping boy won't be enough to keep this place from crumbling around your ears," Grimes said, gesturing with disdain towards the room's stuffy curtains and peeling paint. He squinted mischievously at Winslow. "Nor will it add anything else to your Rolex collection."

His interest piqued, Winslow plucked the cigarette from my fingertips before he said shortly, "Wait outside."

"But I..."

He bundled me roughly in the bedsheets and said, "I'm hungry. Fix me something to eat while you're downstairs." He handed me his empty glass. "And bring more brandy."

I stared at both of them angrily before I stormed out the door, but anyone who knew me knew I wasn't going to make any sandwiches. I pressed the empty brandy glass against the door and listened.

"What are you proposing?"

"That you position yourself for greatness. I have international connections in every hole and industry you could imagine. With my contacts and the right government position, it will be easy," responded the deep voice.

"It's not that easy. It's crossed my mind but I'm not sure how to..."

Ignatious Grimes cut him off. "The path to success is not brightly lit and lined with daisies. It's rocky, twisted and littered with the debris of subterfuge. I seldom leave the darkness of that path but whenever I do, it's a miraculous and storied occasion. The first thing you'll need is a seat in the cabinet. Which one do you want?"

Confusion coloured Winslow's voice. "I'm not sure I follow."

"It means that I can get you any seat you want. The easiest one to get is the Ministry of Land's seat that fat fellow has."

"Elton? Why him?"

"Because he's easy to scare off. I'll send someone to deal with him in the morning. His name will soon cease to be relevant. I'll make it so that by noon tomorrow, he will be no use to James and Land will need a new minister."

The bed creaked and I heard the sharp crack of skin against skin as Winslow and Ignatious Grimes shook hands. "Now...tomorrow morning, this is what you'll tell James so that you're in a prime position by the time lunch rolls around..."

The mere thought of what they discussed was completely against everything my daddy and James wanted for the country. I knew that if James got wind of anything they discussed that Winslow might never work in Barbados again. I turned and hurried away from the door, deciding that perhaps making sandwiches would be a good distraction after all.

Chapter 23

June 23rd , 2015

Ancil put a bowl of oats in front of Lia and said, "We going out today. You want me to bring you anything?"

"Some internet would be nice," Lia groused.

Ancil laughed. "You could try the community centre 'round the corner. I think dem have computers there."

Lia perked up immediately.

An hour later, Susan and Ancil had gone on their way and Lia decided to take the short walk as Ancil had suggested. It was a lovely day for a stroll through the retirement village, past neatly mowed lawns and well-kept homes. Quite a few people were also headed in the same direction. They too were taking advantage of the weather to use the Olympic-sized swimming pool or play shuffleboard in the warm sunshine at the community centre.

A nice lady at the front desk directed Lia to a bank of desktop computers set against the far wall of the information room. The cheerful yellow room had large posters of exotic travel destinations and log-in instructions taped to the walls. Lia looked at the posters for a moment, mesmerized by photos of crystal caves in Belize, the majesty of Portuguese castles and the breezy tranquility of beaches in Barbados. She smiled for a moment at the photos of her island home, wistfully remembering days spent basking in the sunshine and dipping her toes in the bright blue Caribbean sea.

She sighed and turned to the task at hand.

Lia opened the Internet browser, telling herself she would just check her e-mail and go home. Eight minutes later, she had already finished reading the four legitimate e-mails she had gotten in the time since she had last checked her inbox. She rubbed her forehead. She was not only disappointed but disgusted. She couldn't believe that she had been out of touch with civilization for over a month and all she had gotten were a letter from the human resources department at her old job, a note from her mother, a bill payment notice and a reminder about a dental appointment.

Was this really what her life had come to? Just an empty husk of an existence with no real friends?

"Now what to do?" she muttered as she strummed her fingers on the wooden desk. The information room was empty, save for the front desk lady who was reloading the printer with paper. Lia's eyes strayed to the large glass wall that overlooked the pool deck. Retirees lounged on reclining chairs reading books or sat at picnic tables playing chess. Sunlight twinkled invitingly on the surface of the water and for a moment, Lia considered spending the day by the pool. She kept telling herself it would be a better distraction but she knew in her heart that what she really wanted to do was check her social media pages.

Lia's hands twitched as she contemplated if she wanted to take the risk. Finally, as if they had a mind of their own, her slim fingers flew over the keys tapping in her log-in information at warp speed. She didn't care who tagged her in their cat photos or who she should send belated birthday greetings to. All that mattered was checking her ex-boyfriend's page. Finally, the contents of his life spread out before her like a roadmap that would lead her to salvation. Lia let out a gust of air. She hadn't even realized that she was holding her breath until the page loaded, but what she saw was enough to make her wish she had fainted dead away.

There he was, as handsome as ever in his dapper white suit as he smiled broadly at his new bride.

Chapter 24

October 1966

"You ever realized that people are like colours?"

Kenneth looked at me askance before he exclaimed, "Susie, what madness you talkin' now?"

It was a warm Sunday evening in October. Kenneth and I were walking back to the Bailey house after visiting the library truck. We had left the playing field packed with people from the surrounding districts who had gone to return books and select others. Other people were there to see the grainy film that flicked and flittered in the waning evening sunlight on the broad canvas screen of the mobile cinema. The cinema roamed the island, setting up in rural neighbourhoods like our's every other week. It was usually a treat whenever the mobile cinema showed up but Kenneth and I had already seen that film. So we headed to his house to read our books while everyone else sat on the grass staring at that blurry screen.

Insects buzzed around us as we wended our way through a track bordered on either side by knee-high grass that scratched our bare legs as we walked. A lone cow chewed her cud lazily beneath the shade of a dunks tree, glancing at us with hooded eyes as she swished the flies that hovered around her in a small, buzzing cloud.

Kenneth ambled along behind me carrying five tattered books. Two that I had checked out under my name and one that he had let me borrow with his library card. The only book he had checked out for himself was The Adventures of Huckleberry Finn. Miraculously, he had discovered an unfettered enthusiasm for reading. He used to let me use both of his cards to check out books before, but for about three weeks, he had taken out a book every time the library truck came to our village. His excuse was that reading the credits ledger at the shop got boring sometimes. I had my suspicions about the veracity of that statement but I never turned down the opportunity to have book-related conversations with anyone. The fifth book he carried was my journal. I always kept it with me; I never knew when an incredibly profound thought would strike. I even took it to work occasionally and wrote during lunchtime. Perhaps the only time I tucked it away was when I was with Winslow. He called journaling "an asinine pursuit better suited to gossipy teenagers with a crush on Bobby Darren."

"I like cows," I said dreamily as I watched her long swishing tail.

Kenneth let out an exasperated breath. "Susie, you worse than a scratched record on a broken gramophone. Even my grandmother pays attention better than you."

"What do you mean?" I asked, reluctantly tearing my attention away from the cow.

The cow lowed irritably. Kenneth side-stepped a large pile of still-wet cow dung and shook his head at me. He shook his head at me. "People. Colours. Finish that thought."

"Oh yeah. People and colours. People are colours, Kenneth. If you think about it, personalities evoke a feeling...the same way colours do. Like Joan," I said, rolling my eyes. "Actually, it's her that made me come to this conclusion in the first place. Did you see that frowsy looking dress she was wearing today? It looks like dirty mopping water and my first thought was 'that suits her'. She's a musty grey. She has a sour disposition and she's always sucking the fun out of things."

He quirked one eyebrow at me the way he usually did whenever he mulled over what I said. He always tried to stay out of the long-standing feud between Joan and me.

"Hmm...I know she can be difficult when it comes to you. I guess I can kind of see what you mean when it comes to her being grey. She does kind of act like the world is on her shoulders. What colour would your daddy be?" he asked with a grin.

I skipped along next to him and smiled before I answered. "Daddy could only be one colour: bright red like rose petals."

Kenneth laughed. "How did you arrive at that?" he asked.

"Simple. Daddy is always cheery and positive, but when he's serious he's very serious. He's extremely stubborn about a lot of things and he's got a fiery temper. Plus he doesn't worry about much, no matter how bad things get. Mummy is a vibrant lime green: always fresh and sweet, but she can be pretty acid when she's ready too; like the way she told off Miss Greaves after church last week," I said laughing.

Kenneth grinned. "That's true; your mummy ain't easy when she's ready. What about my parents?"

I smiled and thought for a moment. "Your mummy is a regal purple; she's always pulled together and dignified. And of course, she's super pretty. Your daddy would be..." I stopped to think for a moment before I declared triumphantly, "...pearl white."

Kenneth turned to me, a bit surprised. "How come?"

"Mr. Bailey has a really good heart. He has his ways, but no matter how much your mummy complains, he always gives to the needy. And never the expired stuff that your mummy insists on..." I caught Kenneth glaring at me. "...on... turning into delectable delights." I finished, giving him a too-big smile. A grin tugged at his lips before he replied.

"I can see what you mean about my father. He does have pearl white qualities but sometimes he can be serious and strong like a steel grey. He's strict with me, that's for sure. Yeah, he's generous to people who can't do any better, but he's still a good businessman. Well... he is, otherwise, we would be needy too and my mother wouldn't be too pleased about that."

I laughed. Kenneth smiled and said, "At first I was just humouring you, but I can see where you're going with the 'people are colours' theory. That doesn't mean you still ain't bat-shit crazy though."

He took off running and laughing as I gave chase. By the time we arrived at the Bailey home, we were damp with sweat and the sun was losing its battle with the moon for dominance in the sky. I slapped his arm as I caught up to him, telling him off in a flurry of four-letter words. "Shhh!" he said as he pointed toward the house. Through the window, I could see his parents in the living room sitting next to each other and talking quietly. "You want my mummy to hear you cussing like you ain't got no owner?" We stifled our laughter and tiptoed under the living room window.

We walked through the vigorously weeded garden behind the house until we reached the golden apple tree. The night was rich with the verdant smells of plants and flowers that flourished beneath Mrs. Bailey's stern ministrations.

Kenneth tucked the books inside his shirt and started climbing the tree. I made my way up behind him.

We had outgrown many childish delights but we still savoured the ritual of feeling the scabbed trunk of that tree beneath our work-hardened hands while we climbed. We had settled ourselves properly by the time the sun finally twinkled out of view on the horizon. The wind rustled the leaves, shaking loose apples that fell to the ground with a thud. When golden apples were in season that's what we'd eat. We'd rip away the soft thin skin of the fruit until we got to the bright yellow flesh, being careful not to bite too deeply so the prickly core wouldn't scratch our gums. We would eat those golden apples until our fingers and mouth were sticky with the yellow juice that squirted between our teeth. When the apples weren't in season, we would bring biscuits. I'm not sure why. It may have been their portability but in some ways, a sentimental soul like me liked to believe it paid homage to the first time we sat together in that tree.

Kenneth swore softly, "I forgot the biscuits."

I grinned. "It's okay. I brought some," I said as I dug into my pocket.

Kenneth took one and bit it, exclaiming as he chewed. "Oye! These are really good. Where'd you get them?"

I blushed. "Winslow. A gentleman from the British council gave them to him, but he said they're too sweet and he didn't want them so he gave them to me."

My friend took his time chewing his biscuit but declined the next one I offered him. Crickets chirped as the silence settled uncomfortably between us.

"What colour is he to you?"

I glanced up at Kenneth nervously, wondering if it was wise to answer. His face was impassive beneath the moonlight.

"I think he'd be black...like onyx. He's sophisticated and handsome and strong."

"And secretive, evil and cold."

I opened my mouth to retort but thought better of it. I didn't want to start an argument with Kenneth. It had been a while since that night in the dark track when he had saved me. Whenever I thought of saying something rude to him, I thought twice and realized what he had risked by coming to my aid. I shoved another biscuit into my mouth, chewing so furiously that I tasted blood when I bit my tongue.

"And what colour am I?"

There it was. I hurriedly tossed another biscuit in my mouth and made a show of dusting the crumbs from my hands and skirt. I bided my time until his steady gaze warned me that I could do so no more. I swallowed most of it and avoided his eyes. I shrugged and fumbled for an answer. "I think you're brown."

"Brown?" He snorted. "Now I know why you treat me like shit."

I chewed more furiously.

A chilling cold anchored itself in the pit of my stomach and snaked its way straight up my chest. Pain and shame. Those words hurt. Lately, Kenneth had been moody and sullen. Sometimes I didn't even want to be around him, the way he was acting. I had asked why and he always had an excuse that never held up to any scrutiny. I wanted to say that he was acting like shit, but it was clear that he felt being labeled as brown was an insult. I guess I didn't think about the connotations of the colour brown before I answered. I just thought about the positive. I smiled guiltily before I said, "Brown like chocolate and warm earth. I love chocolate and being outdoors. I remember the days we spent playing in the gully. You're warm and comforting and you make me feel safe."

The moon peeked out from behind a cloud and lit his face with a soft glow. "I guess brown is a good thing to be," was his resigned reply. The moonlight illuminated his eyes; they were usually lively and mischievous but that night, they were devoid of any feeling.

"But black is still a stronger colour." He climbed down from the tree and headed to the house, leaving me sitting in the forked tree branches wondering whatever possessed me to answer him in the first place.

Chapter 25

25th June, 2015

"You going to the community centre to use the computer again today?"

"No!" Lia said a little too quickly. Her cheeks flushed. "Sorry, Ancil. My mind was wandering. I didn't mean to shout," she said quietly.

Since she had found out that her ex was now a married man, she had concluded that living in a pit of ignorance had its advantages. Between that and the lack of contact from any of her hundreds of social media friends, she had come to realize that she did not have any significant relationships. That particular epiphany had left her in a state of depression for the past few days.

Even Susan had noticed and had been quick to comment.

"Cordelia, whatever is the matter? Why are you acting like someone cooked your puppy?"

Lia smiled weakly.

"Hmm...," Susan kept her gaze trained on Lia for a moment before nibbling on her biscuit. "It's about a boy, isn't it?"

Her question was met with a glum nod.

"Ahhh...unrequited love?"

Lia shrugged. Susan nodded her head sagely.

"He loves someone else then. Oh...there, there, child. It wasn't meant to hurt your feelings. Don't cry. It will be okay."

Yet, despite Susan's pleading, Lia kept sobbing.

Through her garbled sentences, Susan was able to pick up the gist of the story. She stroked Lia's hair as she listened to the story, never interjecting to ask questions nor cast judgment.

"Well, I know how hurtful these things can be and I'm sorry to hear that it happened to you. In time you shall see that he wasn't meant for the journey you are on. He didn't leave you, he relieved you of him."

Lia smiled and wiped her nose with her sleeve. It felt strange to cross the professional boundary that existed between them by discussing her personal life, but hearing such kind words from someone as gruff as Susan was just what she needed.

"Perhaps it's better if you take some time off to reflect on this. We can always resume in a few days when you feel better."

Lia shook her head. "I came here to do a job and I'm going to do it." She sniffed. "Besides...this kind of thing makes good autobiographies, so maybe it's a blessing."

Susan slapped her thigh and laughed heartily. "That's my girl!"

Lia straightened up and asked, "Where were we?"

Susan's eyes twinkled. "We're at the part where your life mirrors mine."

Chapter 26

October 1966

Early one Saturday morning, I woke up before the sunlight leaked through the cracks in the wooden siding boards and did my chores at top speed before donning my favourite shirt and skirt to walk the thirty minutes it took me to get to Winslow's house. My parents had already left home to go to the market so I would have the whole day with him. Back in those days, there weren't many telephones. Winslow had one, but my family didn't so it hardly mattered anyway. I assumed it would be okay to drop by. But, you know what they say about the word 'assume': assume is "ass" and "u" and "me".

I grasped the ornate metal knocker on the door but didn't get the chance to use it. Someone on the other side yanked me and the door forward into the entrance hall. None other than Joan Mayers stared back at me with the most infuriating smirk on her face. After her mother had died, she had taken up the fine family tradition of being the village's pounding board just in better clothes. That day, she reminded me of the women from the dress pattern booklets I saw in the notions department in Bridgetown in her black and white dress complete with kid gloves.

"Oh... sorry!" she said with a fake smile before eyeballing me with disdain from top to bottom. Behind her, wearing only pants with no belt, Winslow came down the stairs.

Joan eased her way past me and took her time walking delicately down the patio stairs to make her way home.

I shifted uncomfortably as I watched her leave. Her clothes were lovely and perfectly matched to her handbag and shoes. I suddenly felt ungainly and uncomfortable in the mismatched outfit that I had taken so much pleasure in earlier. I wished that I had tamed my thick curly hair into submission and that I had taken the time to darn the tiny hole on my sleeve.

My heart thudded in my chest and I bit my lip uneasily as I turned to face Winslow. His face betrayed no guilt as he fanned his hand impatiently at me. "You're letting the mosquitos in," he said. Rage ran through me but I steadied my nerves and closed the door.

"Want some brandy?" Winslow asked as he walked to the sideboard and picked up the decanter.

By now there was a deep groove in my lip from where I had been holding it hostage with my teeth. I stared at him silently for another moment before I finally said, "Why were you naked when she was here?"

"I think the better question..." he said easily as he filled two glasses with a flourish, "is 'why are you showing up unannounced?'"

My mouth fell open. "'Unannounced?' Is that the way it's suddenly supposed to be?"

He looked at me skeptically. "This is my house, Susan. Haven't you ever heard the saying "ever so welcome, wait for the call"? It may be wise for you to familiarize yourself with it to avoid further embarrassment." He held out the glass of brandy to me.

"Fuck you and your brandy."

He raised an eyebrow and quirked his lips at my outburst before resting both glasses on the circular table that stood in the centre of the entrance hall.

"What is this to you? I thought Joan was just a mistake that happened once and she kept bragging about it. I want you to stop it. You're embarrassing me." My anger had liquified itself. Hot tears streamed down my face as I searched his eyes for remorse or something that would explain his actions.

"You're making too much of this. She came here to drop off some documents that I needed urgently."

"What documents are those? Why didn't you get me to do it? I thought I was your head secretary," I fumed.

He gestured broadly and said, "All the more reason why you shouldn't be burdened with trivial matters such as those."

My entire body trembled, I was so vexed. I asked the question I knew I would regret. "Are you still having sex with her?"

"Look, Susan. Men have needs. Just because a man expresses those needs doesn't mean he's bad."

"I hate you," I hissed as I turned to leave the house.

"This is the problem with you modern-day women; you don't do what you're supposed to and you get annoyed when you don't get the results you want. You need to be more attentive to your king and take responsibility for your actions. I mean..." he gestured at my outfit. "Look at you; your hair looks like something's been nesting in it and you've got holes in your blouse. A man likes to come home to order: clean house, beautiful woman and warm food. Not once have you brought a plate of Sunday food for me. I'm going places in this country and I should be accompanied by someone who at least looks like they're along for the ride."

I glared at him. He hadn't budged an inch. He just stood there next to the table sipping his drink.

I was humiliated, but I knew that some of what he was saying was true. In my haste to see him, I had neglected to pull myself together the way I should have. Still, that was no excuse for what he had done.

I could taste the blood that seeped into my mouth

from biting my lip. "That doesn't mean that you should treat me so."

He slammed his hand on the table. He was in a rage as he said, "It's time you started acting like my queen. If you don't like her being here, then it's up to you to make sure it doesn't happen again." Too many emotions to describe boiled up inside me and in the end, they felt like too much to bear. If I walked away I knew I'd be alone. Plus, working with both of them at the DPP would be excruciating. In the end, I told myself that being with him and still being in pain seemed like something that I could manage.

So, I did what I shouldn't have: I went to him, looked into his eyes with tears in mine and pledged to do better the next time.

I played the part of Winslow's dutiful wife until noon. I left after I told him I had to leave earlier than usual to help my mother. It wasn't true, but the anger and sadness I had within me needed an outlet and I decided to go home and get my thoughts into my diary. I cried all the way home. There had no-one I could talk to about it. They would all tell me I was being a fool and I just didn't want their negativity. The house was still empty when I got home. I went straight into the bedroom, climbed to the upper gable window frame where I had laid it flat so no-one would see it and took my diary down. I was turning the pages when I saw an entry that made me pause. Sometime around January 1966, I began to notice some serious changes in my mother. The woman who had cared for four children and a husband was now clearly in the throes of some serious melancholia. As the months went on there was always something different to distract me from it: Daddy making me leave school, independence, the disagreements with Kenneth and the stress of Winslow's antics. When I started to pay attention to the bigger hints in my mother's strange behaviour, I initially chalked it up to my father not being home and the children leading lives of their own.

At first, she was just moody but eventually, she began immersing herself in every and any organization the church could think up. I thought it was what people now call empty nest syndrome. Don't get me wrong; my mother had always been a devout woman and she had entrenched each of us as deeply into religious life as she could manage. When we were growing up, none of her children could get out of church service, no matter the excuse.

"Mummy, I'm sick."

"All the more reason to go to church and prayer for God's healing."

"Mummy, my homework isn't done."

"Come and prayer that the Lord shows you how to manage your time better."

"But, Mummy, I don't think …"

"You ain't got to. Church is a time to pray not think."

And so it went, that every Sunday, Mrs. Taylor's matching pair of twins, her tall son John and her hazel-eyed waif found themselves in church singing praises to the Almighty. We wore clothes that we could only wear on Sundays, squeeze into our usual pew in front of Joan's family and sing loudly and lustily until the Pastor deemed we had sufficiently praised God. He'd check that everyone had filled the collection basket and then encourage us to go back home and reflect. In my youth, all I ever reflected on was how much I hated that Joan always used to pinch me while we sat on those hard wooden pews. By 1966, those days were over and my mother often lamented how much she missed her babies.

I had made quite a few diary entries about it but I didn't spend much time mulling over it. My mind wandered back to my problems and I sat there, writing and crying until my family returned home.

I spent Saturday night the way I usually would, shelling peas in a little enamel bowl while I hummed whatever pop song was bouncing around in my head. Until of course Mummy passed and slapped my arm; then I'd revert to a soulful rendition of "Blessed Assurance". She always said no-one was to sing any "banja" in her house. Up to now, I still have no idea what "banja" really means but whatever it was, Grace Taylor gave it no quarter, especially when I was supposed to be preparing the Sunday food.

Sunday food was an intense ritual in every Barbadian home. Not only did the amount of food increase threefold, but everything had to be finished in time to get to the first church service at 8 a.m. In some homes, it might be the one day a week you had fresh meat on your plate after killing an animal you had been fattening up for months. Before the sky grew light on the Sabbath, we would bake the chicken and macaroni pie, boil the rice and peas, make juice using whatever was in season at the time, whether it was lemonade, golden apple juice or Bajan cherries.

The next morning, I woke up to find the house as still as a fly caught in a jar of honey. My mother always lamented that now that we were older, no one went to church with her except me because the men usually left early on Sunday mornings.

Heaven knows where the twins went, daddy probably took out the animals and then went off drinking somewhere to stave off the worms and John was probably with him (but not drinking).

By the time I got out of bed, the peas would be bubbling in a pot with a salted pigtail bobbing along on the top of the water while the chicken roasted in the oven. That day, there wasn't a single pot on the stove. I sighed. If Mummy hadn't started the meal, I would get to the great house well past the stipulated 11 a.m. deadline Winslow set as his lunchtime.

Out the back door, past the pit toilet, through the corrugated metal gate and straight past the pigpen, I stomped my way to the sunlit vegetable patch, growing more agitated as I went.

I pulled a handful of carrots and then bent to pick some tomatoes. That's when I heard it - not the gentle rustling of windblown leaves nor the pigs snuffling around contentedly - it was the sound of sobbing. I stepped away from the vegetable patch and eased slowly toward the low stone enclosure that housed the sows. My heart sank.

My mother cowered miserably in the corner of the pigpen, wailing like she'd lost the love of her life. Her body was smeared with pig food, mud and every other foul-smelling thing you'd imagine would be inside a pigpen. Head down, she rocked back and forth, crying and pulling her hair. At first, I just stood there, completely unmade by the sight. I bit my lip uncertainly. "Mummy...," the gnawing in my stomach intensified. My voice faltered. "Wha' happen?"

She turned to me slowly, those warm brown eyes drowning in their tears. It was like seeing me was too much for her to bear. "Susie?" she asked. I knew things were bad when she didn't correct my broken English.

"Yes, it's me, Mummy."

She rose slowly, slopped across the sodden stone floor and gripped my arms with her dirty hands. Her face was smeared and her beautiful eyes were shiny and vacant.

"I dream 'bout fishes," she said accusingly as she squeezed my arms tightly. "You got to stop it" she sputtered, spittle flying from her lips.

Bewildered, I stared back at her. "Mummy...wha' you mean?"

"The girl!" she screamed, getting more agitated.

I didn't know what to do except cry. "Mummy, stop it! Look at yourself. You ain't right." Before I knew it, she started pounding my body with her filthy hands, cursing me at the top of her voice. I was terrified. I pried myself away from her and ran back to the house.

I flew pell-mell into the kitchen, slamming into Daddy and John. They had just gotten home. As soon as they laid eyes on me, they knew something was horribly wrong.

By the time my father came outside, my mother had resumed her position in the corner, babbling to herself about signs and fishes. Daddy's calm voice was at odds with the look of shock in his eyes. He quietly told John to get the rope he used to stake out his sheep. Daddy then turned to me, fished some coins out of his pocket and sent me to the shop to buy two shots of brandy. He warned both of us to never utter a word of this to anyone as he lifted Mummy in his arms and carried her to the animal trough to wash her off.

I heard everything Daddy said, but I figured it wouldn't count if I told Kenneth. Plus, I had been keeping too much inside me and there was no more room for another terrible thing.

His eyes flew open as he listened and I could practically see the cogs turning in his brain as he said, "Maybe your mummy should go to a doctor."

I felt confused and miserable. I rubbed my forehead. "But she didn't hurt herself. She's just dirty."

Kenneth cleared his throat as he slowly poured the brandy into the small metal hip flask I had brought with me. "I understand that. I meant because she's not acting like herself."

I started babbling then too. "No. She'll be fine. She's just... tired."

He looked at me as he pushed the flask back across the counter. Kenneth's eyes searched mine and he just nodded before telling me that there was no charge for the liquor.

Chapter 27

27th June, 2015

"What would you do if you weren't a writer?"

"Am I a writer?"

Lia smiled at Susan's question. "Why would you question that?"

"Why would you question why I questioned it? Susan countered.

Lia's smile broadened. "You know very well what I mean, Miss Taylor."

Susan shrugged and thought for a moment before she answered soberly, "Well...Susan Taylor only wrote one book. Doing a thing once doesn't make one an expert."

Lia cocked her head to one side. "Perhaps, but then that makes me wonder what you would call yourself."

It was Susan's turn to smile. "A bum. I haven't had a job in over forty years so I'm certainly not a beacon of inspiration for the unemployed."

Lia laughed. "Okay, Miss Taylor. What would you do if you weren't a bum?"

Susan grew serious then. She straightened her shoulders and looked Lia squarely in the eye before she said, "I imagine that I'd want to be a psychiatrist."

Lia was surprised. "Oh, that's unexpected. Why is that?"

"I think I would have liked to help people like my mother. People who are misunderstood by the world because they act a little different. You know, there are times when I wonder if I have the same illness my mother did. Times when

I felt so apart from the world because maybe a creative mind doesn't function in a linear way. Sometimes I wonder if the little things I do are genuinely strange or if I'm just paranoid that I'll end up the same way she did."

Lia nodded her head. "It's funny you should say that. I know exactly what you mean. Even when I'm with people I feel like they don't truly get me or understand the way I view everything around me."

"Yes, yes," Susan said, nodding her head emphatically. "They're always slightly adjacent to your thought processes."

"But that doesn't mean you have a mental illness though," Lia pointed out. She leaned forward, her eyes bright and alert. "Do you think that's why you've secluded yourself for so many years? Because you're strange and secretly afraid that you're bat shit crazy?"

Susan quirked her mouth. "I never thought of it that way, but that may be part of it." Then she looked up sharply at Lia. "Don't haul out the butterfly net for me just yet, young lady. I've got enough money that I can be considered eccentric and not crazy, thank you very much."

Lia laughed again.

Susan sipped her tea, the traces of a mischievous smirk on the corners of her mouth. She grew thoughtful and then turned to look at Lia. "Tell me something; have you ever met anyone that 'gets' you as you like to say?"

"Well, other than my mother, not really. But then again, mothers are supposed to get you. Although, now that I know you've experienced the same thing, I could almost say that you also understand me from that point of view." Lia smiled. "It's nice to be understood, isn't it?"

Susan smiled and nodded sagely. "It's good to know we have that in common."

Lia nodded at the old lady, her heart light for the first time in months.

Chapter 28

29th November, 1966

"It's raining again!" I moaned. The knots in my stomach tightened another notch as I peered through the wooden shutters in the living room. It was almost 3 p.m. and I had spent the better part of the day getting ready. It was no mean feat. I had stood by the hot stove for the better part of two hours, warming that metal pressing comb over and over again. I ran it through my curly hair, my sweaty hands trembling with each pass as I worried about burning myself. Then I spent another half an hour wrapping my hair with strips of paper I had torn off the pig food bag to make a curly style. My family was better off now that all of us were working, but I still couldn't afford curlers and I always fumbled whenever I used those rough pieces of paper. Then I showered, ironed and everything else that went along with it. After those five long hours, I was loathed to let the rain ruin all of my hard work.

"Stop fretting," my mother said, bustling past me. Paper curlers stuck out at all angles unravelling themselves from her hair while she raced around the house. Her bronze skin was flushed and our usually tidy bedroom had been transformed into a jumbled mass of clothes and stockings as she sifted through containers while muttering under her breath. She had been searching for her pearl pin since the night before and the small family heirloom was nowhere to be found. And anyone who knew Grace Taylor knew that she never went anywhere fancy without her pearl pin. "You're too jittery," she chided as she kept up her frantic pace.

Truth be told, all of us were beside ourselves. The Supremes were performing at the independence celebration in Bridgetown that night and Daddy had promised the family that he would introduce us to the singing group at the exclusive after-party. It was being held at the swankiest hotel on the island and Mummy was positively giddy. She floated through the house quivering with delight as she sang her own lyrics to 'Can't Hurry Love' - 'Oh, you can't hurry love, ooohhh...Gracie go-in' be there!"

Her thrifty ways went through the door and she spent Daddy's gambling money with abandon for the first time in her life. As she said, "Nothing ain't too good for the divine Miss Diana Ross." For the first time in months, my mother possessed an energy and enthusiasm that I hadn't seen in her for a while. She obsessed over every single detail of her outfit; sometimes when peeling potatoes she could be heard muttering things like "I goin' make both of those dress patterns... just in case".

Yet, she gave me no quarter if I went to her panicking about what I would wear, insisting that I had to be calm and collected. That was one thing about my mother; she would never have admitted to me that she was more nervous than I was.

James had furnished all of the Taylor men with dapper new outfits so Mummy didn't have to worry about them. Samuel, Eli, John, and Daddy looked absolutely smashing in their new togs. For that she was grateful; she said that she had enough to do "making up exquisite dresses" for the Taylor women and was glad she could devote all of her time to that.

The celebration was a big deal for all of us. And by 'us', I mean every single Barbadian. The entire island had been a hive of activity for months. Kenneth grimaced and I bit my lip in excitement when we listened to the Rediffusion box as James spoke about the impending celebrations and announced Winslow as the new labour minister. Kenneth and I had cheered loudly at the sailing regatta a few days earlier. We looked forward to visiting the big agricultural exhibit that was being held in early December. There was much to see and do and everyone wanted to be a part of it. The hope that permeated the country spared no-one. Barbadians in the dry clay hills of St. Andrew right down to the gamblers who lurked in the dank smelling alleys of Bridgetown all embraced the euphoria that had taken root inside of us. And yet, no event was as anticipated as the flag-raising ceremony that would officially signal our independence at midnight on November 30th.

Despite all of this, the sky continued to spew raindrops with spiteful indifference. I worried that roads would become flooded and impassable and that Independence would be canceled on account of rain. Every raindrop that pinged against the corrugated metal roof above my head felt like an arrow to my heart. I glanced at the brand new dress that Mummy had sewn up for me; a beautiful bright blue that matched the colour of the new flag. I wanted to look perfect for Winslow that night. He would be sitting on the podium with James so we couldn't be together, but I still wanted to be a complete knock out if he glanced my way. The mere mental suggestion that I wouldn't get to debut that dress in all of its splendor was enough to give me palpitations. I moaned again, despair filling every cavity in my body.

Mummy turned to me. "Stop pushing up yuh two lips so. Kenneth picking us up so the rain ain't gonna matter, Susie."

I was miserably aware of that fact, but still wished it would stop raining.

Finally, with the house put back to rights, our hair pinned and tucked to perfection and our stiffly starched dresses on our bodies, Mummy and I took turns putting some of the coral pink lipstick on each other's lips. We had picked it out together at the department store in Bridgetown because it looked like it would work well for both of our skin tones. I felt like such a lady wearing lipstick for the first time. Mummy took one look at me and beamed brightly. "You look so beautiful, Susie."

Those were also Kenneth's exact words when he turned up a few minutes later. I blushed with pride as all of us got into the van and headed out to the Garrison. I would never have believed that my little island could have been transformed like that. Even though a steady downpour issued from the fat purple clouds that hung low in the sky, bright spotlights broke through the deluge illuminating the crowd of people that swarmed the savannah.

The rich scent of manure that always hung in the air over the Garrison was stirred up by rain as thunder rolled overhead and lightning flashed. What looked like a million umbrellas blanketed the circular field, bobbing along and weaving an undulating pattern from afar. It seemed like every single human that lived on the island had found their way there. Children that normally would have been abed by that hour clung timidly to their jovial parents who stopped and chatted with everyone they met. Strangers and friends alike exchanged gossip about what they heard would happen that night. I spied some elderly people propped up by younger relatives as they waited patiently to see the Union Jack lowered for the last time. Their eyes - some of them milky with cataracts - shone in the flashes of lightning that clapped overhead, but even in my naivety, I could tell what independence meant for them.

Mummy opened her umbrella and shouted a quick goodbye over her shoulder before she plunged into the crowd to look for Daddy. Kenneth held our umbrella as we made our way through the multitude, our shoes quickly ruined from all the mud we squelched through.

"Look, over there." I pointed to a big stage in the

centre of the large field ringed by chairs reserved for journalists, dignitaries, and a few select others. A large blank movie screen stood in the middle of the stage beneath a wet Union Jack that flapped loudly in the brisk wind that blew in from the east. My breath hitched in my chest as I looked at that flag for the last time. Suddenly, I was torn between what was familiar and comforting and what was new and unknown. In some ways, I was fearful of the future but I also believed in James' vision so I was excited too.

Daddy had pulled some strings and gotten seats for all of us in the VIP section that circled the stage. I turned to Kenneth and said playfully in my best British accent, "Bless our cotton socks, chappie, I do believe our seats are over there. We won't have to sit with this lot." I cocked my head towards a drunkard who was slumped against a tree.

Kenneth chuckled. "Good on you for spottin' that," he replied in his British accent as he offered his arm to me. "Lead the way, milady." I linked my arm in his, both of us laughing as we inched our way through the crowd.

We kept up a running commentary on everything we saw: the beautifully dressed people, the decorations, the weather. We saw friends and distant relatives as we went along, none of them deterred by the heavy rain and cloying mud that ruined their best outfits.

As soon as we settled into our seats between Kenneth's family and mine, the lights dimmed and a hush fell instantly over the savannah. The crowd swayed between breathless awe and exultant applause as we watched the Barbados Regiment's impressive display, the Living Flag performance and the presentation of the new Coat-of-Arms. Kenneth's mother was particularly moved by all of the pomp and pageantry; she wept during the entire ceremony. I was a little confused by that since she wasn't a Bajan. I wondered if it was because her island home of Dominica was still under Britain's thumb. But I digress.

As the clock drew close to midnight, James and the governor-general made their way to the centre of the grounds. The men walked as briskly as they could through the muck, James looking very dapper in his coat-tails, the governor-general in his ceremonial military garb. James' chest puffed out with pride as he smiled and waved at everyone. All of us held our breath as the lights faded away letting darkness engulfed the entire field. I felt Kenneth's hand close over mine. I squeezed it tightly in the dark. At that moment, I felt genuine happiness exploding inside me. I was just so glad to be with Kenneth for that historic moment. I loved Winslow, but that singular moment was something I wanted to share with Kenneth and no-one else; not John, not Mummy, not Winslow. Nothing could blot out the childhood we shared, the secrets we trusted each other with or the unparalleled friendship we had. A realization settled on me like a heavy cloak. I was truly grateful for Kenneth and I felt like I would lose everything if he wasn't always in my life. I turned to him in the dark and even though I couldn't even see my hand in front of my face, I knew he was looking back at me too. I leaned forward - just a bit - and my lips touched his. We kissed - something long and sensual and not really fitting for friendship - and I didn't even spare Winslow a second thought as I did. My heart didn't riot inside me forcing me to contemplate how my deep appreciation for one person could diminish the love I had for another.

When we pulled away from each other, a spotlight fell on the two flag poles that stood at the centre of the grounds. A Caucasian soldier from the Royal Navy worked in tandem with the black Barbadian lieutenant easing the Union Jack down one flag pole as the brand new blue, yellow and black flag was raised on the other. In unison, every man, woman, and child jumped to their feet and the Garrison Savannah exploded in a burst of cheers and applause that even managed to drown out the thunder that rattled the sky above us. Not since man discovered fire was there such unfettered excitement. "Yeeesss!" Kenneth grabbed me tightly, abandoning the umbrella to hug me as everyone around us celebrated our country's new beginning.

Everyone except Ignatious Grimes, who sat two seats behind us, his grey eyes mirroring the storm clouds above as he watched Kenneth and I embrace.

Chapter 29

June 29th , 2015

Lia sat quietly in the kitchen staring down that wretched porridge. Susan sat across from her, saying nothing as she nibbled her toast. Outside, chirping birds and the steady purr of a lawnmower were the only things that broke the silence in the room. And then like a rainbow breaking through grey clouds on a stormy day, Ancil burst in humming a chirpy tune. Both Lia and Susan cast her withering glances but said nothing. Ancil surveyed the two of them but said nothing as she shook her head bemusedly to herself as she bustled about the kitchen.

"You ready? We gine gotta hurry to get there on time."

"Where are you going?" asked Lia.

"It's Tuesday, baby. I taking Miss Susan to..."

"Out. She's taking me out."

Lia raised an eyebrow but said nothing. Behind her sharp eyes, the cogs in her brain started turning.

Ancil smiled nervously but said nothing as she whisked away the dirty dishes and quickly tidied the kitchen. Lia yawned loudly as she pushed back her chair. "I'm so tired; I think I'll sleep until you get back."

Susan cast sharp eyes on the young woman but said nothing as Lia left the room and made her way upstairs.

Twenty minutes later, hidden behind the white lace curtains in her bedroom, Lia watched the car drive away.

Even though the house was empty, she still took her time going down the stairs, being sure to avoid the eighth stair from the top that creaked. She checked the kitchen and the living room. Her heart was beating furiously as she peered through the small foyer window onto the street. Every breath Lia took felt hard-won as she painstakingly crossed the corridor and turned the doorknob of the Barbados room.

The door squeaked slightly - she had never noticed that squeak before; it resonated through the house with the ferocity of a gunshot - and with her heart thumping in her chest, Lia entered the room.

She stole quickly to the writing desk. Her hands trembled as she glanced through the untidy jumble inside. It was clear to Lia that Ancil was never allowed to touch anything inside the drawer. The creativity that governed Susan's mind was only conducive to keeping things unkempt. Utility bills, old letters, hand-written notes, newspaper clippings...there was absolutely no order to the things inside the drawer.

Lia couldn't tell anyone what had truly driven her to search Susan's things. The obvious omissions about her past were part of it, yes. But something about the way Susan had cut off Ancil's sentence made Lia believe that there was something else to uncover. Something far more dubious. The bi-monthly sojourns Lia had assumed were supermarket trips were clearly a sprat Susan had thrown out to distract from their true purpose.

The seconds ticked by. At least four times, Lia was certain that she heard the door open. Each time, she made a beeline to the front door, terrified that Ancil and Susan would discover her snooping. Eventually, in spite of all of her digging, the only interesting thing she found was an unopened letter. The return address was listed as K. Bailey in Alberta, Canada. Kenneth? Susan had said she hadn't heard from Kenneth since she left Barbados. Lia worried her lip. It was slightly rumpled and had the beginnings of a yellow cast, but the postmark was only a year earlier. Her heart beat faster. Did she dare open the letter and try to reseal it before

Susan came home? Beads of sweat formed on her brow as she calculated how long it would take to extract the letter by steaming the flap, replacing it with blank paper and resealing it until the next time Susan went out. Hopefully, it would remain undetected until then and she could re-open the envelope and put back the letter.

Lia shook her head. Knowing her luck, Susan would decide it was a great idea to read the letter five minutes after Lia swapped it for two sheets of blank paper. Reluctantly, Lia put the letter back. But she was determined to read it no matter what.

The next five hours ticked by. Normally, Susan and Ancil were gone no more than two hours. Eventually, her regret at not seizing the opportunity to read the letter gave way to concern. What if something had happened to them? Uncomfortable feelings warred within Lia. The life she had dreamed of as a published author suddenly felt flimsy in her mind. Susan had never taken her to meet the literary agents or publishers as she had promised. She imagined having to go home with nothing to show for her adventure except for the chance to talk to one of the most maligned women Barbados had ever produced. Her foolhardy adventure paled in her eyes. Lia got the phone book from the kitchen and started calling all of the local hospitals and emergency services asking for word on Susan and Ancil. Her heart beat faster with every phone call as she imagined what she would do if the worst came to pass.

She was on the phone with the fourth hospital when she heard the car pull into the driveway. She chided herself for panicking but knew that it was time to nudge Susan into fulfilling her end of the bargain.

Lia went to meet Ancil at the door as she usually did to help her with the groceries, but this time no bags filled Ancil's arms as she helped Susan into the house. "I was getting worried; I wondered if the two of you had run away from home."

Ancil twisted her mouth in a half-hearted smile and Susan just shuffled past Lia without a word.

"I'll be back down to get some sorta dinner started after I get Susan settled."

Lia helped Ancil prepare dinner but Susan didn't resurface for the entire night. And neither did the groceries from the trip to the supermarket.

It was after midnight when Lia once again skipped the creaky step to go downstairs to the Barbados room. She had spent hours in her dark room contemplating how best to get the letter. Eventually, she decided that the middle of the night would be best. The other occupants would be asleep and she wouldn't have to wait until another Tuesday came around. She had made a stop by both Susan's and Ancil's bedrooms to make sure she didn't hear any movement before slinking downstairs in the dark. She felt like a true thief as she opened the drawer again and removed the letter. She was just about to take it upstairs when a small slip of paper that was stuck to it fluttered to the floor.

Lia picked it up to put it back when she noticed her name on it.

Miss Cordelia,

I know how I left my things. Put it back.

Susan Taylor

Lia swore under her breath as she stuck the note back to the letter and slid it back into the drawer. As she snuck back past Susan's room, she heard a muffled voice say, "One smart dead at two smart door, Cordelia."

Chapter 30

December 1966

Life continued to change around me. Samuel and Eli got a great job opportunity and moved to Canada by the middle of December. My mother grew incredibly cranky after that, picking at everything that happened around the house. She started waking up at ungodly hours, grumbling about having to clean the house again or having to check on the pigs all of the time now that the boys were gone. She suffered from headaches and mysterious aches and pains that never seemed to go away.

That whiny, miserable version of her who complained about everything drove my father and me crazy but we both chalked it up to her missing the twins. I also assumed that she may have been going through menopause and assumed those minor storms would pass.

As for my situation with Winslow, I vowed to never again let Joan weasel her way between me and my man. She was an unconscionable tramp and I knew that she only wanted to disrupt the happy life I lived. I became more attentive toward Winslow and set about asserting myself as his head secretary once again. I was quite pleased with myself. I remember walking into the parliament building next to him for a meeting and feeling so proud of myself. I felt like a partner in his life. But the reality quickly sank in. Barbados was a young country which meant it had to be nurtured. And while I spent lots of time pampering Winslow, nothing changed. He worked long hours, which meant that I worked long hours.

It was an exciting thought to practically be the second lady of Barbados. I liked knowing what was going to happen on a national scale before it happened. Admittedly, I could have heard a lot of it from Daddy too, but it felt different to hear it from the deputy prime minister. Secretly, I was annoyed by the fact that despite being given a deputy prime minister's salary, Winslow spent all of his money on liquor, cigars, cars, and gambling. I consoled myself with the fact that a man will be a man and I could probably encourage him to be a better man if I made a better home for him. I figured it would lay the groundwork for our marriage. So, I became the vigilant little housewife; I cooked, cleaned and even decided to paint the kitchen all by myself.

But it was never enough. Winslow constantly complained about all manner of real and imagined transgressions imposed by James, the media, the public, and various business owners. Yet, ironically, the biggest conflict with his job came in the form of the man who had engineered its existence: Ignatious Grimes.

Winslow had mostly followed Ignatious' instructions to get James to appoint him as deputy prime minister. Of course, Ignatious wasn't the type to do something for nothing. His main objective was to get Winslow to repeal tax and land laws that were "making him a pauper in prince's garb" as he put it. I wasn't exactly privy to their many arguments on the issue but I did gather that one of Ignatious' ill-gotten lots of land was brimming with oil. The island's sole oil exploration company told him that the plot could make him a very rich man. That was all well and good in theory, but the land in question also happened to be the site of the island's most well-known slave revolt and was categorized as a historical landmark. As such, the law deemed that Ignatious was not allowed to "execute or permit to be executed any works for the alterations of the building or the grounds which would compromise the historic character." Setting up rigs that pockmarked the land with deep holes in the search for oil would certainly qualify as compromising the character.

Ignatious Grimes had instructed Winslow to request the Ministry of Land, but Winslow had wanted the Labour Ministry because of the number of bribes he'd be able to milk from it. Winslow took it upon himself to get into bed with British and American firms to start companies on the island but he always found the shadiest people to get in cahoots with. The correspondence from these people had some of the most bizarre questions about the best way to set up business in Barbados. Many of them said outright that they didn't want any paper trail and asked Winslow to be the signatory for quite a few of these entities. Almost every week, the minister of labour was at a grand opening. So many businesses opened in 1966 that it was a wonder to me that Winslow didn't get carpal tunnel from cutting ribbons with those gigantic scissors. The public rejoiced at all of the new job opportunities that were availed to them. The field hands who could read and write got great office jobs with onsite training in air-conditioned offices. Ignatious had been livid when he had found out and his relationship with Winslow had been strained since then. Winslow grew more and more paranoid that Ignatious was lurking in the wings, just waiting for a chance to bring down everything that Winslow had worked so hard for.

The stress of everything ate at him constantly and sometimes he took it out on me. Whenever he started up I found solace in my diary. I had found a hiding place for it in an old desk in the hallway that was covered by a bedsheet.

One evening, Winslow came home hacked off by the fact that James was planning to reshuffle the cabinet. James had not given anyone an inkling about who would be reshuffled either. That added further insult to injury as far as Winslow was concerned. As deputy prime minister, he felt that he should have been a key decision-maker in any reshuffle. The thought of possibly having the Ministry of Labour taken from him was just as disconcerting. Oh, I eavesdropped on many a clandestine conversation between him and business owners who wanted labour disputes quashed. Workplace accidents as a result of faulty equipment? Money would change hands. Paperwork would go missing. Falsified safety certifications would be backdated and slipped into files. Any Barbadian who had the bad luck to be underpaid, wrongfully dismissed or injured on the job, suffered greatly while the Labour Ministry was in Winslow Vaughan's hands.

The day I painted the kitchen, he came in and, rather than being pleased about the fact that the peeling lead paint had been removed and replaced with a fresh new colour, Winslow was livid.

"What did you do?" he bellowed.

I cowered under his fiery gaze. "B-but you said you liked white."

"I'm not talking about the walls. This is what you stayed home from work to do? What the fuck made you think you could just come in here and paint the place as though you live here?"

I floundered as I said, "But I asked you about it the other night and you said you didn't mind me painting the kitchen."

Winslow rolled his eyes and stupsed. "Susan...you never once asked me about painting anything."

By that time I felt so bad about this misunderstanding, I figured nothing could make it any better. "On Friday night when we were in bed, I asked you about it. I asked if you wanted us to paint the kitchen together and you said you're a politician, not a painter and to stop bothering you about it. I told you the kitchen looked shabby and I didn't mind painting by myself and you said 'whatever' and then I asked about white and you said 'fine'."

He sucked his teeth again and turned away from me to pour himself a drink. "I'm a busy man...I don't always hear everything you say."

"I listen to everything you tell me, but sometimes..."

"James Hackett is reshuffling the cabinet and won't even tell us who's getting which ministry. I told him it's too soon and it looks bad, but he's on some sort of agenda that only he understands. Painting a kitchen isn't on my radar." He knocked back the stiff shot of brandy in one gulp. "Did you cook?"

I felt guilty for quibbling over such a minor issue. I walked over and rested my hand gently on his arm. "I'm sorry, I didn't know." I smiled at him brightly, hoping to cheer him up. "I cooked rice and chicken stew for you. I put out some of it for you already."

He raised a hand. "Good. Now get home safely. I'm in a bad mood so I won't be good company now."

I shivered. "Can you give me a ride?" Despite the progress made since Independence, a lack of extensive bus routes still plagued the island.

He sighed loudly. "I'm tired. Leave now and you'll still get home at a decent hour."

I frowned. The memory of my assault pricked the corners of my mind. "I'm not sure I feel comfortable walking around after dark these days."

He raised an eyebrow as he poured another shot. "Scared of the heart man? You're too old for that now, ain't you?"

I gave him a withering look. "No, it's just that...," I shifted my feet nervously. "Well...the last time I was out walking at night, a man tried to rape me."

There it was. I'm not sure why I never mentioned it to anyone but Kenneth. Maybe shame or fear caused me not to before, but I thought I could tell Winslow and he would understand why I didn't want to walk the lonely road by myself.

He never even broke his stride as he turned back to the antique sideboard for another shot of brandy. He shrugged. "Women always bring those things on themselves, but all's well that ends well. Use the phone and call someone to come and get you then." And with that, he left his freshly painted white kitchen with a warm plate of food in his left hand and a fresh glass of brandy in his right.

I'm not sure what kind of response I was expecting, but that wasn't it. And it also didn't solve the problem of my parents skinning me alive unless I got home soon.

I bit my lip nervously. The only family I knew with a vehicle and a phone was the Baileys. I weighed the pros and cons of asking Kenneth versus the fear of walking home alone and getting there before I had to face my parents' wrath. Reluctantly, I walked toward the phone table, picked up the receiver and dialed Kenneth's number.

His tone was stiff, but he agreed to pick me up. Twenty minutes later, when headlights penetrated the stiff darkness of the great house, Winslow was fast asleep.

Kenneth said nothing as the pig van trundled down the dark road. The only thing that punctuated the silence was the rustling of young canes on both sides of the road, waving slowly in the cool night wind. We were close to my house when I finally said, "So you're not going to talk to me?"

Silence.

"If you don't want to do me a favour, just say so."

He kept staring at the road.

"I forgot my diary at his house. I guess I'll have to go back for it tomorrow."

More silence.

My anger grew as Kenneth just looked straight ahead, his attention fixed on the narrow road ahead. "Are you jealous because I'm not having sex with you anymore?"

A mirthless grunt but still no words.

I'm not sure what made me do it. Maybe I misdirected my anger from Winslow toward Kenneth. Maybe I had finally had enough of his sour attitude toward the man that I loved. Maybe it was my unstable teenage hormones that didn't allow me to think straight. Whatever it was, I had finally had enough. I grabbed his shirt and slapped him so hard he yanked the steering wheel, causing the vehicle to plunge straight into the cane field. The van bumped and rattled, flying over the neat rows of young plants, jolting us around the cabin as we both tried to hold on to something. We came to a shuddering stop when Kenneth slammed on the brakes. He was surprisingly calm when he turned me and said, "Listen to me...and listen to me carefully. My father would kill me if I bring back this van with any questionable damages on it. My mother would kill you for stretching my new shirt. I would not be happy if I died before having any children or seeing Niagara Falls."

I broke down in tears. Not so much from almost having lost my life but because I was just overwhelmed. It wasn't Kenneth's fault that I was stranded and needed a ride to get home. Neither was it his fault that I was feeling more and more inept when it came to Winslow. I was angry at the world and I had taken it out on my best friend.

Kenneth didn't know why I was crying either but he put his arms around me and kissed my cheek gently.

"Susie, whatever is bothering you, it will be alright. But, for heaven's sake, you can't hit me when I'm driving. Too many young canes lost their lives tonight because of you."

I sniffed miserably at his jab. He shook his head at me as he restarted the truck and shifted the gears. "Hope you're happy that you deprived someone of two sugar cubes."

I thought the worse of my night was over. My house was right around the corner from where we ran off the road, but I didn't actually get inside the house until almost twenty-four hours later.

We hadn't driven very far before we noticed someone wandering down the side of the road. She was nude and unkempt and walked like she was drunk. She slapped at the mop of tangled hair sitting atop her head like it was a hive of wasps. It was sad to see another woman in such a state. It was even sadder to realize that she was my mother. Kenneth and I looked at one another in shock.

I sprang from the truck even before it stopped and ran to her.

"Mummy?"

She batted me away just like she swatted the imaginary things in her hair. Kenneth stood behind me, embarrassed that he was witnessing the whole thing.

I lowered my voice. "Mummy, why are you naked?"

She stared at me, indignation clear on her face. "Don' worry 'bout me! You got bigger problems than me." She started walking again.

Kenneth stayed a respectable distance away, seemingly unsure of how to approach the naked and ranting mother of his best friend.

I caught up with her, barely able to make out her features now that we stood outside the sharp beam of the truck's headlights. It was a silly thing to think at the time, but I was glad that Kenneth could no longer see her naked. By that time, I was at my wits' end and it showed.

"Mummy, you've got to come home or people are going to think you're mad. You want to end up in Jenkins?"

She rounded on me and I don't think I ever saw such venom in Grace Taylor's eyes before that moment. "Don't judge me. It is you that mad, not me!" She turned and hurried away.

I felt a hand on my shoulder. Kenneth's pressed the shirt off his back into my palms and turned away again. It seemed like the simplest thing in the world but at that moment, it meant everything to me. I kept my eyes on my mother's receding form as I said, "Go and get my father."

"But Susie...I can't leave you out here."

"I know, but what else are we going to do?"

He opened his mouth again, but I cut him off. "Please."

He said nothing, but I saw the outline of his head nod before he ran off. The engine gunned, the wheels spun and the little truck bolted up the road as fast as I'd ever seen it move. As the lights faded away, I was left alone and in the dark, battling my mother's demons on my own.

I walked behind her, my eyes welling with tears as she continued to amble on. The sickle moon that hung high in the sky gilded her lithe body with a faint silvery outline as she moved. She reminded me of a woodland nymph, an inebriated one who had been cast out of the forest. I cried as I called out to her. I felt like a sapling caught in a hurricane of emotions, each one wrought by the woman who was meant to be the source of my comfort and strength.

My anger surfaced at the thought. "Mummy! Stop this now!" I threw Kenneth's shirt over her and tried to pull her arms through the sleeves, but far from being docile, she punched me in the mouth. I tasted blood as my teeth met my lips.

She jumped on me and pinned me to the ground. I could feel the grass, soggy with dew, beneath my skin. All I could think about was the last time someone had thrown me down in the grass not far from that same spot. Everything came hurtling back to my memory: the smell of cigarette smoke, the chill that crawled my skin, the fear...but this time, my mother was my attacker. It was too much to bear.

I screamed as she held on to me. "No, no, no," she muttered giddily. "If I gotta kill you to save you, I gine do it," she muttered. "The dream say that the fishes goin' send you mad." She grabbed hold of my throat and started to squeeze, her clammy hands making a vice grip on my larynx. I had never seen my mother take even a sip of rum before, but that night I smelled liquor on her breath, stale and pungent, as she rasped angrily, "I bring you in, I could take you out. I bring you in, I could take you out." What she said was more frightening than what she was doing to me. The anger that fueled her behaviour was something I had never experienced from her. Terror made my blood run cold and sapped my energy too much for me to defend myself.

I tried to scream again but nothing came out of my throat the second time. I'm not sure how long it went on, but it was long enough. My vision wavered; things became shapes and all-consuming darkness soon enveloped everything around me. I lost the strength to beg her to stop. Soon, even the darkness around me slipped away, replaced by a warm bright light that beckoned me forward. It felt ridiculously simple to just succumb to that easy feeling. So I did.

The details were sketchy for a few hours after that, but what I did find out was that my father and Kenneth had dragged my mother off me. My father was a loyal man, one who always made sure everything was right with our family. I suspect if my mother had tried to kill anyone else, he would have made an excuse for her. He would have tried to bribe them. Considering the advantageous position he held with the political powers at that time, he could have bent James' ear to get them anything they wanted.

But I was his only daughter and even the woman who gave birth to me couldn't escape behind the fortress of reason. What he did do was make sure my mother was admitted under a false name to a private room at Jenkins. Being forced to seek help for a mental disorder in the 1960s wasn't something that garnered sympathy from strangers. Being labeled as "mad" got you pointed fingers and the assumption that all of your closest relatives were mad too. My father also begged Kenneth to never utter a word of this to his father. My father was no fool. As much as Norman was his friend, Norman was also a shopkeeper. Shopkeepers paid allegiance to only two things: profit and gossip.

The next two weeks were difficult. It was hard being home in the house without Mummy. It was even harder to be subjected to the personal questions the doctors asked as they tried to pinpoint a diagnosis. I felt like an utter traitor as I described the religious zealousness, the pig pen and that dark night on the road close to home. I cried like a baby as I recalled how she had tried to strangle me.

I also couldn't help but counter everything with an excuse. "That night? I read this book once about someone who was sleepwalking. I feel that Mummy was having a nightmare and sleepwalking. She would never hurt me." I would leave every interview with the shame of knowing that as much as I tried to help, maybe I was also hurting my mother. Not once did I mention my mother's ramblings about the mysterious fish dream. How could I? I had heard stories about other patients who wasted away in Jenkins. The ones who spoke of the 'little green men' that tried to hurt them. I hoped that my omission would help the doctors to conclude that my mother just had a turn of bad luck so she could come back home.

I remember when my aunt was admitted to Jenkins after Ignatious Grimes' trickery had sent her off her rockers. She was pumped up with pills and electric shock therapy. I don't know why you'd call such a thing therapy, especially when you consider that most of us do our best to make sure we're never electrocuted. I visited her once at my mother's behest. I knew it was the right thing to do but I sorely regretted it. My aunt was a solidified ghost; neither completely gone nor partially present. Her once plump figure reminded me of a pencil eraser that was worn down to the nub; nothing left but the aluminum frame that kept it in place until you were ready to discard it. Empty eyes, pallid skin and a continuous stream of drool that accompanied the non-sensical phrases she regurgitated all day long. I never went to visit her again after that. I didn't want to preserve that image in my memory. So I stayed away and kept her memory fresh by casting my mind back to the time she gave me a Raggedy Ann doll for my birthday. The thought of the bright smile and warm eyes she had when I hugged her replaced the slack, drooling grimace of a woman I no longer recognized.

That was my greatest fear for my mother. I didn't want to say or do anything that would make them treat her like that. So, I stayed silent about many unusual aspects of her behaviour.

Those two weeks of adjusting to life without her were compounded by other factors. As the only female left in the house, I couldn't be as liberal as I once was. I was now the woman of the household, quite a big job at such a young age. On top of that everything else was suddenly thrust upon me: all of the cooking, cleaning, washing and even tending the animals. At first, I still went to work, but by the second week, that became unmanageable. Life was difficult, but as the adage goes "when it rains, it pours."

My biggest fear came to pass. Kenneth tried to keep the truth from me, but John's big mouth had no cover. I overheard him telling Daddy that Joan was tooling around town with none other than the deputy prime minister, Winslow Vaughan. All of the times that I had snuck around with him and he was openly seeing Joan? That made my blood boil.

Earlier that day, on the way to the shop to buy goods, I saw them drive by in Winslow's MG. I told myself he was just giving her a ride, but the vindictive smile on Joan's face was proof enough that she knew what she had done to me. I didn't expect much from her. She was a low-minded tramp with an unconscionable attitude and such a thing was par for the course. Yet, it was Winslow that broke me.

I left home fuming after I heard that. Only half the potatoes were peeled and I hadn't even dressed up the chicken for baking. I told John and Daddy I had to run to the Baileys' for something and neither of them noticed that I didn't carry the canvas shopping bag.

I practically stomped as I walked to his great house.

I banged on the door maybe fifty times before Joan answered it. The top buttons on her blouse were undone and she dared to act aghast when I noticed. "Oh Susie, I didn't mean for you to see that," she said as she made a big show of refastening the buttons.

I can't explain the rage that boiled up in my chest at the sight of her doing that. She didn't ask what I wanted and I didn't speak to her either. She sidled off and took a seat on one of the winged chairs in the foyer, barely able to conceal her glee. Winslow sauntered out of the kitchen, looking neither ashamed nor concerned.

"I need to talk to you."

He shrugged indifferently as he stood next to Joan. "Talk."

Joan's smirk made me so angry I started to shake, but I dug deep and rallied my feelings, trying not to give her further satisfaction.

I bristled, indignation rising inside of me. "You don't want me to say what I have to say in front of her."

"Clearly, you have nothing to say and I'm in a hurry. So you either talk or leave."

His indifference goaded me. I folded my hands across my chest. "Good. Do you want to start with the bribes you take or the laws you break?"

His eyes flew open. He stalked over, grabbed me by the arm and dragged me back through the front door. He slammed it and then turned on me, his face filled with fury.

"You are going to learn the hard way that you can't play with me."

His words only incensed me further. "Play with you? You bring this slut here the minute I turn my back and then act like you've done nothing wrong! I've got all kinds of family problems and you don't even try to find out what's going on, come to see me or even pretend to care. Yet, you do this and expect me to just act normal about it?"

He raised one haughty eyebrow at me. "I can bring whoever I want here. This is my house and you're not even my woman." He shook his head bitterly. "You've been calling in sick for a week now which means you've legally fired yourself. There's work to do and I've got needs to be met. Do you know how hard it is when the person you've come to depend on suddenly abandons you? The same way you could run up here to see who is in my house, you could have come up here to help me."

I was livid. "Losing your precious ministry is nothing compared to what is happening in my life!"

A dangerous smile lit his lips. "I know everything about your life. I'm the deputy prime minister of this country and nothing escapes me. You think I don't know you're double-dipping with that shop boy? Or that your mother suddenly went missing two weeks ago? She's as mad as a hatter and you never once told me. How is she liking Jenkins, by the way?"

His words stung. I felt ashamed that he knew.

"I never told you?" My voice rose and my clenched fists banged the door behind me in anger. "It's none of your business. I don't get the chance to tell you things because you only talk about yourself. You're a selfish, drunken bastard and I'm sick of you."

He was smug as he said, "You're almost as crazy as your mother. You think that shop boy can do what I can do for you?"

"You've never done anything for me and all I've ever done for you was keep your secrets and let you use me. But

I'm done."

"That's not up to you." He gripped my forearms and pressed me against the door. He smiled, but no warmth entered his eyes. His voice was low and menacing as he spoke. "Jenkins is a dangerous place. It's full of medicine that can be 'accidentally' overdosed and machines that can 'accidentally' malfunction. A thoughtless phone call might make Jenkins even more dangerous for your mother. If you love her, you will remember that."

His fingers dug into my arm and a cold numbness settled into my skin where he held me. Every word he uttered flooded me with fear. I would do anything to keep my mother safe, but I couldn't let that threat go so easily.

I matched his smile as I said, "You should remember that prison is a dangerous place for pretty boys like you. I've got so many dates, names, and details of your dirty deals written down, that I suspect you'll think hard about making that phone call. Can you imagine your pretty little Rolex stapled inside a plastic evidence bag?"

Emboldened and bitter, I then whispered, "You keep forgetting that you're just the deputy prime minister. James is like a big roadblock on that power trip you're taking, isn't he? I'm willing to bet that an honest man like him wouldn't want to be caught in collusion with a dog like you. You should hope James never finds out what you're doing because losing the ministry will be the least of your problems when you're in prison."

My words found their mark. His eyes grew wide and his face went pale as he stared at me. My strong voice didn't betray the fear I felt when I said through clenched teeth, "Let me go."

He stepped back and released me and I turned and walked home without another backward glance. Little did I know that I had neither enough wisdom nor respect for Winslow's ego to realize that wasn't the end of it.

Chapter 31

July 1st , 2015

"Do you get along well with your mother?"

"For the most part."

"What does that mean?"

Lia turned to face Susan. As with all of Susan's questions, Lia wasn't sure what her angle was. She tried to gauge the reason for the question, but the author's face gave nothing away. The older lady looked beautiful today. She wore a warm chocolate coloured silk blouse that brought out the rich tones of her light brown skin and the flecks in her golden eyes. The bright Florida sunshine that illuminated the room with shafts of light gilded Susan with an ethereal glow.

Lia didn't feel as uneasy about answering the question as she usually would have. However, there was one thing she was curious about given Susan's knowledge of her life. Lia wanted to clarify that point first.

"You know she's not my real mother, don't you?"

Susan nodded. "Your real mother died when you were eight years old in an apparent car crash."

"Yes," Lia said. "It's sad, but I don't remember much about her. The lady I call my mother used to be my neighbour. I don't know if I have any other family; she's the only person who was willing to take care of me. For that, I'll always be grateful. It's just that she's very different from my mother and me."

"How so?"

Lia quirked her mouth as she racked her brain. She didn't want to come across as either disingenuous or unreasonable. "My real mother's name was Cordelia too. So that's kind of why I was always called 'Lia'. I kind of look like her except her eyes were a different colour. My mother was bright and smart and funny and really pretty. The lady who raised me is more…"

"Dull?"

Lia grimaced. "Uh…I don't know if I'd be so harsh. I'd rather say that the scope of her interests is a bit more narrow than mine."

Susan smirked and sipped her tea. "Let me give you a tip: as a writer, brevity is your friend. Just say 'dull'."

Lia blushed. "Well, she has good qualities. I think that boiling it down to "dull" would be a little unfair."

"So she's dull, but she has a good heart. It's funny how that works out."

Lia studied Susan for a moment. "Is that how it was with Kenneth?"

The teacup clattered on the saucer. The glare that Susan fixed on Lia was neither pleasant nor tolerant. "Kenneth wasn't dull," she said crisply.

Lia raised an eyebrow. "So why pick Winslow over him? It's been fifty years but even I can tell that Kenneth loved you."

Susan grunted irritably as she reached for her tea again. The scent of ginger hung in the air as she took a sip. "I didn't pick Winslow over Kenneth."

"So what would you call it?"

Susan huffed, causing the warm amber liquid to fly out in little droplets onto her wrinkled hand. "I'd call it the poor choices of youth," she snapped. Her eyes flickered up at Lia. She sighed heavily and set the cup down before she twisted her hands in her lap. Her gaze settled outside the French doors and for a moment, it was clear to Lia that Susan had lost herself in a world far beyond the well-tended flower garden just outside of her parlour. "Parents are veritable instruction manuals that children get at birth. They badger children with advice that seems trite and impossibly unrealistic sometimes. My mother was the agent for that. 'Cut pumpkin can't keep.' 'Cat luck ain't dog luck.' Oh boy, she had a saying for everything."

Susan laughed ruefully. "Although, the one that comes to mind right now is 'love who love you.'"

Lia smiled. She had always found that particular Bajan saying to be as asinine as they came. Yet, something about the way Susan said it made it finally seem poignant. "Would you say that you're afraid to love men because of your experiences?"

Susan gazed off into space again as she said, "Afraid? No. They just made the mistake of letting me realize I didn't need them."

Lia's pen stopped racing across the page as she looked up at Susan. "Didn't need them or you felt they didn't love you?"

Susan gave a rueful smile. "Back then, I didn't understand that love meant selflessness. Neither did I equate comfort and easiness with security. I invested my emotions in Winslow because I wanted to live an exciting life and enjoy the privileges that came from being with him. He didn't coddle me. He was handsome and thrilling and let's not pretend that teenagers don't love illicit thrills. When was the last time you read a romance novel about a girl who chooses the cute but safe shopkeeper's son over the powerful and handsome politician? No...young people don't realize that stability is a gift while power has to be fueled by something that is neither stable nor exotic."

Susan sighed. "I don't know if I knew back then that Kenneth loved me. All I know now is that I took his allegiance for granted. But, just like anything else, even Kenneth's devotion was like a wick in a kerosene lamp. I burned it until it ran out."

Chapter 32

January 1967

We're supposed to evolve. As a society, as a people; in so many ways we're supposed to grow. But what I've always found to be cloying and absurd is how crippling the evolution process has to be. I always found that situations in my life had to leave me barren and empty before I learned the error of my ways. And one, in particular, was perhaps the hardest lesson I had ever been given.

Everything in my life was thrown into sharp relief, questioned and turned over to the point of redundancy when I lost my mother to the careless ministrations of madness. As I reviewed the last few years of her life, I saw the inconsistencies that I initially didn't pay any attention to simply because she was my mother. The religious fervor, the strange sleeping patterns, the aches, and pains. Things that I had just chalked up to growing old were warning signs that none of us saw.

And somehow, we adapted. My entire family quickly took up new routines, but perhaps my role was more pronounced than everyone else's because I took over the mantle of responsibility. But there was one chore that I both relished and resented.

Every Sunday, I cooked. I would pack a basket of food and walk down the long winding lane that ran through our village until I reached the main road. I would sit on the low church wall next to a vendor as he peddled his wares, reluctant to make small talk with him lest he ask for my mother and I broke down in tears. I would travel thirty minutes by bus to a busy intersection where I would disembark. From there, it was a fifteen minute walk through the scorching midday sun until I reached the textured soft stone walls and dark green metal gates of the Psychiatric Hospital.

I'd try not to make eye contact with patients who wandered around the grounds or stood by the fences and begged passersby for food and money. Others mumbled to themselves, shaking their heads loosely as they went. One man was known to hack away at the chain link fence with a roughly sharpened pencil, his face screwed up in concentration as he rubbed the tiny lead tip against the diamond-shaped links. I'd always try to scurry past him to the front desk; once he had chased me while screaming that I had stolen his sharpener. That was my Sunday routine.

A few days after Winslow threatened my mother, I got to the hospital a little later than usual. My heart was heavy as I walked through the gates and announced myself to the duty nurse. The hospital was a beautiful building, built many centuries before in the typical Caribbean colonial style. Bright yellow hibiscus bloomed in unruly hedges, hugging the walls of the hospital's unpainted soft stone walls. Jenkins shied away from being poetic by housing the most feared subset of people known to mankind: the mentally imbalanced. People can justify prisoners in jail as being "bad" but there's something intangible about mental illness that makes it hard for people to qualify. Perhaps the only thing that marred the historic buildings and beautiful gardens was the melancholia that shrouded the grounds like a dome of sadness. What a lovely place to be mad.

The matron of the women's ward came to personally escort me to my mother's room. The polished stone corridor was flanked by heavy metal doors on both sides. Some were open, so the rooms' occupants were probably wandering the grounds. Others were locked tight. Mournful crying issued from one of the cells, so gut-wrenching and pitiful that it curled up and settled in the pit of my stomach. I focused on the flagstone walkway and kept going.

"Please..." I laid my hand gently on the matron's arm as she heaved my mother's cell door open. "I just want to know... why are some locked up while others can walk around?"

She smiled at me. "Some patients have such severe mental disabilities that walking around isn't safe for them or others, some are on suicide watch and others are heavily medicated."

My heart hurt a little every time I heard the heavy clanking from the metal door of my mother's cell. The weight of that sound and the matron's words felt like confirmation of my mother's madness.

Sunlight flooded the cell, casting a bright square of light on the floor as the door creaked open. My mother sat on a small wooden bench in the corner, her hands clasped awkwardly in her lap. On the other side of the small room was a plain foam mattress. No bed frame, no sheets. I remember bringing the family's best sheets to cover my mother's mattress just two weeks before. I had starched and ironed them to such perfection that I smiled with pride all the way to the hospital, hoping that my mother would notice and be proud. I found out afterward that patients weren't encouraged to have bedsheets just in case they tried to commit suicide.

Up until then, they still weren't sure what was causing my mother's behaviour. They poked and prodded her, observing her mood swings and trying to pinpoint exactly what triggered them. It was a process they said. That's why they didn't want to overstimulate her by letting all of us visit at the same time. Each of us visited on different days.

A tired sadness clung to my mother and she didn't even glance up when I entered. The matron patted my hand reassuringly and then left us alone.

I knelt at Mummy's feet and grasped her hands in mine. They were cold; both in temperature and reception. I longed to feel her squeeze my hands and tell me that she was fine and could go home with me, but it never happened. Her distant eyes and stooped posture made me feel like I was looking at a vaguely familiar stranger. The doctors claimed to be treating her, but the medicine they administered with frightening frequency only made her listless and sad. They said it was necessary to keep her from wandering around or hurting herself.

"How are you feeling today?"

She didn't answer. Only the wind moving through her hair let me know she wasn't just a pretty wax figurine, so still was she. I chattered inanely for a few minutes, filling her in on what my brothers and father had been up to. I was keeping the house clean and the garden was thriving. The sow was pregnant and the piglets had grown nice and fat. We were going to slaughter some for the market on Saturday. I promised I would bring her the sweetest pork chop she had ever tasted the next time I came. She didn't even appear slightly interested.

I tried another tack. "Mummy, I made chicken stew. See…just the way you like it with all of the tomatoes and onions stewed down in the gravy. Stop slapping my hand… just try some."

She croaked out a surly "no". I put a small bit on the end of the spoon and balanced the hot dish on my lap. She pinched her lips shut and turned away. "Try some, nuh. Mummy, don't be like that." I tried humour, tenderness, coercion…nothing worked. My despair turned to anger.

"What's wrong with you?!" I shrieked. I smashed the dish on the wall, sank to the floor and started to cry. The scent of warm food filled the air that lingered over broken shards of white ceramic. Droplets of gravy and grains of rice spattered my mother's pale blue shift and my dark green dress. I was ashamed. I don't know why I did it. Maybe it was to provoke her enough to snap out of the drug-induced trance that held her in its grip. Gracie Taylor was a formidable woman when she was angry and she would never have encouraged such an outburst. Maybe I had just had enough of feeling alone even though I was always surrounded by people. I realized that my mother was like a shell and might stay that way forever. Heaving sobs racked my body and I felt every last one of them shuddering through me.

I stayed like that for a moment, warm tears soaking my shirt as I cried. Time stood still until I felt a hand stroke my hair. It was a fleeting gesture, so soft and unexpected I almost thought I imagined it. I spun around and looked at her but my mother's eyes were still glazed over and her hands were still knotted in her lap.

Squeaky footsteps from soft white shoes came closer and the matron entered the room. She had heard the commotion and came to see what it was about. She took one look at the scene and chided me for my impatience. She said it was quite common for family members to lose their temper in these situations, but it did no good to act that way.

I said I would clean up but the matron said it would be better if I went home. She guided me outside and closed the heavy metal door. I left my mother and the gravy-stained shards of glass behind.

Sleep was slow in coming that night. The tears weren't. I resolved to do better and to be more patient when I visited my mother the next Sunday.

The next morning, I was cleaning the dishes when my father came back home. He didn't say much at first when I asked him why he was home from work so early. I poured him a cup of tea and started washing the dishtowels before I heard the side door slam as John rushed in. "Morning... I get de message to come home as soon as possible," he said breathlessly as he bounded into the kitchen.

I knew then. I fell to my knees and cried before my father said a word. His face was pained as he explained to us that my mother had died early that morning. He looked straight ahead as he told us that he had to leave immediately to get word to Samuel and Eli in Canada.

I held John tightly as I cried. Time passed that day and the next and I wasn't exactly sure what happened for a while. Only a few footnotes from that chapter of my life's story stood out. I remember my twin brothers were back in the house. They smelled foreign. Like fresh soap and prosperity. I remember eating sometimes. Occasionally my hunger would overpower my brain with the desire to eat. Yet, my grief was great. I ate only enough to sustain myself. I remember people coming to the house to offer their sympathies, but who came and when I can't remember. I heard snatches of whispered conversation between my father and brothers, but I couldn't focus on anything they said. I remember a doctor coming to the house and talking to me on the night before the funeral. My father stood next to him as he mixed a bitter powder in a glass of water and made me drink it. I hadn't slept properly for more than a week and the doctor said I needed my strength for the service the next day. The tonic left my mouth chalky and numb. I still couldn't sleep that night.

The funeral was held on a sunny Saturday. The sky above the church was polka-dotted with bright paste kites that bobbed on stiff breezes. I stood next to my mother's coffin until the undertaker closed it briskly and wheeled her halfway up the aisle. I looked questioningly at my father and my brothers. My father's lip trembled when he saw me looking at him. I practically melted on the spot, wailing at the sight of my mother's casket so far away from God's altar. Tears flowed freely from Samuel's eyes, Eli looked at me mournfully and John came and took me to sit next to him.

Kenneth reached out and squeezed my free hand as I passed his family's pew.

I thought I knew death. My grandmother died when I was a child. I had cried so much that my eyes seemed permanently swollen for the better part of a month. Admittedly, we weren't particularly close and I found her long-winded stories and incessant snuff-pinching to be annoying. And yet, compared to the incomparable numbness that I felt when my mother died, Granny's death was more like a pinprick of unhappiness.

The rest of that day passed in miserable numbness. On our way home from the funeral, John mentioned that he planned to check on the piglets that had been born one week earlier. My brow furrowed and for the first time since my mother had died, something other than sadness and numbness filled me: worry. My mother always said that the world was like a clock. At the new moon, the sea was full of fish, animals gave birth and women's bodies went through a monthly cleansing. It dawned on me that I had just buried my mother, broken up with my boyfriend, was unemployed and still there was more to my problems that night. I was pregnant.

Chapter 33

June 30th, 2015

Lia looked up startled at Susan. Lia had gone through everything she could find about Susan's life in Barbados and not once did she read anything about a baby.

Old eyes locked with young and for an interminable moment, something connected them. Having worked at a newspaper, Lia wasn't exactly a neophyte when it came to encountering people who had endured one hardship or another. And despite knowing that the human condition is something that none of us can or should try to avoid, Lia didn't think she had ever come across the range of emotions that lurked beneath those sharp hazel eyes. Lia wanted to know but she hesitated for a moment.

She cleared her throat and broke eye contact with Susan, looking down instead at her notepad. The silence stretched on again until finally, Lia asked quietly, "What happened to the baby?"

More silence.

Lia dared to look up.

Susan was still staring at Lia with that look in her eyes. Her eyes betrayed a complex cocktail of feelings that Lia's past wasn't haunted enough to recognize. Susan started to speak but hesitated. She shook her head gently and picked up her teacup before replying, "I did what I thought was best at the time."

Heavy with implication, Susan left that sentence looming between them like a thundercloud on a rainy day. Lia could tell that inwardly she had retreated, gone to some safe place in her mind where she could seek refuge from that particular memory.

Lia didn't need to be told that the day's interview was over. She excused herself quietly and packed up her belongings, ready to return to her room. As Lia reached to turn the doorknob, Susan spoke.

"Cordelia..."

"Yes, ma'am?"

"Conscience doth make cowards of us all."

Lia turned to look at her and still, the old lady didn't meet her eyes.

Susan sighed. "I have made mistakes. The problem with mistakes is that so many of them are irreversible. But every new day allows us the chance to do whatever we can to smooth the ripples that those mistakes have caused."

Lia didn't know why but a tear slipped down her cheek as she tore her eyes away from Susan Taylor and quietly closed the door.

Lia was trying to sleep, but a large and ridiculously persistent fly wouldn't let her. It bobbed back and forth, its buzzing amplified by its nearness or just a few feet out of reach, its steady hum taunting her as she swore softly under her breath. As tall as she was, she could never swat it away with the leather-bound book Miss Taylor had gifted her. Finally, it glided away slowly as though tethered to an invisible thread, alighting gently on the walnut stained crown molding.

Lia plopped down on the bed seething with fury as she watched the fly.

Susan Taylor had retreated to her room after those uncomfortable moments but she couldn't hear a peep coming from the cantankerous old woman's room.

Ancil was downstairs singing hymns slowly and solemnly as she went about her work. It reminded Lia of her mother. One of the hymns in particular brought a tear to Lia's eyes.

Despite Miss Taylor's eerie silence, Lia didn't dare emerge from her room. She knew her luck was such that she would come face-to-face with the reclusive author as soon as she swung the door open. So Lia lay quietly on the bed as she listened to Ancil singing those dreadful hymns that poked at her soul and weighed heavily on her spirit.

Almost as heavily as Susan Taylor's revelation that she had been pregnant. Lia had spent the better part of the evening wishing she could use the Internet to find out what had happened to Susan Taylor's baby. Despite researching before she had flown to the US to start the author's biography, this was the first time she had ever heard about a baby of any sort. The young woman's brow wrinkled in confusion. Lia had assumed that her grumpy disposition was the perfect form of birth control.

Immediately, Lia chided herself for such an uncharitable thought. By listening to Susan Taylor's stories about her family and friendships, it was clear to Lia that Susan Taylor was once a vivacious and beautiful soul. Now Lia saw a lot less of that. Something had stripped it all away and left a woman bereft of love for anything.

The other thing that struck Lia as unusual was the fact that Susan had been remarkably upfront about everything else: her sexuality, her close brush with rape, her knowledge that Kenneth had crippled the perpetrator. It seemed incredibly odd that Susan had clammed up as soon as she had broached the topic. Not to mention her parting comment of "conscience doth make cowards of us all." That was perhaps the only thing that Lia had been able to figure out and even that small victory had led to nothing. The quote was from Shakespeare's Hamlet (what was this lady's obsession with Shakespeare anyway?) Hamlet uttered those words as part of a speech that some believed meant that he would seek revenge and others believed meant Shakespeare himself was considering his mortality. Lia found it interesting that Susan chose those words when discussing her pregnancy.

The fly moved again. Lia struck, flinging the book and finding her mark. She jumped up in triumph and retrieved the book to find blood smeared on a page inside the book. She wiped it gingerly with a tissue, remorseful that she had been so callous with such a beautiful book. It wasn't just that the book was beautiful; it also signified the shift in Susan's attitude towards her. But her feelings quickly turned to surprise as she recognized her name beneath the smeared blood.

Curious, Lia turned to the beginning of the chapter and started reading.

The next morning, Lia sat across the coffee table from Susan Taylor scribbling non-sensical notes furiously. Meanwhile, Susan seemed more interested in her ginger tea than she usually would.

Ancil came in with a tray of warm muffins and, for the first time, sat down quietly between the two women. Lia didn't look up in time to see the knowing look Ancil gave Susan or the uncharacteristically imploring look that Susan returned.

What didn't miss Lia though, was when Ancil cocked her head to the side thoughtfully and nodded slowly before she stood and quietly left the room. It was becoming more and more obvious to Lia that Ancil wasn't just domestic help. Lia realized she needed to get Ancil alone. But that wasn't going to be easy considering that Susan Taylor never left the house without her.

Chapter 34

February 1967

"How did Mummy die?"

It was two days after the funeral. John and I were standing next to the pig pens watching the sow pick through the slop-filled trough. The new piglets snuffled around their mother, stumbling over each other as they jostled for prime suckling positions.

The days had grown dry as the wet season abated, leaving the island parched. Cane fires were rampant at this time of year. The sky would fill with curls of grey smoke, making bright daylight look like a watery sunset as the fire raged on. Up to the beginning of February, there weren't any fires but the lack of rain was a sure sign that they would happen sooner rather than later.

Samuel and Eli had returned to Canada. Daddy had traveled with James to the United States and blessedly only John and I remained in the house. They were family but I had always been closest to John. I had felt stifled with all of them around. I was nervous and jittery having so many people nearby, constantly asking me if I wanted something to eat or if I had slept well. I always nodded quickly, afraid that any delayed response would prompt a barrage of questions. That wasn't necessary with John. I could ask him anything.

He glanced at me before he said slowly, "I think you already know, Susie. Making me say it won't make it any less hurtful. Or any less true."

I bit my lip. "Are they sure that's what happened?"

John frowned. "That's what they said."

"Yeah, but how? Where's the proof that's actually what happened? I mean..." Winslow's words echoed in my head and I swallowed the lump in my throat as I repeated them. "Jenkins is full of medicine that can be 'accidentally' overdosed and machines that can 'accidentally' malfunction."

John cleared his throat and said, "But ...it wasn't an accident. Mummy did it herself. She...she cut her wrist with a piece of broken glass."

I turned on him, agitated that he would even say such a thing. "That's foolishness. Mummy wouldn't do that."

He rubbed the back of his neck nervously. "It's not that we didn't want to tell you or anything. But we just figured that you weren't ready to hear it yet."

"Hear what, John?" I asked as fury grew inside me. "Someone killed our mother. Aren't the police investigating?"

John was incredulous. "Investigating what, Susie? They found her in a locked cell with her wrists cut."

When John said that, he made me so angry I could barely stand still. I punched my brother so hard, his head whipped back. I heard my knuckles crack against the bones in his jaw. I trembled with a rage so deep I saw fear in the eyes of a man who was broad-shouldered and brave.

He looked at me for a minute, then shook his head and said, "The doctor said you'd be angry with everyone and we should be patient with you."

I had never felt so betrayed in my life. That was how they saw me: as a child with unstable emotions instead of a woman with conviction. I was pregnant, my mother was dead and my entire family was content to just move on with life as though nothing had ever happened. My family wouldn't believe me and unless I had their support, the police wouldn't believe that the island's deputy prime minister had arranged my mother's apparent suicide. It was obvious that it was completely pointless to continue talking to John. I turned and walked away. That was the last time I ever saw my brother.

The ground smelled like heat. Cracks ran through the earth like exposed veins and a scent like the faintest whiff of burnt bread escaped into the air. The weeds that usually thrived around Winslow's house had shriveled up, their green stems desiccated and bent.

I banged on the front door. My body trembled, I was so nervous and angry.

The door swung open and there stood Ignatious Grimes. "Good afternoon, young miss. What may I do for you today?" was his crisp greeting.

I was taken aback. I had assumed that both men were still mad at each other. I cleared my throat and said, "I came to see Mr. Vaughan, please."

"Surely there's no need to stand on ceremony when I've already caught you lying down for it," he said drily.

My cheeks reddened as I remembered the day Ignatious had found Winslow and me in bed.

He fixed those steel grey eyes on me as he said, "Winslow is not here. He traveled to America this morning."

I couldn't stand that little man, but there was certainly no point in staying. I thought I'd go to the police station to file a report instead and hope I could get enough proof before Winslow came back.

"But..."

I turned to face Ignatious again. "But what?" I snapped at him. "You're going to drop some nasty comments about me again? Tell me maybe I should go and lie in bed until he gets back? Well, let me tell you..."

He raised his hand ever so slightly, but it was enough to silence me.

"It's quite the contrary. He's on a little trip to shore up some direct foreign investment. I saw it as my duty to tidy up his files for him and while doing so, I came across the most fascinating diary." He held up my battered brown journal in his hand and said, "I must say it sparked the genius in me." His face remained impassive as always, betraying neither excitement or sincerity.

In all of the drama of the previous month, I had forgotten I had left it at Winslow's house. I looked askance at Ignatious. As much as I distrusted the man, I couldn't help but want to hear what he had to say. He cupped my journal between clasped hands, almost lovingly, as he spoke.

"Your writing is very good. The language, the imagery, and metaphors...it reads like a novel rather than the trite observations of a teenage girl. It gave me a rather insightful perspective into your life. You have played Tonto to Winslow's Lone Ranger for a long time but you're greater than he ever could be. This diary is the key to a great future for you and a long painful demise for him."

I eyed the book nervously. I used to write everything in that book and knowing that Ignatious Grimes had read my innermost thoughts sent a shiver down my spine. I felt naked in front of him and wanted nothing more than to leave. I thought of grabbing the book and running, but then he simply held it out to me as he said, "Or... maybe these are just the silly rantings of an old man."

My feelings warred inside me as I reached for my journal. He said nothing more as I took it from him. He stepped back into the shadows of the great house and started to close the heavy mahogany door, but I needed to know.

I shoved my foot between the door and its frame and said, "What do you mean?"

He smiled placidly as he re-opened the door and fixed those cold grey eyes on me. "Come, my dear. Let us talk."

I left Winslow's house two hours later. Dusk would fall soon; fireflies dotted the landscape like thousands of tiny floating lanterns as I made my way down the dusty driveway that led away from the great house. The steady hum of sandflies lent a soft thrum to the easy rhythm of the evening.

The heat of the day had abated, leaving behind only arid air to dry the tears that ran down my cheeks. The journal in my hand that was once a conduit to whimsy and inner peace was now a sharpened weapon. It was not only filled with my notes but choice inclusions from Ignatious Grimes as well. My head and heart were heavy with the thought of what I was about to do. The thought of the opportunity that Ignatious Grimes had set up for me filled me with nervous excitement. For the first time, I could put my needs and my future ahead of Winslow's. At least that's what Ignatious said. Truth be told, he oversold it a bit. Having revenge against Winslow was more important than anything else by that time.

Uncertainty, anger, and fear all bubbled inside of me but the thought of ruining Winslow quelled the uneasiness. I had never thought I would be in cahoots with Ignatious Grimes. But then again, I also never thought I would be pregnant for with a man who didn't want me.

The thoughts that swirled in my head threatened to leave me nauseous with their intensity. My mother and how much I missed her. My father and brothers and how much I would miss them. But more than anyone else I thought of Kenneth.

He had been everything to me: a best friend, a lover, a confidante, a muse, a safe haven. I could bear anything in the world if he was with me. I stopped for an instant, taking in the gathering twilight and realized that there wasn't much time left.

My breath caught in my throat and dust swirled in little clouds when I started to run down that dark country lane as though my lifeline lay at the other end of it. I could be brave and leave everything I had ever known if he was at my side.

"Susie?" Kenneth rose from the low wall in his back garden and looked me up and down.

I was sweaty and breathless with my wind-whipped hair looking like a silhouetted mess in the darkness, but seeing Kenneth was enough to reinvigorate me. I jumped into his arms. I hugged him fiercely before he held my shoulders and looked at me curiously.

"What's wrong?"

"I have to leave here tonight. I want you to come with me." I said breathlessly.

He was confused. "Leave? What do you mean?"

"I'm leaving the island tonight. I'm going to the States to publish my diary."

Kenneth shook his head slowly. "What are you on about, Susie?"

"Ignatious Grimes spoke to a publisher in New York about publishing my book. They want to meet me. He arranged for me to go tonight. Look, Kenneth, he gave me this spending money and I want to take you with me."

"Take me with you," he repeated the words slowly, as though they were a foreign language.

"Yes! He says my book will be the biggest thing around." For the first time, I smiled brightly. "We can finally go and see Niagara Falls. We'll be right there in New York and we can see the Falls and the Statue of Liberty and ..."

"Susie, stop."

He turned away. His shoulders slumped for a moment before he started to pace in frustration, running his hands over the back of his neck as he shook his head.
Eventually, Kenneth turned to me, his eyes wrought with worry and confusion as he spoke. "Why can't you stay here?"

"Winslow killed my mother because I threatened to talk about all of the dirty deals he did. He'll kill me too if I stay here."

"He did what?"

"Just what I said."

"Why didn't you tell me so? And I thought your

mother had..." Kenneth broke off and looked away uneasily before he said, "...died in another way."

"No, Winslow rigged it to look like she did it.

He looked at me pleadingly. "Susie, go to the police."

"And tell them that the deputy prime minister killed a crazy woman who walked through the village naked and had to be put in Jenkins? They would never believe that."

He shook his head as though trying to unsettle butterflies that had alighted on it. "Susie, if there is evidence they will find it. You don't have to leave."

I bit my lip nervously. "That's... not the only reason I want to leave."

Kenneth looked at me, the question clear in his eyes.

"I'm pregnant."

He said nothing but the silence suddenly became just as pregnant as I was.

I heaved a breath before I said, "It's Winslow's but I know that you know that."

He huffed. "So you just wanted me to leave a family business - which I'm the sole heir to, by the way - and run to New York with you to play house?"

"No, that's not what I meant. I'm going to..."

Kenneth stood rooted to the ground, but I could feel the angry vibrations that radiated from him as he interrupted me. "Susan Taylor, I have been a good friend to you for as long as I can remember. I almost killed a man for you!" He advanced toward me, his anger growing so rapidly that I feared he would hit me.

His breath came in harsh gasps as he said bitterly, "I've always been here whenever it suits you and not once have you ever considered what's best for me. I've never asked for anything in return. But you expect me to think nothing of going to a foreign country to raise that man's child. You're selfish. How would my parents feel if their only child were to pick up and run off? What are they going to do in their old age when there's no-one else here to run the shop? No, Susie, enough is enough."

"But..."

"Enough 'buts'!" he roared. He put his hands out to steady himself. He took a few deep breaths before he finally said, "God doesn't put more on a man than he can bear. None of this is my problem."

Tears slid down my cheeks. "Kenneth...please, just listen."

He shook his head numbly. "Safe trip." And with those words, he walked away.

Chapter 35

July 3rd, 2015

Lia was crying. Susan was rolling her eyes. "Come now, child. It happened to me, not you and you don't see me wailing as though time stood still."

"Y-yes, but...Kenneth should have gone with you."

Susan sighed. "If he had, he would have done himself a great disservice."

Lia sniffed as she looked at Susan. "Why?"

Susan shrugged and said, "I was selfish and he was right - he was right about everything - because it was always about me. Maybe I was spoiled because I was the last child and the only girl. My brothers and father protected me and my mother felt it was her duty to give me the best she had. Kenneth enabled me a lot, as well. In the end, I learned my lesson the hard way." She sighed. "Since then I've given more thought to what I've done and I've always tried to think of the greater good and not myself."

Lia looked Susan in the eye and asked the question that had been haunting her for days. "What happened to the baby?"

The old woman met Lia's gaze for a moment but looked away before saying softly, "Dead."

"But how?"

Susan shrugged her shoulders and sighed before she said, "Cordelia...I..."

Lia stared at Susan. The reclusive author was always confident and uncompromising and therefore, seldom lost for words. Susan's rare patches of weakness always surprised Lia.

Susan sighed again and shook her head. "We will touch on that a bit later. I feel a bit drained today; rehashing these unpleasant memories is much like bathing oneself in ice water; it's an interesting notion until you do it and everything starts to ache."

Lia nodded glumly as she glanced at the older lady. Susan wasn't just spouting hyperbole this time. In the past few weeks, her slim frame had grown more gaunt and only those hazel eyes seemed to emanate any real energy. She was eating less and less every day and Lia could see how much it physically cost her to tell these emotional stories. She had assumed that if Susan got everything off her chest it would be cathartic, but it had exactly the opposite effect.

Lia reached out and patted Susan's hand. "How about if we finish up tomorrow?"

Susan nodded her head slowly. "Yes, tomorrow is a good day to finish everything off.

Chapter 36

February - July 1967

I was shattered after Kenneth refused to go to the States with me. I stumbled home in a trance. I was mad at the world for taking my mother and my two loves. I thought about the things Kenneth and Winslow had said, the things Joan had done, my rage at my father for making me take a job that led me to Winslow's bed. Every conversation and feeling that had led me to that point played over and over in my head until I grew nauseous and vomited on the side of the road.

I thought about what things would have been like if I had been pregnant with Kenneth's baby. How simple life could have been. He always wanted children. We would have been married and I would have helped him run the grocery until we were good and old. I imagined him indulging me in an exotic trip or two with the children, grumbling about having to close the shop, but resigning himself to making me happy. I cried. I would have been satisfied with such a beautifully constructed life. I could have still written books - maybe nothing incredibly profound or commercially successful. I may have become a teacher. I'm not sure. All I knew is that the fractured reality that stretched before me was frightening and lonely. That long dark road had never felt so long and dark before.

Daddy was at home when I got there. He sat alone at the table with just one lit kerosene lamp in the corner. He had grown quiet and reserved in those few weeks, giving up on the gambling and drinking and sticking close to home. I suspect that he spent those quiet moments trying to make sense of everything around him and never reaching a conclusion that eased his troubled mind.

I wanted to tell him the truth about my delicate condition but I didn't even know how to begin. I thought sadly that I wouldn't even have had to tell my mother because she would have just known. Since her death, Daddy had grown accustomed to seeing me in random fits of tears. He probably assumed that's what my latest episode was about. His grey eyes studied me for a long moment before he said, "Want something to eat, Susie?"

"No, Daddy."

"Want me to make you some sago?"

"No, Daddy."

"What happen, Susie?"

That was my chance. But I couldn't get the words to form. So I lied to cover up my unspeakable truth.

"I got an offer to write a book, Daddy."

He sighed and nodded his head slowly. "So wha' that mean now?"

"I have to go to the States tonight if I want it to work out."

"You leaving me, Susie?"

I bit my lip.

For the first time in my life, I saw two fat teardrops leave my father's eyes.

"I is a hard man sometimes, I know. Your mother was a good woman and it ain't easy right now. But I know she didn't going want me to stop you doing something big with your life. She always know you going be the bright spark."

I cried then too. Never before had I seen my father express a sentimental thought about much of anything.

He sank his head between his hands and just shook it for a moment before he looked up at me and gave me a weak smile. "Get packed, sweet girl. I goin' carry you to Seawell."

I tossed my few belongings in the family suitcase and left a note for John bidding him goodbye before my father hustled me to the airport. We talked a whole lot on the way and I cried even more. I remember dragging my feet as we walked to the ticket counter. I wanted to stay. I hugged Daddy for a long moment and told myself to just spit it out and say it. Then I remembered what Winslow had done to my mother and I knew I had to leave. Nothing else seemed worthwhile but getting back at Winslow. In those days, there was no extensive booking system like how there is now. You could just show up, pay for a seat and leave the country. So that's what I did. I watched the island I called home fade away from me as the plane lifted off and I knew I would never be whole again.

I spent the next six months working with the publisher to get The Unspeakable Truth ready for press. Those were the worst months of my life, all alone in that cold place. I was able to get an apartment with my advance, a nice little walk-up close to the West Indian area. The food didn't taste like home and the place didn't look like home either. I sat by my window and watched New York transform as the trees grew green leaves that turned orange and then fell off again. It was maddening.

The winter was bitter and looked nothing like the drawings I had seen in books. There were no fairytale mounds of white snow perfect for sipping hot cocoa after toboggan rides. All of New York was covered in ugly grey ice that gave me the flu and drove me into a deeper depression than I could ever imagine. That slipped into spring which was still colder than anything I experienced back home. Summer came, bringing warmth with it, but I still felt cold inside.

My publisher sent a copy of my diary to the FBI. They interviewed me to get all of the details about Winslow's nefarious deeds. At one point they assumed I was deeply complicit and I feared I would spend the rest of my life in prison too. I spent a whole night in sleepless misery wondering what I had really done. In the end, they determined I wasn't guilty and instead went digging a little deeper into Winslow's business associates.

By the time the book came out, Winslow had amassed a truly envious cache of material possessions. In less than six months, Mr. Vaughan became the proud owner of a brand new Jaguar E-type convertible, some bespoke Italian suits and a pair of horses that he planned to race at the Kentucky Derby. His temporary custody of them ended when the FBI swooped in like falcons and seized every ill-gotten item he owned. As prophesied, Winslow's Rolex did end up inside a plastic evidence bag. I'll admit that I grinned from ear to ear when I heard that. I like to imagine that my words pinged around inside his head when it happened. I heard he cried like a baby and cussed me black and blue when the FBI led him through the airport in handcuffs. He swore I'd never be able to rest until he got back at me.

As for the rest of the island, they grew to hate me too. All of the new jobs in the new companies that paid so well came to a screeching halt. Each of those businesses slammed their doors shut quicker than the cat could lick his ear. Thousands of Barbadians were on the breadline. Many of them had to shelve their new fancy office attire and go back to the plantations to beg smug White people for their old jobs digging potatoes and pulling weeds. Stores repossessed furniture and appliances. My people were livid and their hate for me was almost greater than Winslow's. 'Pretty-Eyed Susan' was born and eventually, the venom they said it with was replaced with mockery which was no kinder.

The Unspeakable Truth wasn't greeted with adoration and reverence in Barbados. I suspect the only reason Bajans didn't create mile-high pyres of my book in the streets was because they couldn't afford to waste the little money they did have after the scandal broke. The DPP hated me too. They lost the next election by a landslide and even James' benevolence deserted him when it came to my family. I remember a conversation I had with my father right before him and John left to go to Canada. James had fired him in one fell swoop and swore that no-one in Barbados would ever hire him or John again.

I was holed up in my New York apartment, crying on the phone and telling him that all I ever wished for was to write a book, but I never imagined it would have caused so much trouble.

"Susie...it done do as you mummy used to say. But girl, my mother always used to say to be careful what you wish for 'cause you just might get it."

Chapter 37

July 4th, 2015

"Miss Taylor, if you had to do it all over again, would you?"

Susan smiled.

"This is the only reality I've known for almost fifty years so it's hard to imagine any other outcome." The older lady shrugged. "A wish is a funny thing. We tell ourselves that we want something so badly but it's always in isolation. We never think about the rest of our reality; how it will impact our family and friends or a chance at a normal life. I wanted to write a famous book and I did. I didn't wish to live in Barbados or have normal relationships with my family and friends. The book is so inconsequential without those things."

Lia nodded and bit the inside of her lip. She thought of her own dreams of fame and fortune and knew she'd had to ask herself some hard questions. She looked up then and studied the room she was in. Months earlier, she had thought it was just Susan's antiquated decorating at work. Now she realized it was a tomb of memories, a way for Susan to relive the good and bad.

Lia turned to Susan and asked, "You've never adjusted to a life away from home, have you?"

Susan laughed. "This room is testimony to that. I saw the way you just looked around like you had an epiphany. Ah...I don't mind how crazy it makes me seem. I love this room and I imagine I will go to my death bed with it being this way." Susan smiled somberly at the thought.

Lia smiled. "Do you think that telling me this story has

been cathartic for you?"

Susan cocked her head to one side. "In many ways, it has been. I've delved into parts of my personality in a really meaningful way. I've gotten some things off my chest. I had stored up so much anger that over the years I got used to just being that way. Talking has helped me to get some relief."

"Wow. I wasn't looking for that response but I'm really glad I got it."

Susan nodded and smiled at Lia.

"What about your fathers and brothers? What is your relationship like with them?"

"Daddy and I used to talk once a month until he died in 1981. I hear the boys sometimes but they've got children and wives so we're not very close."

Lia leaned forward. "But, seriously...if you had the chance, would you write the book again?"

Susan stared her straight in the eye. "Never."

"What happened to Winslow?" Lia asked.

Susan chuckled softly to herself as she sipped her tea again. "It turns out that the nonsense I knew about was just the tip of the iceberg. Winslow had misused his position as deputy prime minister to launder mafia money through the Barbadian government. He claimed it was "foreign direct investment" to fund "infrastructural improvements."

"What he didn't realize was that racketeering is a federal crime and the FBI's long fingers could reach him even in Barbados. He got forty years in federal prison for his crime; he died there in 2004."

Lia thought briefly that prison was just what Winslow deserved. "And Kenneth?"

"I don't know," said Susan crisply. Lia looked askance at Susan, but said nothing as she scribbled a small note in the margin of her book: "Research Kenneth Bailey."

"Can I ask you a question?"

The old lady barked a laugh. "It's 'may I' and you've insisted that's why you're here, so ask away."

"What's your biggest regret in life?"

Susan's eyes flickered toward the bookshelf on her right before she replied, "Oftentimes, preconceived notions are the genesis of misunderstandings. Even when it becomes clear that a thing is far more accessible than it initially appeared, one can still labour under the impression that accomplishing that feat is not easy. There was once a time when I tried to right a great wrong in my life, but I was unable to correct it before it was too late. I...I tried my best to ensure it never happened again, but even I am susceptible to the fear of rejection and failure."

Lia wanted to roll her eyes. Sometimes, Susan displayed a penchant for talking a lot but saying absolutely nothing.

"So...what you're saying is that you froze when the time came to do something that seemed difficult?"

Susan shot her a withering look. "Young people are too prone to abbreviating things that are layered and complex."

"Nothing in life is that hard, you know. The answer to many things is either 'yes' or 'no'. All I'm saying is..."

"All you're saying is that you ain't see a star pitch yet and you have no idea what real hardships are." Nostrils flaring and hazel eyes ablaze, Susan Taylor drew herself up to her full height as she stared down at Lia. Her Bajan accent was thick now that she was angry, easily displacing the generic no-man's-land inflection she typically used. "You t'ink you cuh come hay an' judge me? De day that you forced to mek a choice between you pride and you child, turn you back on the man that you love or leave the only country you ever called home, then you cuh judge me."

Lia gaped at Susan. She tried to will her mouth to

apologize but she couldn't get the words to materialize. She said nothing as Susan swept past her and slammed the door when she left the room.

Lia said, "You know...it's funny. She's mean and crotchety but still, she has so many insanely wise thoughts just flowing out of her, you know what I mean? I want to be right next to her, but far away from her all at the same time."

Ancil nodded silently, her eyes fixed on the mug that warmed her smooth plump hands. "Susan does say something to me almost every day. 'Wisdom isn't learned; it's earned.'" Ancil chuckled lightly as though remembering some long-forgotten thought.

Lia nodded. "Miss Taylor has a life that sounds so thrilling to write down on paper but if many of us had to walk a mile in her shoes, they would realize it's a life full of sadness and sacrifice." She looked at Ancil and decided that now was the time to ask the question that was burning inside of her. "Ancil..."

Ancil looked up and searched Lia's eyes as though convinced she could see the answer to whatever troubled her just beyond their surface. "You have beautiful eyes, Lia."

"Oh, thank you." Lia stuttered, a bit taken aback by the unexpected turn in the conversation.

Ancil studied her hands intently before she murmured, "You right about Susan and her life. She was real honest with you. I real proud that she trying so hard."

Lia wrinkled her mouth. "Yes, she seems to be trying. But, I get the feeling that she's always kind of 'truth adjacent' if you know what I mean."

Ancil shrugged. "What she's doing is very hard for her. Please don't judge her, Lia." She opened her mouth again but seemed to think better of it. She patted Lia on her shoulder and left the room.

The next day was slightly bizarre. Susan talked non-stop about all manner of things. "The illusions that adults feed children through fairy tales and doctored childhood stories are heartless attempts at forcing failures down someone's throat. Life is a combination of many small steps that can result in a great journey. But one must be prudent because a miscalculation of any sort can leave one bitter and alone. Humanity has gotten high on its own supply. We worship at the altars of technology and commerce always forgetting that life and love are the most important things of all."

Lia listened to Susan rambling on, unsure of where she was going with her story. Once in a while, she would glance at Lia as though the answer to her conundrum stared her in the face. And every time she did, Lia thought Susan would suddenly spill her guts and give her the juiciest tidbit that would catapult her to fame.

None were forthcoming. The inane ramblings went on for the better part of three days. On the fourth day, Ancil told Lia that Susan was feeling poorly. Susan didn't surface on the fifth day either. Lia wondered if Susan was feigning sickness to avoid discussing a truly uncomfortable topic. Lia sulked in her room going over her notes. She snuck out for an hour to go to the community centre, using the shared computers there to try to find Kenneth. She even considered sneaking into Susan's inner sanctum to get the mysterious letter in her desk drawer but knew that despite Susan being sick in bed, Ancil was still likely to catch her snooping around.

On the sixth day, Lia had a dream. A loud wail pierced the predawn silence. Groggy and confused, Lia ran to Susan's room and found Ancil groaning and shrieking as she held Susan's limp hand. Lia called an ambulance. They arrived within minutes. They worked on Susan for a while, before bundling the three women into the ambulance and racing to the hospital. An hour later, the doctors told Lia and Ancil that they "did what they could", but Susan was gone.

The dream was troubling but what bothered Lia the most was that she couldn't seem to wake up. It kept going on and on. It wouldn't stop even after Ancil asked to see Susan again and Susan was still laying on a gurney, looking quite peaceful. A soft whirring noise issued from the air conditioning unit above Susan, gently lifting the curly wisps of hair that framed her face. Her face was serene and beautiful, the years of bitterness and anger erased from her features. Lia got another glimpse of the girl who had run barefoot through the gullies, dreaming beautiful thoughts and fantasies. Lia's eyes were locked on Susan's face and for a fleeting moment, Lia thought that Susan would be annoyed if they woke her. It was one of those silly conflicting notions that human beings have. Lia squeezed her hand but it was devoid of the fleshy warmth it was supposed to have.

The rest of the day passed by similarly, neither real nor imagined, but a hazy muddling of both.

By the time Susan's funeral came around a week later, Lia had started to come to grips with some semblance of reality. The service was held at a small cemetery and presided over by a West Indian minister (Susan had told Ancil that only a Caribbean pastor could bury her). Ancil was there and so were Susan's accountant, her book agent, her gardener, the paperboy, and his father. There was also a tall dark-skinned man in a black suit with a full head of hair whose clever eyes were rimmed with tears.

Susan's tiny cortege dispersed without much fanfare as soon as her casket was lowered into the dark abyss beneath the bright green grass. Everyone kissed Ancil and gave her their condolences. They waved awkwardly at Lia and the paperboy asked if he could still make his deliveries even though Miss Taylor was dead. Soon, the dark-skinned man hugged and kissed Ancil before he turned to Lia. He was very handsome even though he must have been well into his seventies. He smiled at Lia sadly as he held out his hand to her. "Hello, young lady. I know you don't know me, but I grew up with your grandmother in Barbados. She's a beautiful lady with a beautiful soul and she's out of her pain now."

Lia smiled weakly. "Thank you, but she's not my grandmother."

Confusion marred his handsome features. "Oh...but I thought...it's the eyes you see. You have her eyes. And you look a lot like her daughter. My apologies."

Ancil's face turned white. "Kenneth, I don't think that now..."

"Kenneth?" Lia stared at him. "But she said that she hadn't spoken to you for years." Lia turned to Ancil. "And what is he talking about? She said her child died. I thought she had a miscarriage."

Kenneth's brow wrinkled. "No. Her daughter Cordelia died in a car accident in Barbados more than ten years ago." Lia looked from him to Ancil in shock and her body turned numb. Ancil's lip trembled. Her body shook and she turned to Lia with a heavy sigh. "We should go home an' talk."

Chapter 38

1950 - 2005

I met your grandmother when I was a little boy. Our families were close so she was always around, but that's not why I was drawn to her. She was different. She was the kind of girl that boys don't mind playing with. She was up for anything and had as much spirit as any of us. Susie wasn't pretentious or difficult to get along with, but she only got along with who she wanted to get along with, if you know what I mean. She was interested in everything, sharp as a tack she was. There was never a dull moment with her around. Still, despite what I knew about her, I don't think I ever really knew her. Or maybe that's just the way it is when you're young. I don't know.

Her family stayed with mine for a few months after Hurricane Janet hit Barbados in the 1950s. My parents owned the biggest grocery shop in the area and up until then, I don't think I took a serious interest in the family business. I found it to be very dull work. But when Susie came to live with us, I really got into it. It was fun to have someone to talk to while we packed out the goods and cleaned the shop. She was a hard worker, quick to learn and she found new ways of doing things that made the work fly.

It was during those little moments that she and I got to know each other much better, but it wasn't all business.

We would fly kites and make scooters with the other neighbourhood children, running through the cane fields and gullies until it grew dark outside. By the time we became teenagers in the 1960s, things between us changed. I knew I loved her since I was about twelve years old, but I was too shy to tell her. Susie was so wrapped up in her imagination and her big dreams that I don't think she gave a thought to the fact that I might have feelings for her.

That changed when she was about sixteen years old. We went through some life-changing moments together and in some ways, we grew much closer. Then in 1967, your grandmother became pregnant with your mother and she moved to the States to work on her book. At one point she feared what would happen to her and the baby if she went back to Barbados. The baby's father was a powerful man in our country and she felt that he would try to do her harm in some way.

After it became clear that Winslow was facing some serious jail time in the US for crimes he committed in Barbados, he sent someone to my house to tell me he would rip her from stem to stern for what she was doing to him. She gave birth in New York City on September 15th, 1967 and named the baby Cordelia.

She called to let me know and that's when I told her about Winslow's threat. She was frantic. I can't imagine how hard that was for her: sleep-deprived with a new baby to look after and always looking over her shoulder. I still loved her and even though we didn't part on the best of terms, I wanted to be with her. I told her I would come to New York to protect her. Susie said no, but she never explained why. Just a simple 'no'.

Once, she called me crying in the middle of the night from the police station. Someone had followed her. I tried to reassure her that New York was a scary place and it was just a coincidence but she wouldn't hear of it. She didn't want to keep living in fear. She decided to send the baby back to Barbados until the end of Winslow's trial in case he found her in New York. She figured that by hiding the baby in plain sight, that was the last place he would ever look for the child.

Two days before that, I got a call from a cousin I had never met. Her grandfather had migrated to Panama to help build the Panama Canal. His grand-daughter - my cousin, Ancil - was relocating to Barbados and had asked me to help her find a place to stay. Luck had shone on Susie. I arranged for my cousin to collect the baby in New York and bring it back to the island.

It broke Susan's heart to separate herself from her daughter. My cousin, bless her, raised that baby. Cordelia grew beautifully. She became a painter and Ancil moved back to Panama for a while. Cordelia had a baby herself when she was twenty-five. By that time, I suspect all of the guilt Susie felt over her mother's death, the book and everything else had simmered long enough for her to realize that she couldn't live like that anymore. She secretly reached out to Cordelia and invited both of you to Florida. On the day the two of you were supposed to leave the island, Cordelia asked a neighbor to watch you while she went to collect the plane tickets. From all accounts, Cordelia was thrilled to be able to see her mother, but it wasn't to be. She died in a car accident.

Your grandmother was devastated, but she kept watch over you from afar. Since then, she's sent a healthy sum every month to the lady you call your mother.

I'm not sure if it was the stress of those situations or the cancer or a combination of both, but either way, her health faltered. Susie was highly suspicious of doctors and hospitals after her mother died and didn't want to go to a home. She asked Ancil to come and look after her. That was proof to me of how much she trusted my cousin.

I still cared a lot for your grandmother even though our lives took separate paths. I got married and had children but it wasn't the same. When my wife died a few years ago, I reached out to Susan, hoping that we could become friends again. At first, we got along well enough, and even through letters and phone calls, I knew my love for her had never faded. But when I asked her to marry me, she stopped responding to my letters and whenever I called she would never come to the phone. All I can say is that Susie had her ways.

I imagine that this was the way it was always supposed to work out, but sometimes I wonder what would have happened if I had made other decisions, if I had taken certain chances.

Your grandmother always said to me that 'conscience doth make cowards of us all' and I think that's the best way to describe what happened between her and me. I can tell from the look on your face that you're angry at her for not telling you the truth. You're hurt and that's okay. And still, I think you should ask yourself if you're looking at all of the truth. The truth is that she's loved you and looked after you even though you didn't know it. Susie did what she thought was best and I think it's only fear that made her operate in the clumsy way she did. So please, forgive her, because I don't want you holding on to anger and grief your whole life the same way she did.

Chapter 39

July 13th, 2015

Kenneth cancelled his flight to Canada and booked one to Barbados instead. He declared that Susan's death made him realize life was too short. He had had enough of the bitter Canadian winters and he wanted to retire to his island home to live out the rest of his days bathed in the Caribbean warmth of his boyhood.

Ancil ambled through the house like a wraith, her cheerful disposition having gone the way of the dodo birds. There was no singing and laughter and even the scent of warm oats couldn't comfort her. Lia lay in her room wretchedly aware of Susan's absence and her sudden feeling of incompletion.

Eventually, there was nothing left to do but go back home to Barbados. Her dreams of a book deal were shattered and the idea of going back to her mother sat like a hot stone in her stomach. To imagine that her mother had always pled poverty because of the sacrifices she made to look after Lia. Lia would have bet dollars to donuts that her mother had gambled away most of the money. She wondered if her mother had only looked after her because she was being paid.

The previous days had unhinged everything Lia thought she knew about herself and the people around her. She felt like a pawn in an elaborate chess game where all of the pieces were made of smoke. She had no idea who she was or where she belonged.

The bed overflowed with freshly laundered clothes

that Lia slowly folded and packed into her worn carpetbag. Her pile of notes, now dog-eared from so much use over the past few months stood in a neat stack on the night table. They were among her only possessions in the world and suddenly it dawned Lia that it was all she had. No money, no opportunities, no real home. She broke down crying.

There was a gentle knock on the door. "Hold on," Lia said in a choked voice. She rushed to the small ensuite bathroom and splashed water on her face before saying, "Come in, Ancil."

If the older lady noticed the swollen eyes, she said nothing. "I know yuh mad at yuh granny but it so easy to judge somebody until you walk a mile in they shoes."

"I just wan' you to know that she was a good woman, l'il rough 'round de edges, but she had a good heart and she deserve forgiveness."

Ancil sat on the edge of the bed and sighed. "I remember when I first meet her with that little baby. So frighten and protective of de l'il chink that was your mother. Letting me take your mother eat a hole in Susan core but she didn' know what else to do." Ancil shrugged. "I use to be a nurse, you know that?"

Lia shook her head.

"Yes, I was. Your granny wasn't always so hard. But your grandfather leff a stain on her heart. And the cancer didn' help. I find cancer is harder on family than on the patients. Susan get so impatient and bitter in the past year. Always in a hurry to finish everything because she know de days did number. Especially dis."

She handed Lia an old book. The worn brown leather sheathed a thick stack of tattered pages that required delicate handling. Only a trace of faint gold lettering suggested what the title used to be, but the book needed no introduction. It was evident that Susan had kept that diary her whole life and Lia was moved to tears when she held it in her hands.

"She used to write every day. She asked me to give you all of de diaries but that's de main one she wanted you to have."

Lia nodded slowly. Ancil kissed her forehead and closed the door quietly as she left the room.

Lia fell backward on the bed. She was mentally drained but her curiosity was strong enough to stave off the barrage of emotions that coursed through her.

She turned the yellowed pages, slowing scanning them for anything that might jump out at her. Susan's cursive scrawl covered every inch of that diary with notes that covered myriad subjects like love and relationships, unusual dreams, her daily activities and even interesting books she had read.

It wasn't lost on Lia that she had not inherited her grandmother's literary prowess. She had missed the opportunity to learn from a truly great woman. She shook her head bitterly at the thought. She flipped to the end of the diary and saw three notations written on the inside of the old back cover.

It was her name "Cordelia Christina" and next to it was her birthday, December 16th, 1992. Above that were two more notations:

Susan Diana Taylor
Date of Birth: May 19th, 1948

Cordelia Diana Taylor
Date of Birth: December 16th, 1967
Christened: January 15th, 1968

Under that was a litany of neat notes including, among others, the date of Lia's graduation, the date of her first by-line in the newspaper and the date she got her driver's license.

All of this bothered Lia even more. Why had Susan called her to do those bogus interviews, why did she poke and prod into Lia's business? Anger bubbled inside her. Why couldn't she just call Lia and tell her who she was? Why did she make Lia go through the trouble of leaving Barbados to sit and talk to her like a stranger when they could have tried to build a proper relationship?

Lia's brain was whirring. She looked down at the diary again and saw a bright white sheet of paper tucked in among the sepia-toned pages.

By the time she finished reading, fresh tears came to her eyes so hot and strong that she cried herself to sleep, so weary and unhappy was she.

Chapter 40

May 15th, 2015

Dear Lia,

It's my 67th birthday and I'm awaiting the arrival of the greatest gift I could even aspire to imagine. Your plane must be touching down at the airport now and it gives my old heart a tremulous little flutter to know I'll lay eyes on you in person. I've been so anxious I could barely sit still for the past few weeks.

I'm writing this letter, but I pray that my nerves don't get the better of me and force me to give it to you. I'd rather tell you in person that I'm your grandmother, but talking has never been my strong suit. I'm known to be gruff and anti-social at turns, but God knows what's truly in my heart. The intricate vagaries of my mind flow like silk through my pen and all becomes clear when I write, but I've never learned to properly convey my thoughts through speech.

First, let me apologize for being out of your life for so many years. I spent many of them in hiding. I thought I'd be able to keep you safe if I stayed away. The last time I tried to see you, your mother - my only child - died an untimely death and I still hold myself responsible for that. The years have grown sallow and cold and even though my heart still aches for my beautiful daughter, I knew I had to do what was best for you. I have watched you from afar and you've grown beautifully. Maybe it's an old woman's vanity, but I was pleased as punch when I found out that you had hazel eyes like mine. I felt then that we were kindred spirits and I believe it shall always remain so. Your ambitions to be a writer mirror my own at your age and I'll see to it that you achieve your dream.

Since your birth, I have always ensured that you were cared for and that is a promise that will never falter, whether I roam this earth or not. I hired a private detective who collected many of your short stories and I took the liberty of sending my publisher some of your more promising prose. They are masterfully done and she is eager to publish a short story anthology for a very handsome advance. However, I have asked her to hold on releasing them until I'm able to discuss it with you first.

I'm also hoping that you'll stay with me in Florida so that we may become better acquainted. We've lost much time and at my age, it doesn't do to waste anymore. Yet, I'm guilty of putting off this meeting for so long because, in many ways, I'm fearful of you. Fearful that you'll reject me because you may feel that I abandoned you. Fearful that you will blame me for your mother's death. If you've got my eyes you may have my temperament and may not be very forgiving and that unsettles me more than you can imagine.

I'm hopeful that my dream of us forging a beautiful relationship will be realized and I look forward to loving you in person the way I have from afar.

Love always,

Granny (Susie)

Chapter 41

July 15th, 2015

The room was cold. It smelled of new carpet, old books and just a hint of expensive furniture polish. Just behind Lia was a row of walnut bookcases that shelved heavy legal volumes on one wall. On the opposite side of the room, a large glass wall opened up to a skyline view of downtown Miami. The sunlight reflecting off the tall mirrored buildings was so bright that Lia kept her head down and her eyes trained on the polished wood surface of the large table that separated her from Susan's lawyer. Beside her, Ancil also sat quietly.

Lia's leather chair was well designed and very plush, but she was uncomfortable. She had no idea why she was meeting her long-lost grandmother's lawyer and despite cajoling Ancil for the better part of the morning, she still had no inkling.

He was a tall Caucasian man with white hair and a somber face. He eyed the stack of official-looking papers in front of him for a moment before he spoke. His deep voice was neutral and betrayed neither emotion nor boredom.

"Firstly, I'd like to say how sorry I am for your loss. Miss Taylor was with our firm for a very long time after she moved here from New York. Miss Davis, before your grandmother passed away, she left me with quite a few instructions and she made it exceedingly clear that they must be followed to the letter."

Lia stifled a little laugh. Knowing Susan, she didn't expect anything less.

"There are several assets to discuss, and we shall start with her home in Doral. Your grandmother has ensured that the home in Doral will be maintained for Miss Ancil Adams for the duration of her life. Miss Taylor said and I quote - ", he picked up a small note covered with Susan's scrawl and read, "'Ancil will live there until she is good and ready, and who doesn't like, it can lump it.' End quote."

He cleared his throat. "A trust fund has been set up to cover all of Miss Adams incidentals and that is separate and distinct. Other than that, all of Miss Taylor's earthly possessions including the rights to her books, any further royalties, the upcoming movie rights, all bank accounts, and all personal diaries are to be bequeathed to you. Here is a schedule of all items which you can peruse at your convenience. If there are no further questions, I'd like to see you this same time next week so that we can go over all of the paperwork."

Lia was aghast. "Mr. Doleman, are you trying to say that she gave me everything?"

Mr. Doleman nodded curtly. "Of course. You are your grandmother's sole heir and it was the obvious choice to my mind."

Lia exhaled. She felt like she had just had the wind knocked out of her and her mind was spinning at the reality of what she had just heard.

Ancil tapped her hand lightly. "Miss Cordelia, the gentleman asked if we have any more questions."

"Oh, sorry. I don't. Thank you very much for your time."

"Okay. We shall meet again next week. Thank you for your time today and the entire staff here at Doleman, Wiggins, and Burke wants to extend our heartfelt condolences for your loss."

Lia and Ancil stood to leave but on their way to the door, Lia turned abruptly. "Did you say 'books' with an 's'?

"Yes. Your grandmother wrote 'The Unspeakable Truth'

under her birth name, but she's been using a nom de plume since then. She wrote two books every year until she got her diagnosis last year. They're all quite good, I might add. Many of them have topped the best-seller lists." Lia looked at Ancil. She was glad to see that she wasn't the only one who was shocked.

Even in death, Susan still managed to make her feel faint. Lia wondered if she'd never truly get to know the reclusive author. They thanked the lawyer and made their way back home.

Lia watched traffic whiz by on the highways as Ancil took her time driving them home. Horns blared from the other cars trying to get Ancil to speed up, but either she didn't realize they meant her, or she had long grown accustomed to it. Lia rolled her eyes and settled into her seat, letting her mind wander over the journey her life had taken over the past few months. The long drive gave her plenty to think about and by the time they had gotten home, Lia had made up her mind.

Ancil knocked on the door before turning the polished handle and entering the Barbados room. Lia sat at the desk reading one of Susan's unpublished manuscripts. It was a story about Lia. It chronicled her life and background with a dash of artistic license and fiction to hold it together. Lia loved the way Susan portrayed her: gritty and smart with a hint of whimsy. She loved the nuance and beautiful flow of the writing.

There was a bright smile on her face and she didn't realize Ancil was in the room until she felt a hand on her arm. "Oh!" she grabbed her chest and looked up at the other lady.

"Sorry, Miss Cordelia, but you taxi outside."

"Thanks so much, sweetie," Lia said as she pulled Ancil into a warm embrace.

"Why you don' stay here with me? Can't believe you gine leave me in this big house all by myself," Ancil sniffed as tears settled in her eyes. "I gine miss you, young lady."

Lia sniffed too. "I'll be back, Ancil. I've got to go back to Barbados for a little while but I'll see you again in a few months."

Ancil nodded and wiped the moisture from her cheeks. "I understand, but it gine be real lonesome without yuh here to keep my company. You can't handle your business from here instead of going back?"

Lia smiled. "Not really. I think it's time to sort out some things with my mother. I appreciate her raising me, but I don't like that she lied to me about so many things. I'd like to get her some help for her gambling problem. I want to travel the world and write books and I'd like to be sure that she's okay before I do that."

She took up Susan's thick manuscripts from the desk and tucked them into an envelope. "Plus, the publisher said I need to edit the short stories Ms. Taylor sent to her if I want them published. So I've got a lot to do."

"You know," Lia mused, "this has been the best experience I've ever had in my life. So much of Miss Taylor's life mirrors situations I've had and for the first time, I feel like I understand myself. I was upset at first about her lying to me, but in a way, I can understand why she was so afraid."

Ancil smiled sadly. "She was a great woman, but she had some hard breaks in life."

Lia nodded. She hefted the envelope. "Miss Taylor - my granny - has inspired me more than she will ever know. I don't want to live my life as a reclusive author with so many regrets when I die. I want to live fully, breathe freely and love deeply."

Lia hugged Ancil again and made her way out the door to get into the waiting taxi. She looked around at the neat lawns and beautiful homes she was leaving behind. It felt like a lifetime had passed since she had arrived. And in some ways, it had. Meeting Susan Taylor had shifted Lia's life in such an unexpectedly, beautifully complicated way that she had been reborn. No longer was she afraid to face problems that she had been so quick to run from. No longer did she feel alone. Susan's unfinished story about Lia's life was like a roadmap for Lia to follow. Lia imagined herself fulfilling her ambitions with grit and vigor just like Susan had prophesied. Lia looked at the manuscript in her lap and smiled.

Don't forget to leave an Amazon review.

Hi there,

I hope you enjoyed 'The Girl with the Hazel Eyes'. It's been a labour of love for me in so many ways. I started writing this book in May of 2015 and it was initially intended to be a short story for a regional writing competition. Suffice it to say, something about Susan and Lia intrigued me and I couldn't get them out of my head. Eventually, I spent many dark nights huddled on the floor of my room letting these two women take me on a remarkable journey. Delving into decades of my country's history through months of research opened my eyes to Barbados' beautiful culture and really made me treasure it so much more.

As a self-published author, nothing is more valuable to me than feedback and I hope you'll be kind enough to leave an honest review on Amazon and Goodreads. Leaving feedback helps me to become better at writing and publishing so that I may enhance your reader experience. It also helps other readers make informed decisions about if they may enjoy this book.

Thanks once again.

X,
Callie

About the Author

Callie Browning was born and raised in Barbados. She is an avid reader and has been writing since 2009. She has won awards for her short stories and her first full length novel, The Girl with the Hazel Eyes, was a finalist in the JAAWP Caribbean Emerging Writer's Prize. She lives in Barbados with her family.

Follow Callie on Instagram, Facebook and Twitter
@BajanCallie

Credits

Cover design by Ebook Launch. Special thanks to Dr. Ashlia Lovell for her assistance with information on the historical treatment of mental illness in Barbados.

Copyright

Follow Callie Browning @BajanCallie on:
Instagram
Twitter
Facebook

CPSIA information can be obtained
at www.ICGtesting.com
Printed in the USA
FSHW011257160920
73837FS